# THE SIEGE OF REGINALD HILL

## CORINNA TURNER

Copyright © 2018 Corinna Turner

First published in the UK in 2018 by Unseen Books*

The right of Corinna Turner to be identified as the Author of the Work has been asserted by her in accordance with the Copyright, Designs and Patents Act 1988.

All rights reserved.
No part of this publication may be reproduced, stored in a retrieval system, or transmitted in any form or by any means without the prior permission in writing of the copyright owner or, in the case of reprographic production, only in accordance with the terms of licenses issued by the Copyright Licensing Agency, and may not be otherwise circulated in any form other than that in which it is published and without a similar condition being imposed on the subsequent purchaser.

Cover design by Corinna Turner

*Psalm 49:1-2, 7-15, 17* from The Jerusalem Bible © 1966 by Darton Longman & Todd Ltd and Doubleday and Company Ltd.

*Psalm 73:21-23* and *Psalm 130:1-2a* from the New Revised Standard Version Bible, copyright © 1989 the Division of Christian Education of the National Council of the Churches of Christ in the United States of America. Used by permission. All rights reserved.

*Psalm 130:6* from the World English Bible (Public Domain)

*Songs 8:7* from The Holy Bible—Knox Translation—© Westminster Diocese, published by Baronius Press, *www.baroniuspress.com*. Used by permission.

*Colossians 1:24* from the *Open English Bible* (Public Domain) Revised.

A catalogue record for this book is available from the British Library.

ISBN: 978-1-910806-78-4 (paperback)
Also available as an eBook

This is a work of fiction. All names, characters, places, incidents and dialogues in this publication are products of the author's imagination or are used fictitiously. Any resemblance to actual locales, events or people, living or dead, is entirely coincidental.

* An imprint of Zephyr Publishing, UK—Corinna Turner, T/A

*Many thanks to the developers of these beautiful Open Source fonts:*
*Quattrocentro Roman, Source Sans Pro, Note This,*
*WC Rhesus A Bta, Rosario, TOP SECRET, and EDO.*

## PRAISE FOR CORINNA TURNER'S BOOKS

**LIBERATION**: nominated for the **Carnegie Medal Award 2016.**
**ELFLING**: 1st prize, Teen Fiction, **CPA Book Awards 2019**
**I AM MARGARET** & **BANE'S EYES**: finalists, **CALA Award 2016/2018.**
**LIBERATION** & **THE SIEGE OF REGINALD HILL**: 3rd place, **CPA Book Awards 2016/2019.**

### PRAISE FOR *I AM MARGARET*

*Great style ...like The Hunger Games.*

EOIN COLFER, author of *Artemis Fowl* and former Irish Children's Laureate

### PRAISE FOR *THE SIEGE OF REGINALD HILL*

The Siege of Reginald Hill *is a powerful story of sacrificial love—the kind very few are ever called to. Kyle is faced with unbearable pain and suffering, but he handles it in an amazing, almost unfathomable way. ... If you've enjoyed the* I Am Margaret *series, you will love this story.*

THERESA LINDEN, author of award-winning *Battle for His Soul*

*There are a few stories that I'll never forget even though it's been years since I read them. Henry James'* The Beast in the Jungle *and C. S. Lewis'* The Great Divorce, *and now Corinna Turner's* The Siege of Reginald Hill. *An extremely powerful example of what it really means to love our enemies, this novel provokes a whirlwind of emotions.*

T. M. GAOUETTE, author of *For Eden's Sake*

*What an eloquent priestly figure is given us in* The Siege of Reginald Hill! *No time is wasted by the young priest on his awesome journey to reach the lost sheep. Fr Kyle's example reminds the reader that our sufferings lead to victory when united with the sacrifice of Christ.*

FR ARMAND DE MALLERAY, FSSP, author of *Ego Eimi – It is I: Falling in Eucharistic Love*

The Siege of Reginald Hill *is another suspenseful and moving work by Corinna Turner. Fans of* I Am Margaret *will love the continuation of the story!*

REGINA DOMAN, author of *The Angel in the Waters* and the award-winning *Fairytale Novels* series.

# ALSO BY CORINNA TURNER:

### I AM MARGARET series
*For older teens and up*

Brothers *(A Prequel Novella)*\*
1: I Am Margaret\*
*1: Io Sono Margaret (Italian)*
2: The Three Most Wanted\*
3: Liberation\*
4: Bane's Eyes\*
5: Margo's Diary\*
6: The Siege of Reginald Hill\*
7: A Saint in the Family\*
'The Underappreciated Virtues of Rusty Old Bicycles' *(Prequel short story) Also found in the anthology:* Secrets: Visible & Invisible\*

I Am Margaret: The Play *(Adapted by Fiorella de Maria)*

### UNSPARKED series
*For tweens and up*

Main Series:
1: Please Don't Feed the Dinosaurs
2: A Truly Raptor-ous Welcome
3: PANIC!\*
4: Farmgirls Die in Cages\*
5: Wild Life
6: A Right Rex Rodeo
7: FEAR
8: A Different Kind of Camouflage
9: A Different Kind of Freedom
10: What's Done is Done†

Prequels:
BREACH!\*
A Mom With Blue Feathers†
A Very Jurassic Christmas\*
'Liam and the Hunters of Lee'Vi'

### FRIENDS IN HIGH PLACES series
*For tweens and up*

1: The Boy Who Knew (Carlo Acutis)\*
2: Old Men Don't Walk to Egypt (Saint Joseph)\*
3: Child, Unwanted (Margaret of Castello)\*

Do Carpenter's Dream of Wooden Sheep? *(Spin-off, comes between 1 & 2)*

*1: El Chico Que Lo Sabia (Spanish)*
*1: Il Ragazzo Che Sapeva (Italian)*

### YESTERDAY & TOMORROW series
*For adults and mature teens only*
Someday: A Novella\*
*Eines Tages (German)*
1: Tomorrow's Dead†

### OTHER WORKS

*For teens and up*
Elfling\*
'The Most Expensive Alley Cat in London' (Elfling *prequel short story*)

*For tweens and up*
Mandy Lamb & The Full Moon\*
The Wolf, The Lamb, and The Air Balloon (Mandy Lamb *novella*)

*For adults and new adults*
Three Last Things *or* The Hounding of Carl Jarrold, Soulless Assassin\*
A Changing of the Guard
The Raven & The Yew†

† Coming Soon
\* Awarded the Catholic Writers Guild *Seal of Approval*

Let no power,
visible or invisible,
grudge me that I should reach Jesus Christ.
Let fire and the cross; packs of wild beasts; lacerations,
breakings and dislocations of bones;
cutting off of members;
shattering of the whole body—
let all the dreadful torments
of the devil come upon me:
only let me win through
to Jesus Christ!

*Saint Ignatius of Antioch, Letter to the Romans*

*KYLE*
No blazing sunset covered the sky now, just starry blackness. As the muzzle of the pistol ground into my spine, the memory of that setting sun's beauty filled me with three times the appreciation and thankfulness I'd felt earlier. While I took those few steps from the church to the waiting vehicle—shiny and black in the darkness, like a four-wheel drive hearse—I drank in that night sky and all the starlit beauty of the savannah.

What form would my perception of the physical world take once I was dead? I'd no idea. But it would not be the same. To waste a single glimpse of God's creation felt, at this moment, akin to sacrilege.

A hand yanked painfully on my bound arms, rough fingers pushed my head down, shoving me sideways onto the leather seat of that very expensive hearse. The door slammed, tinted glass stealing the world. But not its Creator.

Him, they could never take from me.

# THREE HOURS EARLIER

*KYLE*
The sun set like a diver disappearing over the horizon. A blaze of red and orange, and it was gone. As I stood there in the church doorway, I still found it hard to believe how quickly it happened, even after all these years in Africa.

I looked back down the earthen track leading into the village in time to see the girl going into her house. Just after evening Mass ended Sikudhani had come to the church crying about a fight with her brother. It'd taken me ages to calm her down, but she was bouncy enough now and freshly absolved from her own responsibility in the childish row.

And safely home. So I could snatch a few minutes with Our Lord, say Night Prayer, and go to *sleep*. Never mind my missed meal; it was Friday, after all. And please, Lord, I wouldn't have another sick call tonight. When my primary motive for that appeal switched from concern for the sick person to concern about getting into my own bed, there'd been too many. Three nights in a row in the wee hours was positively...zombifying. It was one thing if the congregation fell asleep during a homily, but when the priest *giving* the homily started nodding over his non-existent notes...

Well, they'd all been very nice about it, but I'd rather it didn't happen again.

I went back inside the church, leaving the doors wide open to admit the breeze, which was cooling blissfully as darkness settled over the savannah. A lion grunted in the far distance. A hyena whooped from over near the recycling area. No doubt someone who lived closer would chase it away.

I headed up the aisle, my feet scuffing against the wooden floorboards. Most of the houses in the village were modern, made of strong, heat-repelling breeze blocks, with waterCool roofs that provided hot water and air conditioning all through one simple, natural process. But the church, formed of five circular huts, was constructed in the traditional way. Not that 'hut' really did justice to the skill and artistry involved.

I passed through the small porch-cum-foyer hut and entered the big nave. The raised sanctuary stood exactly central, sheltered under an intricate canopy of carved and interwoven branches, and along the far wall stood three small hut-chapels—the central one the Blessed Sacrament chapel, with a Lady Chapel on the right and the Chapel of Reconciliation—where I'd spent my evening so far—on the left.

A dense thatched roof topped it all off, its small, discretely placed waterCool panels less effective than the standard full-roof set-up, but enough—along with that thick thatch—to keep the church significantly cooler than outside. Thank the Lord.

This had been my parish for six years now, and I rarely gave it all a second glance. But when I did, a wave of admiration for the craftsmanship invariably struck me—and a stab of homesickness for the priest holes and concealed sanctuaries of my childhood, growing up in the EuroBloc. Before my little sister gave the EuroGov a nice, peaceful thrashing and forced them to decriminalise belief in God. Go, Margo!

My eyelids dragged downwards, wanting to close. Settling in the front pew of the Blessed Sacrament chapel, I opened my Office book to Night Prayer. I'd do what I *had* to first; I really wasn't sure how long I could stay with Our Lord tonight. I was just so tired.

Nowadays, of course, EuroBloc-born priests—both the survivors of the long persecution and, increasingly, the younger ones for whom the danger and secrecy was just a dim memory from childhood—also worshipped openly, in real church buildings—supplemented by an army of African priests. There hadn't been a *lot* of survivors. Some of the buildings were even original church buildings, finally wrestled back from the EuroBloc by the Underground. Well, mostly by my stubborn sister—though she'd be furious with me for saying so.

At thirty-three, I belonged to the half-and-half generation. I'd answered the call to the priesthood expecting 'giving my life to God' to be literal—brutally, agonisingly, bloodily literal. But before I could even be ordained—let alone martyred—my sister happened. And everything changed. No more persecution. No more Conscious Dismantlement. A long, normal life ahead of me. Sometimes it still seemed unreal.

*Thank you, Margo, thank you so much.*
*Thank You, Lord.*
*Ah...I'm supposed to be praying, aren't I? I'm sorry.*

I dragged my mind back to Night Prayer, but having mastered that distraction, I fell asleep twice instead. Eventually I stood up, completing it on my feet.

*There, Lord. Done. I'll stay with You for just a few minutes, and then I hope You'll allow me to deposit my frail human body into my bed for a night's uninterrupted sleep. Please? Or I'll be fit for nothing in the parish footie friendly tomorrow, for one thing.*

Yes, I wanted to be on top form, because it could be a tough match. Karangwo had fielded a strong side last time. Hopefully I could score, though. Okay, so I usually scored, but it would be nice to score several times.

In my mind, I was sprinting down the pitch, dust flying under my feet, the goal ahead... I kicked the football and it was one of those perfect kicks, where the moment the ball is in the air you just *know* it's going to go in...

*Whoa! Kyle, come on. This is prayer time! Get down on your knees, man!*

Pushing away the daydreams, I lit the two candles that stood on either side of the altar, then unlocked the tabernacle and opened the little double doors so that I could see the glass case in which the Host stood, ready to be slotted into the monstrance for public Adoration.

Kneeling at the altar rail, I determinedly fixed all my attention on it. On Him. God Himself, concealed under the form of mere bread. That familiar sense of peace and warmth filled me, as it sometimes—all right, as it *often*—did. Of being loved. And for once, a twinge of disappointment stirred. If I'd experienced nothing, I could've nipped off to bed with a clear conscience.

Guilt followed close behind.

*Sorry, Lord.* I pressed my forehead to my clasped hands, ashamed of my response. Many people—including my devout sister—could only dream of being blessed with the feeling of closeness with which Our Lord so often—in His unfathomable goodness—chose to bless me. Yet I would choose my bed over my Lord's company? *Really?*

No. I would stay as long as He wanted me to. That sense of being cherished held me too tightly to allow sleep, anyway. *Forgive my weakness, Lord.*

*Let's see...please watch over Mum and Dad, keep them safe...* A serious storm was bearing down on the state in which my parents lived and worked, way across the continent. The danger wasn't grave—buildings were pretty storm-proof nowadays—but it would still be a stressful few days for them, with plenty of clean-up to follow.

Thoughts of the rest of my family thronged into my mind. My sister, the famous Margaret Verrall; her husband, Bane—and my five nephews and nieces, who would swarm over me on my all-too-rare visits to Vatican State, drowning me in love. I missed them so much. In unwary moments—like now—the feeling overwhelmed me with deep, painful longing.

As always, I tried to fight free of it. I loved my parish. I loved my parishioners; my beautiful church, the beautiful land in which it stood. This ache in my chest was stupid. I had given my life to God and this was where He wanted me. Silly to wish that He needed me in the Vatican instead.

Of course, my sister was the reason that I was here in this foreign land. Though Margo had taught the EuroGov plenty of manners over the last twelve years they still remained in power. And the slow, steady civilising of the bloc's laws only made them hate her more and more.

They couldn't get to her, safe in Vatican Free State. But if I had a parish in the EuroBloc? Well, they'd have no trouble getting to her brother. So no parish in the British department for Father Kyle Verrall. A nice safe African parish instead.

Which I loved. I did.

I let out a long breath, trying to release the restless thoughts with it, and focussed on the tabernacle again. Enough meaningless fretting. It was the Lord that mattered.

My head knew that for truth, but my heart still throbbed unhappily in time with my banished thoughts. Why couldn't I concentrate tonight?

Actually, I'd been inattentive in prayer all week, now that I stopped to think about it. And the cause wasn't hard to find. Tiredness. Skipping off to bed after the bare minimum of time before the Blessed Sacrament. Lack of fervour—for whatever reason—bred lack of fervour. Fact. Like a poisonous serpent devouring its own tail, circling deeper and deeper into desolation, shrinking away...

*Calm down, Kyle. You only snatched a couple of early nights. And you've got to sleep. You should be in bed right now, in fact.*

I turned my mind enquiringly towards my Lord and Maker to see if he agreed with this argument, hoping to be dismissed for the night.

Nope.

No words—I never really heard words. But a definite sense that my presence was desired.

I had a sick call tonight, after all, didn't I? Only this time, I was the sick soul, to be tended by The Great High Priest Himself. I rested my chin on my hands and settled in for...for the duration, if the Lord willed it so. It was probably good for my humility to fall asleep on my feet in the pulpit and play poorly in a match.

Some great lessons in humility coming up tomorrow, then.

Quietness slowly settled over the village itself as my parishioners went to their beds. No actual silence reigned, though. The animal kingdom filled the night with life. The lion grunted again, a bit closer. Maybe it was time I closed the doors...

*...stay...stay with me...*

Or not. Lions never came right up to the village, anyway.

*...The Lord loved the lion. He loved all the animals I could hear. He loved me and all the sleeping humans in the village...*

*I will stay with you forever, if you will have me*, I told Him.

*...good...*

My soul soothed, settling under the Divine caress like a contented housecat, I nestled into His lap, safe and warm...

Finally, a noise dragged me from this snug cocoon. A vehicle was pulling up outside the presbytery. *Oh no, a sick call? Seriously, Lord?*

*Well, now who's contrary? You didn't want to stay here tonight, and now you don't want to leave.*

*I wanted to go to* bed. *That's not the same.*

Someone knocked on the presbytery door—the floor creaked as they went inside. I should get up and go out to them...

*...stay...stay...*

*Okay, I should go on kneeling right here, feeling decidedly rude. Huh.*

Footsteps creaked back over the presbytery's wooden veranda. "He's not here." A woman's voice, speaking in Esperanto, the artificial European language, though with an English accent.

"There's a light on in the church." A man's voice, this time, the accent...Scandinavian? "Let's try there."

Both were totally unfamiliar and clearly foreign. *Was* it a sick call? Maybe they were travellers. Surely, I should go out...

*...stay...*

So insistent. Like the Lord wanted to keep me with him every possible moment tonight.

I sighed and stayed, keeping my eyes obediently on the tabernacle even as footsteps trod straight up the aisle and into the chapel without any pause to genuflect. My visitors weren't Believers? I ought to be making them twice as welcome...

They were right behind me. Surely, I was allowed to turn to them now?

Before I could, something dug into my ribs. Hard.

"Get those superstitious hands up!"

I looked around, my eyes darting from the muzzle of the lethal pistol rammed into me to the woman holding it—plump and middle-aged—and on to a tougher-looking man of a similar age, who stood at a safer distance covering me with a nonLethal in a way that suggested the Lethal was just for show. He held a video camera in his free hand—pointed my way. My heart slid down into my sandals.

Slowly, I raised my 'superstitious' hands. EuroGov assassins? Or atheist fanatics? So much for a nice safe parish in Africa...

"On your feet!" The woman panted for breath, whether from unfitness or from sheer excitement at having me there at the point of her gun.

Unbidden, my eye picked at the word on the medical ID bracelet around her wrist—but I couldn't make it out.

"*Get up...*" A painful jab into my ribs with the too-solid muzzle.

I bowed deeply to the tabernacle and crossed myself, ignoring their sharp warnings—they were probably going to kill me regardless, so I felt little temptation to be irreverent. Then I got to my feet. All sleepiness had left me. My heart thudded too fast, adrenalin sharpening my vision.

I should lock the tabernacle... No, actually, I probably shouldn't call attention to my Lord's physical Presence. *Don't you touch that tabernacle, don't you touch it!*

The woman couldn't have heard my fierce thought, but thankfully she showed no interest in the fancy strongbox on the wall. She probably had no conception of the fact that she stood two metres away from God Himself. "Walk..." Squaring her jaw, she jabbed the gun into my ribs again, hard, drawing an involuntary flinch. The man just watched me impassively, the hand holding the nonLee remaining even steadier than the one holding the video camera.

I'd have to leave the tabernacle unlocked. If they realised, who knew what they'd do to Him? I headed down the aisle, my back tingling in chill expectation—the back of my head even more so. But...a nonLethal. Perhaps they didn't mean to kill me on the spot.

*Lord...* I thought, as we passed the altar, but then I wasn't sure what to say next. Save me? No... *Your will, Lord. Just...keep me close to You. Keep me true to You. Please?* I didn't really want to die, but I wanted to fail Him even less.

I reached the entry hut without any deadly scrap of metal smashing through either head or spine, and the woman pulled my hands behind my back, yanking a cable tie tight around my wrists. After that, I was unsurprised to see a shiny black jeep waiting when we got outside. *Ah, the beauty of the night sky!* I drank it in as the man switched the lights off and carefully shut up the church for the night.

All too soon, he opened the back door of the hearse-coloured vehicle and shoved me within. The man and woman got in one on either side, pinning me between them. And their two guns.

The heavy, ugly tint of the glass in the closing door blocked the stars from my appreciative eyes, to my momentary dismay. But...

They could take the beauty of creation from me.

They could take my life.

But they could never take God. The knowledge lodged in my chest like a small hot water bottle—or a captive sun.

"Put his seatbelt on." A cold—and oddly familiar—voice spoke from the front passenger seat. "It would be *such* a shame if an accident befell him."

The menace in this apparently benign statement sent a chill down my spine—the woman laughed, a sound of cruel anticipation. I was getting a bad feeling about this whole thing. Okay, an even worse feeling.

Hunched awkwardly in the seat with my hands behind me, I stared at the man who'd spoken as they fastened the lap belt around me, trying to make out his face in the dark. Did I know him? He sounded quite old. Well-spoken. But so cold.

"Your sister would have known my voice at once," the man remarked, as I continued to peer at him. "But then she and I have actually met, several times. Your slowness on the uptake is understandable."

A shadowy hand rose to touch the overhead light and I squeezed my eyes half-closed as brightness filled the vehicle. Squinting, I made out a lined face...

My stomach didn't drop this time. It plummeted.

"Hello, Kyle," said Reginald Hill, the EuroGov's universally feared Minister for 'Internal Affairs'. "It's so nice to meet you at last."


*MARGO*
"No, I can't do that week." I balanced the phone between cheek and shoulder as I checked my diary, then glanced at my study door as I heard Polly's and Lizzie's voices, raised. Uh oh. The children had come in from school a while ago but there were some things I'd wanted to finish before knocking off for the day.

"Are you sure, Margo? They're a major TV station in—"

"Sister Mari, I know, but *no*. That's when Kyle's visiting. There's got to be another date they can do." I put the diary back on my desk, ear still cocked towards the door. Did I need to go out? No, I could hear Luc's voice now, speaking at a normal volume. He was only eleven, but good at keeping the peace.

Sister Mari sighed. "Well, I expect they can be persuaded; they're very keen."

*Thank you, Lord, for that,* I thought, as we said good evening and rang off. Not only because Kyle's visit wouldn't be spoiled by me having to work, but also because I dreaded waning interest. Waning interest in *me*, I would love, *except* that interest in *me* and interest in the *cause* remained inextricable. Every time I thought I'd resigned myself to a life under the public spotlight, I found myself thinking wistfully of the quiet anonymous life in Africa I'd once imagined for Bane and myself.

I pushed the phone back to the corner of the desk and drew my laptop to me.

Simply not being able to live in Africa didn't bother me, mind you, though it would've been nice to see the place. Eduardo, still the Vatican's head of security and as cautious as ever, always vetoed us going to see Kyle out there, on grounds of 'security challenges'. If only Kyle could visit more often.

Of course, he'd been here only three months ago. A vice closed on my throat, just thinking about it, and my hands went still, my laptop lid unopened.

As soon as he'd heard about little George's diagnosis—*anencephaly*, the word made me shudder—Kyle had arranged to be with us for the birth—and he'd come in good time. And what a blessing, since Georgie, impatient to reach heaven, had arrived—contrary to all the predictions—so early that Mum and Dad hadn't got here yet, and Jon had still been in South America on a research trip.

Our little baby had looked so perfect in his soft white hat, lying there in Kyle's strong arms as my brother baptised him. How tenderly Kyle had laid him back on my breast afterwards. A few agonisingly wonderful minutes were all I'd had with him—then Doctor Carol noticed how much blood I was losing. Little George was hastily bundled into Bane's grasp and I was rushed away, crying and screaming for my poor doomed baby. Emotional and overwrought, I'd had a serious failure of both reason and upper lip.

But Bane and Kyle and Luc and Polly and Javi and Lizzie had all held little Georgie. Even Joey had held Georgie, with Bane holding them both. All recorded on video for me, since by that point I was unconscious in the operating theatre. And by the time I woke again, our precious little boy had fallen asleep in his father's arms, for the first and last time, with his uncle and brothers and sisters gathered around him.

I'd cried almost non-stop for three days. Or so it felt. For months I'd known Georgie had been fast-tracked for heaven, but to miss those last few precious hours with my little one... I suppose it was all exacerbated by hormones and sheer exhaustion from the blood loss, but it broke me in a way nothing else had. Kyle sat with me in the hospital for hours upon hours, praying or just holding me as I sobbed—and sobbed and sobbed—while Bane tried his best to maintain some normality for the children.

Once Mum and Dad arrived, they took over the child

care, so Bane—always my tower of strength—took over most of the hugging. Kyle kept on with the praying, though. My big brother had always been a lot more...spiritual...than me. For years it'd felt like every time I saw him, he'd made new strides in his prayer life, while I was running in one place, just trying not to go backwards. I'd have blamed the demands of family—and fame—except Kyle was busy enough himself. He didn't know how not to be—especially with an entire parish to look after.

Since finally working through the old, old trauma of Joe's death, Kyle had bloomed even more, both emotionally and spiritually, so much that—honestly?—I'd struggled not to be jealous. Now, I was just so grateful that he'd been there with his unshakeable faith and trusting calm, right when I needed it.

We'd talked often on the phone, since—something else I appreciated, since he wasn't great at calling, usually—if he'd nothing else to do, he'd be too busy praying to phone, these days. But I was really looking forward to his visit, in a month's time.

And I was having *all* that time with my brother, not with a TV station, however major!


*KYLE*
The cable tie bit painfully into my wrists. Maybe if I could shift my position...but the guards sat so close, the woman a warm, plump mass, the man all wiry muscle. *Ignore it, Kyle.* Hill remained turned in his seat, watching me. He knew I'd recognised him and awaited my reaction. His snow-white hair—only thinning slightly—looked ghostly with the light above it, his pale skin only adding to the impression.

No point asking Hill what he wanted with me. This man had caused nothing but pain to my sister and my family. He was the one who'd signed Margo's death warrant, all those years ago. He'd tortured Bane for three long days. He'd 'interrogated' Lucas brave-but-batty Everington for three whole *months* and later allowed him to carry out the deadly transaction that had helped Bane so much, but at the cost of such grief to Margo. He'd sent poor old Georg Friedrich to kill Margo, then turned around and tried to execute him for it, for the sake of public relations.

As the so-called 'Minister for Internal Affairs,' hurting, coercing, and betraying people was something of a speciality of his. And killing. Let's not forget that.

No, I'd no need to ask what he wanted with me. The famous pre-vote debate, Margaret Verrall vs. Reginald Hill, in which my sister had got the better of Hill in such a humiliating way, snatching Georg Friedrich from death with less than an hour to go, remained one of the thousand most watched videos online. Oh, I knew what Hill wanted with me and it had nothing to do with *me* at all. *Revenge.* Pure and simple. Simple, anyway. I was just a tool in his hands, a weapon that could hurt my sister.

"Mr Hill," I said politely, focusing on that shadowed face, "there's really no need for this. If you'd like counsel or baptism, you're very welcome to just come in and ask for it. It's about time."

After a second's silence, Hill barked a laugh. "So, you're a bold boy. No surprise there. Not that I ever actually got to measure your sister's exact quantity of guts. But I hope to make up for it with you."

That...did not sound good.

"Well, what are we waiting for?" demanded Hill.

My body tensed...

"Let's get moving," Hill went on, glancing at the driver—tall and more youthfully fair-haired than Hill; that was all I could see from behind. "We've a long drive."

I tried not to relax too obviously.

*Silly Kyle. Why would they put you in the car and then kill you? That would just make a mess all over this smart vehicle.*

For now, this was only a kidnapping. My heart was still thudding painfully, though. *Lord, keep me close to You.*

The jeep began to move, bumping gently as it gathered speed along the rough track. We weren't taking the main road out of the village. What were the chances anyone had even seen me taken? That they had realised what they were seeing if they had? I refused to despair—*despair* hardly being an appropriate reaction to death anyway, not for a

Believer—but suddenly I didn't fancy my chances of beating Our Lord's record when it came to the length of my earthly life.

*How* I would die—and how *long* it would take—was a fear far less easily soothed. I should probably start praying for that nice clean bullet to the back of the head. From Reginald Hill? I should be so lucky.

Hill glanced around again and scowled. "*Excuse me?* Are we forgetting something back there?"

The male henchman's face betrayed nothing, but I glimpsed his fingers tighten around the camera. Then he put it aside and pulled a cloth bag over my head—close black weave filled my vision. Short stubby fingers touched my neck on the other side, as the woman drew the bag's drawstring tight and fastened it. Tight enough to hurt, though not to strangle. I tried not to shrink from her touch, but in the next moment her hand was running over my chest.

"You don't recognise me, do you, handsome boy?"

I think it was meant to be a purr, but it came out too grating.

"Should I?" I spoke as calmly as I could.

"My name's Gladys. Major Gladys Wallis, EGD Security. *Retired*. Thanks to your sister."

Oh dear. The girl's warden from the EuroBloc Genetics Department Facility where Margo had once been imprisoned as a New Adult. Great, another person who hated Margo. Was the guy ex-EGD as well? And the driver? How official *was* this little operation of Hill's?

"I hope you were able to find other employment, Major Wallis?" I said civilly.

"Think that's so easy, do you?" Her nails were suddenly biting through my cassock. "After your sister made me out to be a...a..." She broke off, breathing hard as though suffocated by her rage.

"I remember how much my sister encouraged people to offer former EGD Security personnel a second chance."

"Oh? But what did she say about *me*?" snarled the angry woman.

"The truth."

*Smack.*

Pain flared across the side of my face. Yes, Margo had said this woman was quick to lash out. The truth indeed.

"You won't disprove what he said that way," chuckled Hill, as though in echo of my own thought.

A silence followed, as though the Menace (how Margo always referred to this woman) didn't dare talk back to Hill—but it was a baleful silence.

"Mr Hill," I ventured, "this seems a rather...imprudent move...on your part. With the elections coming up."

"The election is my business, Kyle."

"Yes... Um, you know, you're not close family—or even related to me at all, to the best of my knowledge. So it's Father Kyle, if you don't mind."

Hill laughed harshly. "I'm not endorsing your superstitious lunacy, Kyle."

"I still think you should just let me out and forget this happened if you want to be re-elected. I can walk back, and I won't hold a grudge."

Hill laughed again, but...there was a slightly manic edge to it. Yes, I should be *listening*. This man, for all his crimes, was just that, a man. Like any of my parishioners. I should be listening, not just to what he said, but to what he *meant*, what was driving him. Anyone who could do the things he did had to have serious spiritual problems.

"You *are* a brave one. No crying. No begging. Well, I didn't really expect it. Always makes a nice change. But no struggling, either. A strong young man like you. But you're not putting up a fight at all."

I could tell from his smug tone that he was simply probing me. "As you know, Mr Hill, I am not allowed to fight. I am a priest."

"But you carried—and used—a weapon on your sister's so-called Liberation missions."

"I carried and used a *nonLethal* on *Bane's* Liberations, yes. To save innocents—and with Papal approval. Facility guards and soldiers, well, they're not going to have an undiagnosed heart problem, are they? All the same, I don't think I would fire even a nonLee merely in my own defence. Just in case."

Hill laughed yet again. "Do you really think it's smart to

tell us that, Kyle? In your position?"

I shrugged, the bag tight around my neck. "My sister's the smart one. I just care for people's souls."

"Souls don't exist." Hill's voice took on a sharper note. "You've wasted your life caring for non-existent things. How does that feel now?"

"I have no complaints about my life." My voice sounded so...serene...to my ears, and...yes, what I said was true. I did wish I could've seen more of my sister and family—but not so much that I regretted—even remotely—giving my life to God.

*Giving my life to God.* Synonymous with martyrdom when I was growing up. I needed to get back into that way of thinking. And quickly.

"No complaints..." Hill's tone was vicious. "What a poor fool you are, Kyle Verrall."

"But a content one. What about you, Mr Hill? Do you have...complaints about your life?"

"Enjoy your last night alive, Kyle." On the heels of his cold words came an electrical whine, then he spoke again, harshly, but not to me. "If you want to cross your legs—well, that's just too bad. Pass me that blanket."

From the sounds, I guessed Hill had reclined his seat almost onto the Menace and was tucking himself in for the night. When he said long drive, he clearly meant it.

Well...it would give me time to prepare. Compose my soul, as the old saying went. After all these years of safety, I was reeling in shock to find my life suddenly demanded of me after all. Part of me, screaming and wailing in protest, sought to cling to this world like a child throwing a tantrum. Like any tantrumous child, my fingers needed gently but firmly prying apart so that I could be carried away to something better than that to which I clung in such small-minded foolishness.

*Joe, little brother, pray for me? I think I'll be seeing you soon. Dear little Georgie, pray for your uncle. Blessed Peter, Father Mark, Lucas, pray for me, please?* Any help my family's—mostly uncanonised—saints could give me would be welcome indeed.

To have a whole night to do the finger-prying was

certainly a great blessing. How many people were simply struck down so suddenly they could think of nothing in those last brief moments but the pain and the fear? How many people suffered that even more dreadful fate, a silent departure as they slept, passing to God just as they were when they so blithely plonked their heads down on their pillows? No, although my heart still thud-thudded in my chest and sweat covered my brow under the smothering bag, I was very blessed indeed.

But I had others to pray for first. *Lord, please comfort Margo. Please comfort them all. My parents, especially them. They're not as young as they were, and this will be such a shock. But above all be with Margo, Lord. She's still dealing with losing little Georgie. Please enable her to grasp firmly and unwaveringly that it is* Hill *who is responsible for this. I can imagine all too clearly how awful she will feel, knowing that he kills me because he cannot get to her. Or maybe simply because he knows it will hurt her more. He's cunning enough for that.*

Okay. I'd pray more for my loved ones later. But now I'd better do the bare minimum to put my own soul in order. The bag, though hot and claustrophobic, was another blessing, really. A perfectly private prayer-space.

I started by examining my conscience as closely as I possibly could, listing to my heavenly Father with brutal honesty every sin of act or of omission I'd committed since my last confession. No mortal sins, thanks be to God, though in truth I couldn't remember when I'd last committed one of those. But I wasn't going to sit around patting myself on the back about that. After all, *of him to whom much has been given, much will be demanded.* The Lord had surely blessed me very greatly, which made even the smallest failure of mine a very serious matter.

Only when satisfied that I'd called to mind all I could, did I make a fervent Act of Contrition.

*I'm so sorry, Lord. I wish I'd done better.*

Then I said a rosary for Hill and everyone else involved, since their need for prayers was probably greater than anyone else's, including myself, my predicament notwithstanding.

*Pray for us sinners, now and at the hour of our death...* The words went through my mind again and again, and each time I felt I'd never heard them before, despite having given talks on them too many times to count. At the hour of our death...at the hour of *my* death...

*Pray for us sinners, now and at the hour of our death...* A second rosary for my loved ones.

*At the hour of our death...* A third for my parish.

*At the hour of our death...* I was onto the fourth and last set of mysteries—for myself—when sleep began to snatch at me, weighting my eyelids and trying to suck my mind into blackness. *Seriously? I'm being driven to my death and I'm nodding off?*

*...sleep. Rest, Kyle...*

Well...if the Lord wanted me to sleep...and I'd that nagging sense he did...I *was* exhausted. And despite the joy waiting at the end, tomorrow promised to be a thoroughly beastly day, possibly the worst of my life—Hill would have to work hard to top the day Joe died, but I'd a feeling he was going to try. Undoubtedly, I'd face it better after even a few hours' rest.

I made a few more limping efforts to reach the end of the rosary, but under that gentle encouragement and the not remotely gentle pressure of my over-tired body, I quickly gave it up for a lost cause. I'd just get to the end of this decade, then...


*MARGO*
I kissed Bane, my hands sliding under his pyjamas...

"Margo! Cut it out; don't torture me!" He fended me away. "You know what Doctor Carol said."

Bother. I flopped down beside him, my head on his chest. "I'm feeling heaps better, Bane, you know that."

"Has she actually given you a green light?"

I sighed into his pyjama top. He knew perfectly well she hadn't. Doctor Carol had been quite clear that we shouldn't have another child until I was a hundred percent again—and to be honest, I still felt far too emotionally raw to seek that, yet, even if we discerned it was the Lord's will to try for another. But tonight, I just actually had the energy to want... Well. Bane wasn't going to co-operate, and no doubt he was right. I was being irresponsible.

"I saw your chart," he scolded me. "It's a cuddle night, right?" He hooked his arms securely around me and drew me close, which had the useful side-effect, from his point of view, of pinioning my naughty hands.

"Yeah, it's a cuddle night," I grumble-agreed into his chest. Thwarted, my body retaliated by crashing from energised to exhausted. Thus proving Doctor Carol's point, I suppose. I let my eyes close.

"A very *short* cuddle night, this one..." I heard Bane mutter, but I'd drifted too far into sleep to respond.

"Mummy?" A familiar, plaintive little voice from outside our bedroom door started to drag me back up from almost-sleep. *Lizzie...*

But Bane pressed a quick kiss on my forehead and disentangled himself. "Go to sleep, Margo. I'll take care of it."

I dropped back into sleep so fast, I never even felt him get off the bed.


*KYLE*
A sharp blow struck the back of my head and a grating voice sounded right in my ear. "This cocky young pup's gone to *sleep!*"

I blinked, momentarily disorientated by the darkness and the scratchy fabric that flopped against my face as I jerked upright. My back, shoulders, and wrists ached fiercely.

A harsh voice spoke from very nearby, low and furious. "This *old* hound is sleeping too, so *shut up.*"

Ah. Reginald Hill. My unfortunate predicament flooded my mind.

Silence from the Menace. With my hands secured behind my back, my hunched upright position was pretty uncomfortable anyway. So after a futile attempt to ease the pain in my shoulders, I bent to rest my chin back on my knees—and she whacked my head a second time. I ignored her, closing my eyes, but my heart pounded so hard from my abrupt awakening that sleep had fled far away. Still, probably better to pretend slumber. Pretence might turn into reality.

The Menace clipped my head yet again. I'd a feeling I knew exactly how to put a stop to it, but...*turn the other cheek, Kyle.* I went on peacefully not-sleeping on my knees. Surely she'd get bored before long.

*Whack.*

*Whack.*

I offered up each little pain for her salvation and tried to ignore her. Until she slipped her hand inside my cassock, her fingers running over my chest.

"Handsome boy like you, wasted in that chastity belt around your neck?" she breathed in my ear. "Should be a crime. *Was,* until your stupid sister messed everything up..."

Her hand kept moving—I abandoned my cheek-turning and kicked Hill's seat as hard as I could.

An explosive—and truly obscene—word broke from the old man. Sounds of rustling fabric and shifting came from where he sat, then light flooded the car behind my black weave. The Menace snatched her hand out, but was too slow.

"You stupid sow!" Hill bellowed. "You think any pathetic little thing you can do means the tiniest thing compared to what awaits him? Just *leave him alone!*"

Leave him alone and let *me* sleep, in other words. No doubt in daytime he wouldn't care *what* she did—the worse, the better. Well, hopefully we'd get where we were going before Hill was well enough rested to reconsider.

Sullen silence from beside me. I closed my eyes again, fighting for calm. The Menace's behaviour—and Hill's ominous words—had chased sleep so far from me I wasn't sure it would ever return.

*Gird me, O Lord, with the cincture of purity, and quench in my heart the fires of sin, that the virtue of chastity may abide in me.* I'd recited those words first thing in the morning as I fastened the wide cloth belt around my cassock and again only hours ago while tying the rope-like cincture in place among my liturgical vestments before offering Mass, and I clung to the prayer now. *Lord, be with me.*

My skin prickled where she'd been pawing me. I wanted a shower more than I'd ever wanted one in my life. How I had *wept* in the confessional, in rage and in grief, as penitents tried to confess to *having been* assaulted by someone or other. How vehemently I had denied that they had done anything wrong, that anything needed to be forgiven. Not for *them*. At this moment, I understood more clearly than ever why they made such a heartbreaking, irrational accusation against themselves. In fact, I felt in need of my own counsel.

*Nothing she does to you means a thing,* I reminded myself firmly, *if she does it against your will.*

Poor consolation, but some consolation was better than none.

How long had I slept before the Menace took exception to my slumber? How long had I now been kidnapped *for?* No way to know. I wanted more than anything to go back to sleep, but my body thrummed, adrenalin keying me to painful tension.

Right. I'd pray again.

Another rosary for my captors.

One for me, since I never did finish it.

Another for my loved ones.

One for my parish...

*...I held the host between my forefingers and thumbs, ready for the consecration. My parishioners were all there, and Margo and Bane and the children and my parents. Joe knelt in the front row, as well, just beside Margo. Uncle Peter—Blessed Peter—was next to him. Shouldn't he be up here concelebrating with me? And Father Mark, too. Oh well, too late now. Maybe they'd arrived after the beginning. Concentrate, Kyle...*

*My attention snapped back to what I was doing, to this most awesome reality taking place in my consecrated hands, to this most precious of my priestly tasks. My heart swelled. Nothing could compare to the joy and the honour of saying Mass.*

*Adoration was more relaxing, it was true, and came a close second. No need to concentrate on words; no possibility of, heaven forbid, dropping something. Or Someone. Just me and Our Lord in the silence.*

*But Mass still won...* Concentrate, Kyle! What's wrong with you today? *I was never distracted* now.

*I finished the words of consecration and Our Lord was there in my hands, hidden. I'd just started to raise Him—still gripped ever so carefully between my thumbs and forefingers—when an unseen force seemed to throw me forward...the Host flew from my hands...in slow motion, I grabbed for Him, desperately...but my hands wouldn't move, my arms seemed to be pinioned behind me and suddenly black fabric covered my face, blocking the church—and the Host turning so slowly through the air—from my frantic vision...* NO...

Black fabric...the distinctive sloped shape of a car's seat under me, the bite of the cable tie around my wrists...

*Oh.* I'd been dreaming. I hadn't just dropped the Host—thank heaven for that small mercy—the car had simply come to a halt, yanking at my already well overstrained shoulders and back. I wanted to play dead—well, play *asleep*—but the pain drew me, against my better judgment, to sit upright. I bit back any sound as fire ran down my neck and through my shoulders. Clearly not a recommended sleeping posture.

"How are we doing, Croft?" Hill's voice.

"Only another twenty K, sir." That must be the driver, speaking for the first time. He sounded a lot younger than the others, his accent English, like Hill and the Menace.

"Good. You assist me. Jonas, deal with dear Kyle."

Deal with...? I didn't tense up much, though. Would they seriously have driven me all night just to shoot me dead on some... Well, wherever we were.

All that happened was that the imperturbable 'Jonas' ordered me from the vehicle—though his mutters grew irate as he struggled ineptly with my cassock. But soon enough he'd enabled me to take advantage of what was clearly a comfort break.

"Stay there and wait your turn," Hill snarled to the Menace as she tried to follow me out of the vehicle. Clearly, he was still peeved enough about his disturbed sleep to put punishing *her* above tormenting *me*. Or maybe it was his own privacy he was worried about.

But...if Jonas was helping *me*, was the driver 'assisting' Hill? Was he...sick? How sick? Sick enough not to give a fig about the forthcoming election? A cold shudder ran down my aching back as fear washed over me. A strange dual fear—for myself, and for him.

For myself, because if so, there was no way his proven political cunning would kick in at the last minute and save me. Huh, some part of my mind had clearly been hoping, hadn't it? *Just let go, Kyle. The Lord is waiting. You already gave your life to Him, remember? First at Confirmation, then on that Salperton road when you faked your death, and most irrevocably of all, when you were ordained. So don't...cling.*

For *Hill*, because if he was dying, he was dying in *such* a state...and about to compound it with yet another act of torture and murder. *Lord, have mercy on that man.*

"And if you need to do any medical stuff, do it now." Hill spoke to Wallis again. "We're not stopping specially."

A faint snicker from near Hill, then Croft the driver spoke in a—daringly?— familiar tone. "Are you sure these two has-beens are up to being on active service, sir?"

Hill merely sniffed slightly. "They were *available*."

Jonas gripped my wrists hard enough to hurt as he marched me back to the car.

As we set off again Hill and Croft exchanged a few more relaxed—but inscrutable—words about our route. They must've worked together before. Much good that observation would do me.

The surface of the road grew rough. Every bump and jounce yanked at my shoulders. Sleep was impossible, but I felt considerably refreshed. I must've got quite a few hours, in all. At least I'd have my wits about me, now. Not that screaming in agony required much in the way of wits and that was, no doubt, all Hill and his video camera wanted of me.

The jeep decelerated at last, the tyres crunching over a gravelly surface. And then we stopped. My heart rate rose again. Had we arrived?

Yes. Doors opened, and everyone got out. Jonas ordered me out too. Sweat dripped down my forehead, even though the light behind the black weave was dim, dawn-pale, and the air still cool against my hands. I barely noticed the shoulder-pain, though it hadn't gone anywhere. *Lord, be with me. Joe, pray for me.*

Jonas and the Menace—firm, steely hands and soft, hot ones, I was pretty sure it was those two—gripped my arms, marching me along between them. Everything darkened, and our steps echoed slightly. We'd gone inside. We turned left...right...down some stairs...right again... I tried to fix the sequence in my memory, just in case the Lord did have an escape in mind for me, but it was hard to concentrate.

Finally, a door closed firmly behind me and hands fumbled at my neck, loosening the drawstring. I closed my eyes to protect them as the bag was yanked off. I dreaded opening them again.

What did Hill have in store for me? All the horrors of Hollywood flitted through my mind. Scorpions. Snakes. Jellyfish. Crocodiles. No, all too quick for Hill's liking. Burning? Drowning? Suffocation? Poison? Or some fiendish combination of them all?

But when I looked around, Jonas was just closing the door behind him. And then I stood alone in a small windowless storeroom. So. A makeshift holding cell. They weren't...ready for me yet.

I checked the door, but I couldn't have got it open, even with my hands free. Metal, and very close fitting to its frame. I looked the walls and floor over, and remembered to inspect the ceiling above me, but it was all concrete. Yes, we'd gone down some stairs, hadn't we? This was the basement. No way out. Only one way to pass the time, then.

I knelt on the hard floor and began to pray again. Several hours sleep or not, a big lump choked my throat, and my eyes burned. Part of me definitely wanted to break down and bawl. I struggled to calm myself, determinedly casting my mind back to those cosy hours I'd spent last night with the Lord.

*That's why you wanted me there, wasn't it, Lord? So I could remember now and be comforted. Thank you.*

Gradually, my heartbeat slowed, that embarrassing desire to cry eased its grip, and I was able to rest quietly in the Lord's love.

But not for long. Footsteps soon tramped up to the door. *So. Here we go, Lord.*

The door creaked open in an appropriately sinister manner. The Menace and Jonas—still wielding the video camera. As they took my arms, leading me off along a utilitarian concrete passage, all those imagined horrors began to teem in my mind again. Why had I watched so many adventure films in my life? Why hadn't I only watched stuff about happy little kittens?

We approached a door... *Dissolved in acid?* my mind offered helpfully. *Buried alive?*

*Shut up!* I told myself, as they opened the door. *I don't care what it is, just so long as it isn't—* Then we'd stepped through the doorway and my thoughts trailed off in a silent wail of dismay. Close followed by a wave of self-mockery. Of course, it was this. What else would Hill choose?

Hygienic-looking equipment filled the ugly concrete room.

A fancy many-doored chiller cabinet.

Wheeled trolleys spread with carefully laid out medical instruments.

And in the centre, a gleaming metal gurney, complete with restraining straps.

My stomach convulsed, attempting to force its contents up my throat and out of me, but thankfully I hadn't eaten now for over eighteen hours and a firm swallow sent the mouthful of bile burning back to its rightful place.

*Oh Lord, stay with me!* A silent scream.

Hill sat there in a wheelchair—yes, he was sick all right—looking decidedly smug. "So, Kyle. From the way that tanned young face just faded to the colour of silver birch bark, I take it a lengthy explanation of the procedure you are about to undergo would be a waste of breath on my part?"

My body trembled, limbs quivering unstoppably. My mind roiled, lurched from side to side, as though seeking some escape, physical or otherwise, but there was nothing. Jonas and the Menace stood right behind me, Croft just behind Hill, a nonLee in his hand. Yes, Croft was young, not much older than me. His sunny face might've inspired hope, but a cold competence filled his eyes.

Three white-coated men waited in the corner, but I struggled to take them in, except as a statistic. I was outnumbered, outgunned, helpless. Like every other priest, sister or Believer who'd ever stood where I stood, looking the same death squarely in the mouth.

No, Hill had absolutely no need to describe the 'procedure'. We'd studied it in seminary, all its hideous stages, from start to finish, because taking away the uncertainty of what was to happen lessened the fear—at least slightly—freeing more attention for prayer. Or so the theory went. Whether it was possible to pray much—or at all—while in that level of pain was a question...I was about to learn the answer to.

*Lord, stay with me!*

"You're very quiet all of sudden, Kyle." Hill smiled. "No bold words? Don't fancy another nap?"

Somehow, I unstuck my dry lips, though I had to moisten them before I could get words out. "Maybe in a minute. When I'm lying down."

Hill grinned in appreciation. "Oh, this is going to be fun, it really is." He made a gesture to Jonas—a *snip* and the cable tie fell from my wrists.

Gingerly, I tried to bring my arms forward—such pain shot down them and through my shoulders that my stomach churned again. Holding them still, I simply tried to relax them, concentrating on flexing my fingers instead.

"Smarts a bit, does it?" said Hill evenly.

"It doesn't take a very highly developed knowledge of anatomy to know that arms aren't meant to stay in that position for so long." What was I really getting at with that remark? I could barely think, my mind paralysed between pain and fear. Except this wasn't really pain. This was *nothing*. A mere *twinge*.

Part of my mind gibbered—*no, no, no, no*—and I fought to stop it overwhelming me. But... *This isn't supposed to happen anymore! This isn't supposed to happen to me! Not now...*

Not for over ten years. But I'd accepted it, back when I first accepted the Lord's call. Just because I'd got used to the—apparent—fact that it would no longer be necessary didn't change that.

*This is what you signed up for, Kyle. Maybe not the new priests, but* you—*this is* exactly *what you signed up for. So don't whine. Just deal with it.*

Yes... *Lord, I won't refuse you now. But...but for pity's sake,* stay with me*!*

I focussed on Hill again as he spoke.

"Ah, I can see you standing there, making up your mind to be brave and true. I've seen it so many times. Well, I'll let you in on a secret. The majority of you most terminally insane ordained or consecrated types always did hold firm. I imagine it's those gruesomely graphic lessons they gave you during your, what do you call it, 'formation'? Those weeded out any faintheart who somehow managed to get that far without fully grasping the realities of what they were doing. Only the really strong ones got as far as *this*. No, we never broke many."

"Then why did you even *bother* with this viciousness?"

Hill smiled unpleasantly. "Oh, *I* always knew *exactly* how to increase the rate of apostasy, but the other members of the High Committee, in their collective dimness, believed that high numbers of gruesome deaths would best crush superstitious behaviour."

"Clearly they never studied Church history."

Hill barked another laugh. "Indeed. Martyrs don't crush superstition, I told them a thousand times. Apostates walking around alive, claiming to believe but not prepared to truly live it—or die for it—are what cause superstition to wither and die." He sighed regretfully. "But no, they never would listen to me."

"Well, if you're looking for sympathy about *that*, you've come to the wrong store."

"I don't need sympathy from anyone." Hill's voice was sharp. "But aren't you going to ask me how I would have done it?"

"Done it?"

"Increased the rate of apostates so exponentially."

Uneasiness curdled my insides. "I've got this feeling you're going to tell me whether I ask or not."

"Clever boy. So I am. Well, as you know, the traditional format of a Full Conscious Dismantlement is that the condemned gets a final chance to make the Divine Denial once they're on the gurney. If they don't make it, they get the paralytic, and then they *can't* make it. Their last chance gone. But if they do make it, they walk out, free, all charges dropped. Highly attractive, yet less taken up than you might expect. Received wisdom was that the condemned's dread of not being able to make the denial once they wanted to would lead many to apostatise.

"Of course," Hill rolled his eyes, "the reality was that at that point they still *didn't* want to make it, so most didn't. And my dear colleagues were happy with that, because they wanted to ensure high numbers of gruesome executions, and the system did that very well.

"I, on the other hand, could see quite clearly that the way to increase apostasy to...well, I would posit about *one hundred percent*, in fact...would be to administer a different drug that paralysed sufficiently to allow successful dismantling, while still permitting speech, and then allow the victim to make the Divine Denial at any time during the procedure. Life—perhaps slightly maimed, but life all the same—still their prize, if they made it soon enough, or later on—the still greater inducement—a quick, clean death."

A lump of ice had just dropped down the back of my collar and was running slowly down my spine. Surely such a drug simply...didn't exist?

"I," Hill went on smugly, "even commissioned such a drug. It took some time, but at least a decade before your sister blew everything out of the water, the serum was available. But it was not to be. At least, not until today. You, dear Kyle, get to be the test subject for my new, improved, one-hundred-percent-rate-of-apostasy system."

He beamed as though he'd just told me I'd won a prestigious award, but a buzzing filled my ears and a fog damped my mind, and for all I could tell, that was what he *had* just told me.

"I...I don't understand..."

"Oh, I think you do. You're going on that gurney for Full Conscious Dismantlement, and when you want it to stop—when, not if—then all you have to say are four simple little words. There. Is. No. God. And the pain will be gone. I'm only offering you the second prize for saying them, I'm afraid, but I have my reasons—not least my little cinematic debut to think about." He gestured to the camera, now mounted on a tripod nearby, recording everything for poor Margo.

The ice reached my stomach, freezing everything up to my Adam's apple. My arms and legs and neck grew long, so long, I teetered a million miles above my body...and my distant legs were spongy, insubstantial...

My knees struck the hard floor, my palms smacking down in front of me. I pressed my spinning head to the cold concrete and tried to breathe. Was I about to faint? *Lord I...I don't want to faint...please...* I'd wake up on that gurney...

From the rushing sensation in my head and my sharpening wits, blood was returning to where it needed to be. After a few more moments, I dragged myself up into a kneeling position, clasped my hands and responded to the situation in the only possible way. I prayed.

*Lord, I entrust myself entirely to you. Please save me...or keep me firm. Somehow, enable me to stay true to you... Please, I beg you...*

But was it even possible? Possible to hold out throughout an *entire*... What would happen if I broke? If I gasped those words, rejecting my Lord and God?

Oh, I'd surely regret them with my next breath, repent, an Act of Perfect Contrition would fill my mind...but I wouldn't *get* a next breath, would I? Hill would be waiting. Hill would see me dead or unconscious the very instant the last word left my lips. He'd make quite sure Margo could see that I'd had no time to say *Sorry, Lord, I didn't mean it, forgive me. This* was his revenge: he wasn't content to merely *kill* her brother, he wanted to *damn* her brother. Evil, evil man.

Whether I would actually be damned... Well, God was very forgiving. If I had really, truly tried my best...*maybe* not. But the very possibility would be unimaginable torment for Margo and my family. And the thought of leaving this life with the last words on my lips words of apostasy rather than words of praise... Unbearable.

There was only one thing I could do. One thing to spare Margo and save myself. Hold firm. *Somehow.*

I pressed my forehead to my clenched hands and prayed harder. *Lord, Lord, please be with me. Keep your weak servant faithful. Keep me close to you. Help me, Lord...*

"Have we finally rattled the bold Father Kyle Verrall?" Hill's mocking voice penetrated my mind. "Not *afraid*, are we?"

I dragged my eyes open and focussed on him once more. "I'm flesh and blood, with nerve endings, just like you. Of course, I'm afraid."

"Really? But won't your *God* save you?"

"Yes." I looked at the camera, not at Hill. *Hear me, Margo.* "He will. No matter what."

Hill sighed. "Still so brave. Well, we had better get started. I hear your dear sister actually *forgave* Lucas Everington, after he tortured her. Apparently, *I* exceeded her capacity. Yours too, I imagine."

"If you've read her blog over the years—which you have," I pointed out tiredly, "then you know perfectly well the only reason she didn't is because you lot left the room too suddenly. She's said she forgives you often enough since."

Hill snorted. "Like I care."

That thread of bitterness. Like he cared about *nothing*. Nothing truly *worth* caring about.

An odd surge filled my heart as I looked at him, sitting there in that chair: so old; so evil; so broken; so...alone. A warmth. A caring. A...love. I loved him. Just another poor sinner who needed my care.

I pushed up off the concrete and got to my feet. My legs still felt like sponge cake, but somehow I stood straight. I headed for Hill, not wobbling too much, and Croft raised the nonLee a fraction. But I just took Hill's hand between the two ice blocks that were my own and pressed it tightly.

"Whether you care or not," I told him, "I do forgive you. And I'm very sorry that you're sick—I'd surmise *very*—and I pray with all my heart that the Lord will heal you—and heal that poor soul of yours too."

Hill's eyes, as I looked into them, were a surprisingly pleasant shade of blue. Yes, nothing God made was *inherently* evil.

He stared back, motionless, for several long moments, then finally yanked his wrinkled old hand from mine. "You think I need your *imaginary friend* to heal me?" he sneered, more genuine emotion in his voice than I'd ever heard. "Science is all *I* need. And *that*..." He poked my chest hard with one bony finger.

Poked it right over... "You want my...*liver*?" I hazarded. Is that what he meant by 'having his reasons'?

"And I'll have your heart while I'm at it; my old ticker isn't too good these days. But absolutely no need for any superstitious nonsense, you see," he said nastily. "A simple transplant will do. Except you and I, you know, are a rather rare tissue type."

"Oh," he shook his head dismissively, "nowhere near as rare as the precious Jonathan Revan. But rare enough that this whole 'voluntary donation only' business doesn't work well for us. Easy enough in the good old days. A few extra Borderlines of our tissue type would simply fail, who might otherwise have passed. Shortage dealt with. But not now. Not after what your sister did." His tone had become truly vicious. This whole subject seemed to have rattled him.

So...Hill had seen what must have appeared the most glorious opportunity to steal what he needed while simultaneously wreaking the most horrible vengeance imaginable on my sister. Well, he'd always been cunning. And *economical*.

"We're going to need you to get on that gurney now, Kyle." Hill's voice was smooth again, faux-pleasant, that glimpse of genuine emotion locked away once more.

No more stalling. Apparently, celibate or not, I had a date with Lady Destiny. I swallowed hard. Hill's eyes watched, watched every betraying movement of my body, savouring my fear. What must it be like to be him? I couldn't really imagine it. To believe the things he believed—or to pretend, even to himself, that he did? To have done the things he'd done? How could he repent? Accept that much guilt? What would it take?

And just what could *I* do for him, now?

Oh. A familiar verse slipped into my head. *I rejoice that I can suffer on your behalf, and in my own flesh I supplement the afflictions endured by Christ, for the sake of his body, the church.*

Of course.

*Lord... Lord, I offer all the small sufferings of this last night, and all the great ones still to come, for him. For his conversion. For his salvation. I offer every second of this terrible death. For him. Let me take my chances with Your mercy; I trust in You. I offer this all for him.*

So... Oddly, I actually felt calmer now. Giving this horror a good purpose, beyond simply *not giving in*, had steadied me. From this moment on, every pain I suffered helped someone who needed it, needed it *desperately*.

*Lord, stay with me.*

I walked to the gurney. Forced myself to sit on the cold edge. The gleaming metal dazzled me. *Is this what surrender is, Lord?*

Would it be enough? Could one death, however horrific, really be enough to help Hill? Or would it still be for nothing? Nothing but Hill's revenge...

Well, one single death had *already* saved Hill's soul outright, if he would only *accept* it. One Infinitely Perfect, Utterly Innocent Life laid down for him. I couldn't match that. I could only offer my small, insignificant, sinful life in the hope that it might help Hill to accept that Ultimate Sacrifice...

"What peculiar thoughts are going through your peculiar mind, Kyle Verrall?" Hill's bemusement, when I looked at him, seemed genuine.

No doubt he hadn't actually expected me to walk to the gurney by myself. "Quite honestly, I don't think you'd want to know." Struggling inside myself for willingness, willingness to make this sacrifice with a generous heart, not merely grudgingly, I lifted my legs up onto the gurney and lay down. Closed my eyes.

*Lord, be with me.*

*Lord, will it be enough? If it is not, if despite all, he*

*continues to lock you out, what will become of him?*

A strange feeling of dread swept over me that had nothing to do with *my* predicament. An utter aloneness. A sundering. A loss so searing and absolute that the full pain of it would have obliterated my physical mind...but some merciful hand shielded me and it only brushed past. Even so, a couple of tears sprung from my eyes and trickled away.

"Dear me, not getting weepy already, are we, Kyle? We haven't even got your skin off yet."

I started and opened my eyes. Hill's chair now sat right beside the gurney, his face close to mine.

"I'm not crying for me, I'm crying for *you*, you fool!" The words flew out before I could edit or soften them.

Hill stared at me. And stared at me. And stared. It took my fuddled mind ages to realise that he was trying to figure out whether, contrary to the evidence of his eyes, I was having him on. I closed my eyes again and prayed for him. That glimpse of his soul's future had only stoked my determination. While I still had life and breath, I would do everything for this poor sinner that my Lord had granted me the grace to love. Everything.

Hands touched my limbs, adjusting their position, fastening the restraints around them. My heart sped up even more, pounding away so fiercely it *hurt.*

For all my resolve to turn this to good, I'd never been so scared in my life. Actually, it was clear I never had been scared in my life, not really.

Not on that Salperton Road as I faked my death. Not as Joe and I sat in that lorry, watching red and blue lights approaching. Not when I stepped foot on EuroBloc soil with a dog collar around my neck the very first time for the Liberations. Not as held my sister's hand and waited for the EuroArmy to burst into the Citadel.

Nor on that day during the drought when I'd been limping morosely along after crashing my bicycle on route to the neighbouring village—twisting my ankle and busting my tyre—and I suddenly heard chuckles and cackles circling me in the surrounding grass and realised a pack of hyenas were sizing me up for their dinner.

No, I'd never been scared before. Just slightly nervous. Now I was scared.

Hands were cutting my clothes away; inserting tubes and needles into various parts of me to keep me alive and sanitary throughout the 'procedure'. I knew all the details from seminary, but I tried to turn my mind to the Lord instead. Knowing what they were doing right now wasn't important. Distracting myself from the fact that the Menace, alas, still stood there, almost certainly ogling me, was. Stupid thing to worry about, in the circumstances, but my cheeks grew hotter and hotter as I lay so helplessly exposed.

When they cut my Angelic Warfare Confraternity cord from around my waist and whipped it away, I felt three times as naked. I hadn't taken that off since the last one fell to pieces. Come to think, a new day had dawned, hadn't it? Reciting the daily confraternity prayers for chastity helped keep my mind off things for a few minutes.

"Well, I think they're nearly ready, Kyle." Hill's voice. "Are you going to smile for the camera? Say a few brave words for your sister? I promise not to cut them out. You'll give the lie to them soon enough, after all."

What could I say to Margo? To my poor, poor sister who'd already suffered such heartbreak recently? I wasn't going to say, *this isn't your fault*, because that ought to be so beggaringly obvious I didn't even want to dignify it with words. Perhaps I should just say nothing. Refuse to play along with Hill's sick games.

No. He might well leave it in. I drew a few steadying breaths, fighting for calm. Opened my eyes. Looked at the camera.

"Margo, I love you," I said softly. "Mum, Dad, I love you. Bane, Luc, Polly, Javi, Lizzie, Joey, I love you. Everyone else, I love you too. I even love Mr Hill, here, and Major Wallis and Jonas and Croft and these other people whose names I don't know. I forgive them for what they are about to do and so must you. And I forbid any of you to worry about me, not one iota. My life and soul belong to the Lord—He alone will decide my fate and there is nothing Mr Hill can do to thwart *Him*." The mere thought brought a slight snort of laughter from me.

Then I focussed on the camera again, sobering. "Well... goodbye, then. I'll see you all again—in the Lord's time. I love you..." I closed my eyes, turned my head away. I was done. A few moments could never be enough for all I wanted to say, so I wouldn't babble. I wouldn't speak to the camera again, either. I'd *wanted to*, this time, but I wouldn't play along with Hill any further.

All the same...my words had stirred another deep, deep thankfulness in my heart. That Hill had *me*. Not Bane—again. Not Mum or Dad. Not—and I could barely even bring myself to think of it—one of the children. *Thank you, Lord.* This was better. It would be horrible for Margo, for them all, no mistake, but...better than *that*.

"Well, I think it's time to get started." Hill's voice remained calm, oozing confidence that I'd eat every word before the end.

*Lord, please prove him wrong. Please...*

I couldn't help peeping from below my lashes as hands touched my arm again. The Dismantler was attaching a tube to a cannula needle they'd already inserted and taped in place. Lifting the camera from the tripod, Jonas quartered the room, taking would-be artistic close-ups of the trays of instruments and other equipment.

The Dismantler, now holding a syringe, located a vein on my opposite arm.

Hill leant close and smiled—if such a cold and evil expression deserved to be called a smile. "Just my little insurance policy, Kyle." His voice was so soft and self-satisfied I hardly caught the words.

I watched as the pale blue liquid disappeared into me. Insurance policy? What was that supposed to mean? I didn't feel anything other than the sharp sting of the needle and the pressure-pain as the stuff went in. But the Dismantler already wielded another syringe, full of grey fluid. He stuck this needle into the cannula. "Inserting prototype serum now, sir."

*Yes, it* was *a prototype. How well tested was it? Perhaps it would just kill me. Please, Lord?*

A quick death wouldn't help Hill, though. The longer I stayed conscious, the better...from that point of view. I quelled a shudder, just. Actually...I tried to move my hand... Ah. No more shuddering from me. I couldn't really move anything. Except my eyelids and, presumably, my tongue and vocal chords.

"The other improved thing about this serum, Kyle," Hill told me, as though partially reading my mind, "is that it contains a highly effective mix of stimulants. You'll remain conscious for far, far more of the process than with the old paralytic. Wonderful, hmm?"

My stomach churned more icily than ever. Terrible news, so far as holding out went. Great news for Hill—as long as I actually *could* hold out—though not in the way he thought. I closed my eyes tight again and retreated as close to the Lord as I could. *Let me hide myself in your robe. Let me cling to you like a frightened child. For that is all I am...*

"You said you wanted to direct the sequence, sir?" The Dismantler's voice again.

"Yes. Start with the skin as usual. Just legs and abdomen for now." Hill's voice moved as though he'd turned back to me. "I'm sure your sister has told you how pleasant these early stages are."

*Ignore him, Kyle.*

*Lord, preserve me. Lord, save your servant.*

*No, remember your training, Kyle.* All these disjointed prayers were no good. I needed to get settled into something familiar and repetitive. Well, that wasn't hard.

*...Holy Mary, Mother of God, pray for us sinners now and at the hour of...*

Pain seared across my thigh, shocking pain, startling as a slap in the face, like touching an electric fence, only long and drawn out. Like nothing I'd ever suffered before. And that was just one pass of the skin peeler... *Oh Lord, help me!*

*...Pray for us sinners...*

Pain

*...Pray for us sinners...*

Pain

*...Pray for us sinners...*

The strokes seemed to come so rapidly I could hardly breathe; I was gasping, gasping as though the skin peeler was stripping the oxygen from the room, and I fought to ignore it all and focus on praying, praying, praying, *Lord, Lord, Lord, I'm yours, I'm yours, I'm yours...*

Eventually I managed to pick up my rosary again. Time lost all meaning. There was only the prayer and the pain.

At some point—realisation filtered dimly into my mind—no new pain-strokes had struck for...for... Well, they'd stopped coming. Just the fiery agony that covered my legs, burning on and on. A voice murmured in my ear: "Enjoying yourself, Kyle?"

I'd a vague feeling I shouldn't reply, but that was okay. The thought of mustering words was...

I went back to praying. Who was I praying for?

"You, go and make me a cup of tea. Yes, *now*."

Oh, for the voice. For Hill. And for me. I couldn't help praying for me too. That I might hold firm...

The pain-strokes began again, across my stomach, creeping up towards my ribcage. I could feel tears of pain oozing from my eyes and trickling down into my hair. Clearly my tear ducts weren't paralysed either.

"Anything you want to say, Kyle? Any more motivational words for your dear sister?"

Yes, the camera...I should stop crying, I really should. It made my suffering too obvious. But *I* wasn't crying, my body was. I couldn't control it.

"What next, sir? It's usually the eyes..."

My heart clenched up in instinctive dread, for all I'd been keeping my eyes firmly closed anyway.

"No, we'll save those for later. It will make a better film. Where is the *milk*, you fool? Let's see. He does love his football, doesn't he? Take a few muscles out of one of his knees."

"A few *muscles*? But...transplanting muscles back into knees is a really tricky business, almost impossible. Much better to just take the whole joint, intact... Oh. Right. Okay. I'll just take a few out."

Football? I'd never felt less worried about football in my life. Still, Hill was a cruel blighter, no mistake.

How *long* was this stage going to take, done like this? My

knee tingled in fearful anticipation, dread knotting up my insides.

But it didn't matter how long it took, did it? Every minute helped Hill more...


*MARGO*
*Beep-beep-beep-beep...*

My alarm. Fighting sluggishly up out of sleep, I got my reaching hand tangled in the sheets, extricated it and finally managed to shut the sound off. Mumbled, "Sorry, Bane."

Silence.

"Bane?" I turned my head. Huh. No Bane. Up already? Or...hmm. I had a double memory from last night, of him kissing me and telling me to go to sleep. But the second one? *I've got to go to HQ, love; I'll see you in the morning.* Or something like that.

Well. Hardly the first time. He got called in to work at all hours to consult on little problems occurring in far-flung corners of the world. Hopefully he was back already. I was quite capable of getting everyone up and to daily Mass more or less on time—*I was!*—but another pair of hands certainly did help.

By the time I'd dressed and woken Polly, Javi, Lizzie, and Joey, and asked Luc—being the oldest *and* an early bird—to help Javi get ready as soon as he'd finished his rosary, it was clear that Bane was still out. Oh joy. Last night's brief burst of energy was just a memory.

"Polly, get out of bed," I yelled at the wall, trying to run a brush through Joey's wispy two-year-old hair.

"How d'you know I'm still in bed?" came the ear-piercing reply from eight-year-old lungs. "You're in the next room—you can't see me!"

"Well, you *are*, aren't you?"

I listened hopefully for the thud that would accompany Polly pouring herself out from under the covers.

Nothing.

*O Lord, only you can get us all to Mass on time today!*

KYLE

...*Pray for us sinners...*

...*Pray for us sinners...*

...*Pray for us sinners...*

"That's the third muscle out. Should I harvest the rest?"

Only when I smelt the incongruous sweetness of breath mints did I register the coppery smell that had filled my nose for...for too long. Blood. I sensed Hill's face close to mine. Studying me?

"I don't think we'll bother just now. We don't seem to be making much impact on dear Kyle. Not so much as a scream. Or even a groan. Ah, there you are—*get* me a biscuit, how many times do I have to tell you? Let us see. Take his... Yes. Take his thumb and forefinger. From both hands."

*No!* My heart felt like it shuddered in shock. *No, don't take those! Please! How will I say Mass?*

I fought to control my foolish reaction. They were going to kill me. I'd never say Mass again anyway. And my priesthood was an indelible mark embedded in my soul—no scalpel could remove it. But my insides quivered in misery, and my throat constricted with incipient sobs. I swallowed hard, fighting them back, but the next moment Hill's finger was stroking my Adam's apple.

"Not quite so happy now, are we, Kyle? Well, you know how to stop it. Four little words, that's all."

*Why would I say four little words that would lead directly to my death and possible damnation out of fear of never being able to say Mass again? I can't say Mass dead, let alone damned.* But I kept my mouth shut and my eyes shut too.

"Take the joints and the corresponding bones from his hands," Hill was instructing. "Remove it all."

...*Pray for us sinners...*

Pains began in my left hand... Each new one began to seem less—the only mercy of the accumulation—compared to the sum of the whole. My knee, my legs, my abdomen, they were all vying for my attention. *Lord, save Hill...*

...*Pray for us sinners...*

"Wait..." Hill's voice again. "Crush each bone before you

draw it out. Make a thorough job of it."

"But then I'll need tweezers...it'll take ages... Right. Right. As you wish, sir."

*Lord, help me...*

I tried to return to my rosary, but the pain that struck next was unlike anything that had come before. My body actually jerked slightly against the restraints, then flopped, twice as limply, as though its last shred of muscle strength had been spent.

Lesser pains followed and I struggled to orientate my mind, to reach my rosary again...

*PAIN*

It hit again. No movement from my captive body, this time, but a low, thin sound came from somewhere under my chin, involuntary, unstoppable...

"Well, a moan is something, I suppose." The voice sounded cross, so I prayed for it some more.

Or tried. Praying was becoming so hard. Thinking was becoming hard. A fog of pain hid all, smothered all... I could barely remember who I was, or what I was doing.

*...Hill...save Hill...*

"Four little words, Kyle..."

Kyle...that's who I was...

"...and the pain will go away..."

Oh God, I wanted the pain to go away, I wanted it so much... But...*God...*

"There. Is. No. God. That's all you have to say..."

The voice wanted me to deny God. But God was...*everything*... I mustn't. I knew I mustn't...

*PAIN*

A strangled scream wrenched from me. *Lord, let me die, please...please!*

*I can't do any more for Hill, I can't! Just take me, please! Somehow...*

But my mind cleared a little—unhelpfully—and told me that I wouldn't die any time soon, not from losing the little things I'd lost so far. I was...hours...from death. Hours and hours.

Despair choked me...

*PAIN*

*Aaah...* They hadn't even moved to my second hand yet... Hadn't even...all the rest...

*I can't, Lord...I can't...I can't bear this...I'm not strong enough, I'm not...*

God forgive me, Hill was right. It wasn't a question of *if.* Only *when.*


## MARGO

Thank the Lord—or thanks *to* the Lord!—we'd all filed into our usual pew in Saint Peter's just before the bell had rung to signal the start of Mass. With Joey in my lap and Lizzie and Polly wriggling on either side, Mass hadn't exactly been a prayerful experience—not in the traditional understanding of the word—but at least Javi had sat quietly beside Luc, sharing his missal and following his older brother's finger with his usual placid interest.

Javi, our third oldest after Luc and Polly, didn't read as well as Luc had at seven, but he was coming on. Luc was eleven now—how was that even possible?—and still an advanced reader. He'd already worked his way through the letters of Saint Pier Giorgio, several books by Saint Thomas More, along with all the major works by Saint Maximilian Kolbe, and had just started reading the Catechism. The full-length version. Bane had tried to make a bet with Jon over whether Luc would read the *Summa Theologica* before he was fifteen, but Jon refused to take it.

"Lizzie, stop that..."

But, thank goodness, with a final prayer request for a priest in Africa who'd been kidnapped, Mass was over. I offered up a hasty, distracted prayer for this unfortunate cleric—I mean, how many priests got kidnapped in *Africa?*—and started gathering up children. Time to march this lot home for breakfast. And if Bane didn't show his face soon, I'd have to call Eduardo and demand my husband back! Bane was supposed to be off-duty today, and I had a full schedule.

Leading and carrying my precious exhaustion-inducers—and trailing their 'Uncle' Georg, my duty bodyguard, who determinedly ignored them—I headed back towards the doorway into the rest of Vatican State. Where I met...

"Jon! I thought you were supposed to be on your way to Kazakhstan for your conference?" The tall, russet-haired priest was the last person I expected to see that morning.

"I don't need to go right yet. I can take a later boat."

"Oh." His eyes looked through me, as ever, and his face was pretty expressionless, but I read tension in the lines on his brow. "Everything okay?"

"Umm. Eduardo wants you to pop down and see him, though. Uh, just you." He waved towards the noisy horde around me.

"Ah. Well, is it urgent? Because Bane had to go to work and it's just me. Could you look after them for half an hour?"

"Actually...I was going to head back down to HQ with you." His fingers clenched around his white cane, tight and pale.

"You were?" A faint ominous prickle—rarely experienced these days—began down the back of my spine. Jon was... much tenser than I'd originally realised, actually. Putting a good face on, but...something was far wrong.

"Bane!" I gasped.

"He's fine." His hand reached reassuringly for my arm, though I was too far away. "Quite alright. Why don't you, uh, send the kids to...hmm..."

"Jane?"

Beside me, Georg Friedrich gave his head a tiny shake. Jane was on duty. "Well, Unicorn, then?" Another shake. Okay, something was far wrong indeed if Eduardo had a husband and wife on duty together. Anxiety churned leadenly in my stomach. Exactly what was going down? That involved *me*?

The penny dropped, leaden and ice-cold. "Kyle!"

They hadn't said an *African* priest, but...a priest in Africa.

Jon's lip twisted slightly. No denial this time, but he gave his head a tiny, warning tilt towards the children.

"What *about* Uncle Kyle?" Luc was already demanding. Sensing the tension.

"Nothing, Luc. Take your brothers and sisters up to Aunty Calla and ask her to give you some breakfast, would you?"

"Mummy! I can't just knock on Aunty Calla's door and

demand she feed us!"

The children stared up at us. Polly's face mirrored Luc's anxiety, Javi looked curious, Lizzie just smiled at the thought of breakfast with Aunty Calla, while Joey went right on sucking his thumb.

"You don't have to demand, just go along and ask if it's alright if you play there for a little while and when she asks if you've had breakfast... No, no, just tell her Uncle Georg sent you for breakfast, okay? *Go on*..."

Their Uncle Georg gave the tiniest nod. Luc's notion of good manners satisfied by this, he took Joey from me and herded the other three away. But he shot an unhappy look back over his shoulder.

"It's Kyle, isn't it?" I turned to Jon as soon as they were out of earshot. "Who took him? Where is he?"

Jon spread his hands helplessly. "I think for once they're rather clueless down in HQ, I'm afraid. Eduardo certainly had no idea this was in the air."

I grabbed his arm and towed him with me, heading off at a near-run. "Why didn't Bane *wake me*?"

"What, having you worried *and* tired would help in some way?"

Hitting priests was a big no-no, however old a friend they might be, so I didn't slap him. I just towed him even faster.


### KYLE

My left hand was a burning mess of agony. My breathing was noisy, so noisy, gasping, wheezing whoops too closely related to sobs. Utter despair enveloped me. What was the point bearing any more of this? Hill was done for. And so was I. Because I couldn't hold out until the end. I simply couldn't...

"You can't hold out, Kyle..." The devil whispered in my ear... "You can't hold out, so why not give in now. Make it easy for yourself. Let the pain go..."

Why not? How had I ever thought I could be strong enough? Frail, sinful me?

"There is no shame in accepting the inevitable. No one

could hold out, Kyle. *No one.*"

No one... Certainly not me...

The hands touched my right thumb. I screamed and tried to buck against the restraints, but barely twitched. My breathing came fast, faster, too fast, it was about to begin again, that terrible, terrible pain, that desecration of my consecrated hands, that destruction, that agony...

"No one could hold out. Let go, Kyle. Just say the words. You don't have to *mean* them..."

No one...

No one?

That...wasn't true. Was it? *Someone* had suffered a death as bad as this...worse. And held resolute to the end. To save me. Frail, sinful me.

I couldn't hold firm. I wasn't strong enough.

But He was.

*Lord, I am yours. I am yours.*

I surrendered. I dropped barriers I'd not known I had, I opened doors I hadn't known I kept closed, I yielded parts of me I'd not realised I held back. I gave every fibre and cell and particle and thought and memory to Him.

He filled me. He enveloped every fibre and cell and particle and thought and memory with Himself. He'd wanted to do this since...forever. But He needed me to let Him in.

Pure joy permeated my entire body, expanded my mind. I'd never felt such peace, such love, such awe...yet even as I relaxed in His embrace, I knew this for a mere pinprick, a mere fraction, of what I would feel when I entered His presence face-to-face. Such a longing gripped my swelling heart that again I struggled to breathe.

Or perhaps that was the pain. The Dismantler worked on my right hand now. I could still feel it, all that pain piled upon pain, but it just didn't seem to...matter. If the only way to keep this awareness of my Lord was to endure *ten times* this agony, I'd have accepted unhesitatingly.

I floated on a sea of Love, drowned in it, deliriously. *Why had I shut Him out so much for so long? What a fool...* I laughed at myself, and it came from my half-paralysed throat as a rattling cackle.

The whispering in my ear stopped abruptly. Yes, Hill, Hill was there. I opened my eyes—or rather, winched my eyelids up—there he was. Frowning at me. *Yes, Mr Hill, I laughed. I am so happy right now you just wouldn't believe it, and I simply cannot wait to die, but not for the reason you think!*

The grey concrete room seemed Technicolor, as though I'd turned into a mantis shrimp and suddenly had sixteen colour-discerning cones in my eyes instead of a mere three. Hues overwhelmed me, beauty overwhelmed me, and Hill... Confused, selfish, evil old man he might be, but his soul remained beautiful with potential, un-actualised but still waiting, waiting for one drop of the Spirit to seep in and let it bloom...

My puny love for him was swallowed up by a roaring torrent of LOVE—pure, unadulterated—filling my heart to bursting. *Lord, please, save him, I beg You, don't let him be lost, my beloved brother, Your beloved child...*

"Care to share the joke?" Hill asked.

The Dismantler stared at me as well; they all stared at me. Could they see Him shining in my eyes? Or merely joy?

Well, I had something terribly, terribly important to tell them. "Do you kn..." Okay, speaking was...possible, but incredibly difficult. It came out a feeble, mumbling rasp. I dumped the lengthy, eloquent homily forming in my mind—way over the heads of this particular congregation, anyway—and simplified: "God...loves...you. Really loves...all of you. So do...I... And He...wants you...to love Him..." I trailed off in physical exhaustion, though mentally and spiritually I'd never felt so energised in my life.

"He's still thinking about *God?*" Wallis. "I always assumed they'd forgotten all about that nonsense by this point!"

"He's lost his marbles!" Jonas.

"He's a flaming priest!" exploded Hill. "He didn't have any marbles to start with! Dismantler, carry on!"

I tried to smile at Hill, at Croft, still hovering behind him, at Jonas, at the Dismantler, but my mouth muscles weren't working terribly well. In the interests—or at least the spirit—of modesty, I ignored Wallis. Letting my eyelids close again, I floated contentedly with the Lord as they continued to rip apart my other hand. My awe at God's awesomeness swelled and swelled inside me, until I just had to let it out. I started to sing a *Te Deum*.

"*We praise you, O God...*" The worst, most quavering, most stumbling, gasping, *Te Deum* I'd ever sung, but the most...appreciated? *Yes*.

"*...The white-robed army who gave their lives for Christ, all sing your praises...*"

"This is ridiculous," snarled Hill. "Dismantler, if you've slipped him a painkiller I will put *you* on this gurney, do you understand?"

Terrified spluttering from the Dismantler...

I opened my eyes again. "It...*does* really...*really*...hurt," I assured Hill as earnestly as I could. "Don't...be angry...with... him..."

"Then *why* are you *smiling and laughing and singing* all of a sudden?"

"Because God...is good...all the time!"

"You think God is good *now*? Lying there? You were screaming in agony a moment ago, and there's plenty more of that coming up, I assure you."

"He is...glorious. He is...love itself! He loves...you. Please repent...Mr Hill...please do..."

"Argh!" Hill threw his hands in the air in frustration. "Perhaps the old paralytic had its good points after all! Dismantler, back to work. Thumb and forefinger, come on, finish off..."

I let my unenergetic eyelids close again and nestled in Love, letting them get on with it.

"*... You overcame Death's power, and opened the Father's kingdom to all those who believe in You...*"

My body wasn't important, I understood that now. The Lord would give it back to me one day, whole and undamaged, and until then my soul would be safe—to say nothing of radiantly, indescribably happy—in His keeping. There was no need to worry. About anything, anything at all...

"What next, sir?"

Silence. "Take a few toes. If that doesn't make any impact on him, we'll try the big guns. Or rather, the big gun. Even a priest's got to get a little upset about that."

That horrible, excited titter came from the Menace. Was she enjoying this? From what Margo had told me about her, probably. Whereas, Hill? His satisfaction came from the revenge and from a job well done—this was his profession, after all. Interrogation. Changing people's minds. 'Re-educating' them. *Breaking them.* He only enjoyed watching me suffer because my suffering hurt Margo. Because it got him what he wanted. It almost seemed worse, in a way.

Someone who gave in to their own dark and twisted desires always seemed worthy of pity, while the person who coldly did evil purely for their own gain... Surely a much more calculated, conscious sin? Still, I offered up another prayer for Wallis, as well as yet another for Hill.

The dismantler started on my big toe. Same leg he'd stolen the muscles from. It didn't feel very nice. But the Lord was still with me—oh, how He was with me—so it was easy to bear. In fact, my jubilant mind began soaring to the music of a favourite classic worship song. How well it expressed what I felt now:

*You lead me up above the clouds,*
*To the unseen mountain's peak*
*There in the mist I meet with You*
*Give You my heart to keep...*

Huh, it turned out I could still hum. Badly, but I could. Easier than singing...

*I fix my gaze on You as the storms roll in,*
*Your breath strips away black clouds of sin,*
*On the bare mountaintop, I cling to You,*
*You hold me tight in Your arms and never let go...*

"If one of you did slip him morphine, I mean it, you are *dead*..."

"I don't know what's the matter with him, sir, but he *hasn't* had anything, I *swear*... I mean, you would have seen! It would be on the *video!*"

"Well, you can be sure I'm going to check. This is turning into a *farce.*"

*Lord, I long to stay with you upon the heights*
*Dwell forever on Your highest peak,*
*Yet lead me deep down into the depths,*
*Where You will, I'll go, high or low,*

*In places dark my heart will grow
Ever closer, one with You,
My Saviour and my God...*

"Fine, leave those toes. It's time for something even he can't ignore."

"Yes, sir." The Dismantler sounded relieved, clearly confident things would proceed as expected from here on.

*They're not thinking this through, are they? They've made it quite clear they're going to kill me, so what does it matter what order they do it all in? I'll never miss any of it once I'm dead.*

All the same, certain parts of my anatomy would have clenched up in helpless anticipation if I'd had enough muscle control. *Lord, you are with me. Let them do what they will.*

I sensed the dismantler leaning over me again but kept my eyes closed. Seeing would only make things worse. They'd trained us well...

"Are you keeping an eye on his heart readings?" Hill's voice again. "They don't look too sharp to me."

A pause. Dismantler checking the monitors...

"He's okay, sir. It's almost time for the next dose of serum, that's all. Now, if we could only get Sorting up and running again, we'd have a machine to take care of all that."

"Dream on. The High Committee dance to his sister's tune these days and no likely end in sight."

A sigh from the dismantler as he turned back to me...

*Clang*...confused sounds—shouting, scuffing, clattering—several thuds. An odd silence...no, the sound of heavy breathing. All very strange.

I'd just started to consider cranking my eyes open again when strong hands seized my shoulders—but very gently—and a familiar but choked voice called my name, speaking in a language that struck strange—but sweet—against my ears after all the Esperanto. *Latin.*

"Kyle? Kyle, bro, talk to me, come on..."

I got my eyes open and focussed as quickly as I could. "Bane! It's lovely...to see...you. Wasn't expecting...you..."

"You've got yourself kidnapped by the most evil man alive and you weren't *expecting* me? You wound me, bro."

But as his brown eyes darted down the length of me, then back up to my face, his usual dark gold skin tone faded to a washed out grey. "Oh Kyle, we got here as fast as we—"

He sounded so anguished I wanted to comfort him, only— "Hill! Where's Hill?"

"He can't hurt you anymore, you're safe—"

"No, no...is he...*alright?* You mustn't...shoot him. Bad heart! You...didn't? *Did you?*" Horror gripped me at the thought of Hill dead on the floor, and his soul... His *soul*...

Bane's expression turned sour. "A chance would've been a fine thing." He sounded wistful. "Old buzzard didn't give us one. Stuck his hands up in the air so fast."

"Sure? You mustn't...hurt him."

Brow wrinkling, Bane stepped back and to the side, gesturing reassuringly.

Ah... My panic eased. Hill sat there in his chair, only now he had his hands up, and a guy in commando gear held a nonLee trained on him. One of Bane's squad, no doubt. Two guys had Croft rammed against a wall as they fastened restraints onto his wrists—I couldn't see Jonas or the Menace, so they were probably flat on the floor, unconscious. The dismantling team huddled nervously in a corner, covered by several more of Bane's men.

Something about it worried me, but the thought wouldn't coalesce.

*How on earth had they even...* No, thinking was too hard. I was just going to lie quietly with the Lord. He could take me if he wanted or leave me here for poor Bane to try to put back together. Still, despite my stupendous longing for that total union, right now, I needed to stay here. Stay with Hill. Save him...

Another Vatican Secret Service agent—that was the department my brother-in-law's operations officially came under—had just plonked a large first aid kit down on a nearby trolley, his face as ghastly as Bane's. Yes, a mite underequipped—and probably undertrained—for this, unfortunate man.

"Let's grab the...parts...and get him straight to hospital," said the medic. "He needs proper surgeons."

"Yes, but for pity's sake give him some morphine!"

"Love to," the medic was already opening his bag, "but he might've had some already. He seems pretty with-it, and an overdose or a strange cocktail of drugs could kill him."

Bane swung back to me, swiping a distracted hand through his short matt black hair. "True... Kyle, mate, have you had morphine?"

"Morphine?" I murmured. "That would rather...defeat the point...right?"

"Well, what have they given you?"

"Something grey..." Speaking was getting harder and harder. Exhaustion welled up from the depths of my belly, swallowing every part of me. Everything echoed strangely in my ears. I couldn't get a proper breath.

I was dimly aware of Bane, swinging around to Hill, pointing a nonLee, his voice gone menacing. "What's he had?"

Hill looking back coldly. Saying nothing.

"Listen, you!" snapped Bane, switching to Esperanto to give Hill no excuse not to answer. "Despite years of trying, I am *not* as nice as my wife, understand? And even leaving past history aside, may I remind you that is my brother-in-law you've been torturing. Trust me when I say I would simply *love* to shoot you a couple of times with this thing and see what it does to that weak heart of yours..."

"Bane...no..." I whispered.

"...so I suggest you tell me right now *exactly* what you've given him!"

Hill smirked. "Nice bluff, Bane—you really should be on the stage—but I'm not buying it. Dear Kyle just told you—and I'm confirming it now, in case you'd any doubts—that I have a rather dicky ticker. I also have my hands up and am behaving myself completely, so there's simply no way you're going to pull that trigger. You don't want another death on your conscience, not even mine."

"I *really* hate you!" Bane muttered under his breath.

Anxiety flooded me at that...that ugly word. "Bane..." I protested weakly, catching his attention this time. "Bane, you mustn't... Mustn't *hate*..."

"Kyle, *seriously*? Take care of my soul later, for pity's sake!" Bane swung to face the dismantling staff this time.

"So, you lot. Any of you fancy a reduced sentence for being cooperative?"

Their eyes shifted from Hill to Bane a few times, clearly weighing up the pros and cons. Then one of the assistants spoke up. "He hasn't had morphine. Mr Hill accused us of giving him some, because he was singing away so happily, but he really hasn't had any."

"Singing?" The VSS medic looked flabbergasted.

So did Bane. "Kyle, bro, you were singing? What are you on?"

I managed to smile at him, just slightly, despite the dark shadows crowding my vision. "Holy Spirit," I whispered. "Jus'...Holy...Spirit..."

"I don't like his vitals," said the medic. "We've got to do *something*..."

"He was due his next dose of the serum," said the cooperative assistant. "It's full of stimulants. Without it, his body's going to crash into shock, hard and fast. I'd say he's starting to go."

"Look, let's forget the morphine," said the medic. "He's going to pass out soon. I'll do what I can, but let's just get him to hospital ASAP. They can check what's in his blood and dose him accordingly."

*Hospital...* That niggling worry solidified. "*Bane!*" He reappeared at once. "Wallis! Medical...condition. *Bracelet...*"

Bane squeezed my shoulder gently. "Calm down, Kyle. We checked it. Diabetes. So the nonLee won't have hurt her. Just relax, okay?"

The room was swaying. The gurney was swaying. I still couldn't breathe, and I was so cold, so so *cold*... The medic bent over me, doing things, while Bane took a few MedPacks from the cooler and transferred them to portable freezer units.

"Right, and where are his fingers and thumbs?" Bane's voice, coming from a long way away.

Silence.

"Well, where are they?"

The dismantling team's frightened faces swam in my vision.

*"Tell me where they are!"*

"Sir?" The medic's voice; uneasy, queasy. "I think I've... found them. What's...left of them."

"Argh, no! Do you think they can...put them back together?" Incredulous silence from both medic and dismantlers. "Right. Stupid question. Argh! Alright, let's get him out of here. You three, with us; we're going on ahead. You six, bring Hill and the others—and that insulin."

*Bring*...no... "Bane..." The room had gone very dark indeed. I could hardly make out Bane's face as he leant over me. "Bane...keep...Hill...must...keep...Hill...with...me... *Have...to*..."

He might've been frowning, but it was too dark to be sure. "What do you mean, *have to*? Is there...some kind of booby trap, or something?"

"Or...something. Promise... *Promise, Bane? Please...*"

"Alright, alright, I promise. Hill stays with you. Just calm down, okay? You're safe now..."

*I was safe before*... I meant to whisper it, but I'd misplaced my mouth...then the darkness swallowed up everything...

...except Him.


...Blazing sun...blue sky...bumping...

...jolting...jarring...pain...an engine...intense, un-cooled vehicle-interior heat on my skin...but so cold...so cold...

...corridors...anxious faces, dark against light green gowns...white habits and veils...faces...faces...faces...lights... so bright...something pressed over my mouth and nose...strange air...all swimming, blurring...

...dim noises...voices...beeping...creaking...gentle hands...

...Quietness. Well, gentle beeping, nothing more... But, no. Birdsong. A familiar wild chorus from...somewhere.

A dim ache enveloped me, along with a great sense of well-being. Not the well-being He brought...that...was still there as well. Fainter. But still He cradled me. *Oh Lord*... My heart expanded in love...then crashed earthwards. Bitterest disappointment gripped me, with that awful realisation. I was earth-bound still. Alive. So far from Him.

If so, that was His will. Something important... There was a reason why, and it was important... I struggled to tame my reaction, to console myself, resign myself, before I broke down and bawled.

Yes, I didn't want to do that. I'd scare the...nurses? Was I in hospital? The beeping said so. And the smell of disinfectant, tingling in my nostrils. Dim memories crowded in, sharpening rapidly...of pain, injury...the Lord holding me... Yes, I'd been hurt. I must be in hospital.

Hurt... *Hill!*

My eyes tried to fly open... *Okay, patience, Kyle.*

I inched my lids up, a fraction of a millimetre at a time. The pillow tilted my head just enough for me to see... A small, light room. A big bay window taking up much of the longer wall. Door across from it. Dark blue privacy curtains currently drawn almost all the way back—the same for the bed on the other side of the window—the only other bed, standard hospital equipment beside both—a two-bed room. And, was it? Snow white hair, lined face... *Yes!*

Reginald Hill lay in that other bed. Hard to see from this angle, but...asleep? Were there...? Yes, two sets of gentle beeps pierced the room's early morning quiet. Hill lived. As did I, like it or not. I relaxed again, my head snug in the pillows.

"K...Kyle?"

My eyes moved much faster than my head as it tried to turn towards that dear voice. "Margo! What...what are you doing here?"

My sister smiled—bravely? "Bane said you didn't need *him* anymore, you needed your sister. He went home to look after the children, so I could come."

"I'm so pleased to see you." I smiled back at her, trying to share some of the radiant happiness that still choked me. Yes, being dead would have upset so many people I loved. Maybe this wasn't so bad. I'd believe it if I repeated it to myself often enough, no doubt.

She smiled at me again, but the smile wobbled. She swallowed anxiously, her green eyes remaining fixed on my face. Why so tense?

Oh. Some of those memories coalesced, forming the answer. *That.*

Steeling myself, I raised an aching, leaden yet too-light hand. Looked.

Despite knowing what I would see, the sight hit like a fist to the stomach, a jarring, wind-ing disorientation of not-rightness.

Half my hand was just...not there. Up to my middle finger and down to halfway across my wrist, everything was gone. Bandages swaddled my palm and wrist but couldn't hide how much was missing.

I dragged my left hand up...yes. The same.

They simply looked so...odd. So...wrong.

I flexed the three fingers on my right hand. The ache intensified slightly but not too much. Ah...a needle ran from a cannula in my left wrist to what I easily recognised from all my visits to hospitalised parishioners as a morphine machine. That's where the non-Divine sense of well-being came from.

My eyes returned, as though magnetised, to my hands. To what remained of them.

*How can I say Mass, now?*

A tiny noise escaped my sister, like a smothered sob. Oh. Yes, I wanted to make her feel better, didn't I? I'd been staring at my hands for far too long.

I turned my head back to her—moving things was getting easier with practise—and smiled again. "Look, Margo!" I wiggled all six fingers at her. "I've still got three fingers on each hand. Isn't God good?" He was. And most people got through their entire lives without ever saying Mass. To have said Mass even once was an honour of...divine...proportions. *So don't whine, Kyle.*

Margo mustered a shaky smile. "Yes, Kyle, God is good."

The faintest of snorts from the bed opposite—if Hill had been asleep, he'd woken up when we started talking.

"You're...you're alive, anyway." Margo's voice still trembled. "Sounds like it was quite a close-run thing."

I stared at the clean white ceiling as my slowly-moving brain caught up with things. Bane had come. Rescued me.

Brought me to this hospital. My gaze shifted to the wide window. Sunlight spilled in, warming my bed on the left side of the window, not reaching Hill's, over there on the right. I was still in Africa. I knew that from the singing birds and the view outside the window—the outskirts of a town with distant savannah beyond—and my dim memories of the doctors and nurses leaning over me. But...

"How did Bane find me? How did anyone even know I was missing? I mean, so *soon.*"

Margo looked relieved, as though she expected me to burst into tears and start sobbing for my missing body parts and felt I'd handed her a brief reprieve. Hmm. I peeped down towards my feet, but sheet and blanket were raised up on a frame to keep them off my skinned areas and I couldn't see if both my big toes were present and correct. Ah well. If it only did Hill some good, I didn't care. *Well...* I could bear it, anyway.

"They found out very quickly, actually. Someone went to get you for a sick call shortly after midnight. No sign of you in the presbytery, but in the church, although the lights had been switched off and the doors closed, he found the tabernacle wide open and candles burnt down. Well, he knew you would never, ever leave the tabernacle unlocked willingly, so he dashed all around in a panic, afraid you'd been taken ill and collapsed somewhere, but nothing.

"Despite the closed door, he then thought an animal must somehow have got in and dragged you off. So he fetched the village's best tracker out of his bed. The tracker scoured the church and all around it and the presbytery too, and concluded that the beasts that had dragged the parish priest away were two-legged, at least two in number, and had come and gone in a very expensive, unfamiliar vehicle. At which point they got onto Eduardo as fast as they could."

A faint smile twisted my lips. The irony! The very sick call I'd prayed so hard to be spared had saved my life!

Margo wound a strand of her long brown hair around her hands as she continued. "Eduardo had nothing to go on other than what the tracker could tell him—sounds like he was ripping what's left of his hair out or would have been if he was one to get in a tizz. Bane set off for the African continent with his team, post haste—but had no idea where to go upon arrival. In fact, by the time anyone actually bothered to tell *me* about all this, they were still pretty clueless."

Margo's lips tightened, as though in memory of several very bleak hours. "But finally our prayers were answered and your location just fell into our lap from heaven. Well, via a far more unsavoury source, but thank God, all the same. Eduardo, wonderful man, had actually traced the vehicle fifty kilometres or so by that point, but it was slow work and..." Her eyes flicked down me, then jumped back to my face. "...clearly there wasn't any time to waste."

"What source?"

Margo finally smiled, slightly. "Mr Hill should have been nicer to his subordinates. Or maybe she was always hoping to fund her retirement by selling him out. Anyway, dear Gladys phoned Eduardo and offered to sell your location."

A dim, dim memory registered. From during the worst part of it all, before I let Him in. Of Hill demanding a cup of tea. Forcing the Menace to leave the room to put the kettle on. She kept popping back in-between each stage of the tea-making process, desperate not to miss anything, and he kept sending her out again. Still punishing her, vindictive old man?

At what point had she snapped and decided she'd rather be avenged on *him* than on Margo—and line her own pocket while she was at it? Or maybe she *had* always planned it. Maybe she figured by the time Underground forces could arrive, I'd be dead or as good as, and she'd have her revenge *and* her money. Tempting.

Clearly, all that forgetting the milk and then the sugar and then the biscuits had just been an excuse to keep going out and bargaining with Eduardo. In fact, she'd even eventually popped out—voluntarily—to wash up, hadn't she? Getting on to Eduardo, for his final decision? But...

"Eduardo didn't *buy* my location from her, surely?" The thought of that stuck in my throat.

Margo...smirked. "He didn't need to. Dear Gladys, being no better off for brains than she is for loyalty, didn't do a good enough job of making her call untraceable. She just relied on typing in that number you can dial to hide your caller ID, can you believe? About as much use against Eduardo as a wet paper bag against a shark."

Margo smirked again. "Eduardo strung her along nicely, of course, but about thirty seconds after she first made contact, Bane had the location and was on his way. Eduardo's tracing of the vehicle had already put Bane and his squad within striking distance, otherwise Eduardo would have sent security forces from the nearest Underground Free Town instead."

"Hmm. No revenge and no money. I imagine poor Major Wallis is not a happy bunny this morning. I hope someone at least gave her some painkillers for the post-nonLee headache." *Hang on...* Ah, yes, Bane sent the insulin.

Margo grinned rather less sympathetically. "And facing the foreseeable future incarcerated in the 'touchy-feely farm', as Georg always refers to the Underground's prison. I'm sure she's ecstatic. Well, you never know. Maybe they can reform her. They do good work there." She glanced over her shoulder with a more genuine smile.

I followed her gaze to where a well-muscled guy, about my age, with a tough-looking buzz-cut and uber-watchful eyes, stood in the doorway. Ah. Georg Friedrich, on guard, and Hill was still alive. Well, Friedrich was a disciplined VSS agent and a committed Believer, these days—and as unfailingly devoted to Margo as ever. "I don't think the prison can claim most of the credit for *his* conversion," I said softly.

Surprise, surprise, my sister turned beet red and changed the subject. "Anyway, Bane and the squad rushed you here—well, half the squad rushed you here. The other half took the assorted underlings direct to the rehabilitation farm. Turns out this little jaunt of Hill's was totally unofficial. The rest of the High Committee are absolutely furious with him and scrambling to distance themselves from the utterly appalling publicity.

"Well." She smirked yet again. "I shouldn't say the *rest* of the High Committee—he's not Head of Internal Affairs any more, as of yesterday. There's a warrant out for his arrest and they're even trumpeting that they've frozen all his assets. Public relations damage control, you know. Personally, I think we should get a psychologist in here to examine the man; he must've taken leave of his senses."

Reminded, I managed to lift my head a fraction and look across at Hill. His head was turned away, but his eyes were open, and he was surely listening.

"No, he's not mad," I told Margo. "He's just in rather serious need of a liver—and ideally, a heart. He's finding them hard to come by and mine are a match. I suppose revenge on you was just a bonus. They are looking after him well, aren't they?"

Margo gave me a strange look not unlike the one Bane had turned on me...yesterday?

"He's been offered all the medical care the hospital customarily provides, but he refuses to be so much as examined. He even grumbled about the standard heart monitor—though he's had to lump it as far as that's concerned. Doctor Fathiya put her foot down."

"Demanding a lawyer and his own medical team, then?"

Margo shook her head, frowning slightly. "No."

"No? Is he...waiting for something?"

Margo shrugged, still frowning. "The Lord only knows. I don't. He just lies there and refuses to speak to anyone. Politely, anyway. There have been a few rude words. Well, cold ones."

I frowned, as well. Hill's physical well-being was of intense concern to me, knowing as I did what would become of his soul if his mortal form came to its end just now, but if he wasn't demanding health care or his liberty, then he must be waiting for *something*. What?

Glancing uneasily at my sister, I thought of all the patients and nurses and doctors that must be within these walls. "How secure is this place?"

Margo shook her head, dismissing my worry. "Eduardo sent a large contingent to the hospital itself, plus the authorities have placed heavy guard around both hospital grounds and the entire Free Town. Too tough a nut for mercenaries to crack, and for the EuroGov to break in and snatch Hill, they'd have to send a force so large it would be impossible for it to be construed as anything other than a declaration of war on the African Free States. They're not going to do it. Right now, the only reason they'd want him back would be to kill him themselves, anyway. So I have no idea what Hill is waiting for, but I doubt it's that."

But...what, then?

"Look, Eduardo let *me* come here, right?" Margo saw my continued concern. "So it's got to be secure."

True. My sister was the Underground's Golden Goose and had to be protected accordingly, something she'd gradually grown resigned to as the years passed. I gave up worrying about some sort of commando invasion. "What day is it?"

"Tuesday." Margo tensed.

"Tuesday!" I'd been snatched on Friday evening. I'd figured I might have lost a day since my rescue, but not two.

Her eyes darted to my hands, then jerked back to my face. "You were in a bad way from shock and that nasty serum when you arrived here. Despite the need to get you to surgery as soon as possible, they had to wait almost twenty-four hours before they could get you sufficiently stabilised. You slept a lot after the general anaesthetic, never waking properly. Some reaction with the serum? They finally got it all out of your system—or passing time did—and here you are, awake again." She smiled—but her lips trembled.

I looked down towards my hidden toes again, tried to wiggle them. Tried to...count. No good. Too much morphine. "How many big toes do I have, Margo?"

Margo's eyes were round and worried. "One. I'm sorry, Kyle..."

"It's not *your* fault. They put my skin back on, I imagine? But what's the situation with my knee?"

Margo's face grew pale and even unhappier. Oh dear, maybe I shouldn't have made it so clear I remembered everything.

"Yes, they were able to put your own skin back on—which was really lucky, because donors for white skin of your type wouldn't be too easy to find around here. The knee... Well, it's...the surgeon put the muscles back in as well as she possibly could. And she says if you don't move it while it's healing, then there's a good chance you'll be able to bend it again, walk on it again. But...oh, Kyle, I'm so sorry, she says you'll never run again. No chance at all. I'm *so sorry...*"

"Why are you apologising, Margo?" I kept my voice calm and firm, though her words felt like a dull blow administered to my sternum, and a choking heaviness settled over me.

I would never run again. Never play football again. Probably never cycle from village to village again. Not that *that* would matter. Since I couldn't say Mass any more, I was finished as a parish priest.

I struggled to push the feeling of dullness away. It didn't matter. It *shouldn't* matter. The Lord was the only thing that mattered. Oh, that closeness I had felt... I still felt it, but nothing, nothing like as much. Was I already ceasing to surrender? Was my grief for my lost hobby a symptom of that? Finding myself alive, were those earthly bonds already knotting back into place, those doors closing inside me? How did one live in the world and yet keep *everything* open to Him? So easy when you were about to die, but when you had to *live*?

"The Lord is in charge, Margo," I told her, since she still stared at me in mute misery. "All will be well."

Another snort from Hill. Yes, *Hill.* My attention sharpened. Why was I lying around moping about football when I had precious work to do? Hill's soul needed saving. What could I do, right now? What could even I *offer*, now?

Hmm.

I eyed the morphine machine. Flexed the three fingers on my right hand. Could I lift my arm? It weighed an awful lot, missing digits or not, but yes. I fumbled, trying to position my middle fingertip on the button, though my brain tried to send my hand too far to the right, to position my absent forefinger there instead...

"Kyle, what are you doing? Are you in pain?"

"Oh...no. No, the opposite, really. I think this thing's turned up too high."

"Too high? The head doctor set that up herself. You should probably leave it alone."

"I'll only drop it a fraction." *While you're sitting right there, anyway.*

I didn't need to look at my sister to sense her scowl, but I lowered the dose by a modest three bars, then took my half-hand away and tried to look as though I had no further interest in it. Margo would pop out to the loo eventually.

Now, Hill. What to do with Hill?

"Can we take Hill off to his own room now?" My sister's thoughts were running along slightly similar lines.

"No!"

She stared at me. "Why not? Unicorn has been over the pair of you—medically, chemically, physically, you name it—and he's quite certain that there is no booby trap that will operate if you are separated."

"Uh...I never mentioned any booby trap."

"No, Bane said you were pretty evasive, but with you being addled with pain, Unicorn had it checked anyway. So can't we take him away?"

"You don't like having him around?"

"Kyle! Of course not."

"I thought you forgave him?"

"I've forgiven him for the old stuff. The latest stuff is a work-in-progress. Anyway, forgiven, yes, doesn't mean I *like* him. He's a horrible man."

"Liking him isn't necessary. Just loving him."

My sister glared. "Kyle, couldn't you at least wait until you get the bandages off before insisting I love that man?"

"But what if you drop dead before I get the bandages off?"

"Patience, Kyle," she muttered. "I'll get to it. Just give me time, okay?"

"It's not healthy, Margo," I persisted. "To wait, I mean. Can't you love him *now?*"

"Can you?" Margo's fists were clenched.

"Well...yes."

Margo drew in a long, deep breath that quivered slightly. "Kyle..." Abruptly she rose, bent over and kissed my cheek. "Kyle, I love you, but I'm going to the canteen for a cup of coffee. Back soon."

"*Margo...*" But she rushed from the room, taking Georg Friedrich into orbit at the doorway like a nucleus collecting a missing electron. A couple of guards I didn't recognise remained—to protect me from Hill, no doubt.

I stared after her, my head spinning with confusion and a vague guilt twisting my insides. *What did I do, Lord?*

*...gently, Kyle. Gently...*

Did I push her too hard? Was I insensitive? Maybe she was finding it very, very hard to forgive this time. Well...had she ever found it easy? Had *I?* It just seemed different, now.

Now, okay, I loved Hill too much to even feel any *need* to forgive him, but before? Say, with Joe? With Snakey? With *Bane?* Oh, *how* I had struggled to forgive the EuroGov. To forgive Friedrich. To forgive my own brother-in-law. I'd almost lost my vocation over it. I'd got myself straightened out in the end, with plenty of help from other people, but it had been so *hard.* At times it had felt *impossible.*

If Margo was struggling like that now, with Hill, no wonder she was peeved with me. Or maybe I'd made her feel guilty, like she was failing... Oh, no, no, no, I didn't want to make her feel like that. She already kept apologising, and I wasn't sure if it was the usual 'sorry' people give with bad news or if it was what I dreaded, that she felt some deeper responsibility for all this...

"I hoped she might slap your smug face." Hill's voice broke in on my thoughts, speaking English, his native tongue. "Shame. Would have been entertaining."

Oh help. Even Reginald Hill could see I'd planted my big toeless foot in it. *Sorry, Lord. Sorry, Margo.*

All the same, while Margo was out of the way... I raised my leaden hand again and knocked another five bars off the morphine dosage, since I could hardly feel the previous reduction, then turned my attention to Hill. The foot of his bed lay only a couple of metres from the foot of my own, yet a vast expanse of clean blue linoleum loomed between us, like an unbridgeable sea.

*How do I get through to you, Mr Hill? How do I pry open that little chink in your armour—armour un-breached all the long years of your life—and allow the Holy Spirit to slip in?*

No one else had ever managed it, evidently. Was it pure arrogance to think I could? No. Just pure necessity. I was here, I was the *only* one here who cared and Hill was running out of time. I might be Hill's last chance and that was simple truth.

Problem was, I knew an awful lot *about* Reginald Hill, but I really didn't *know* the man at all. So that was probably the first thing to change.

"Would you like your family to visit you, Mr Hill?" I asked him, shifting my head on the pillows so I could see him better. I used English, since it was my (earthly) native tongue as well—though more as a courtesy than anything. Hill might rarely have cause to *speak* Latin, but he understood it fluently. "I'm sure that could be arranged. Your wife is still alive, I believe? And you have three children?"

For men as powerful as Hill, a third child was the ultimate status symbol. *Look how rich I am, I can afford the Third Child Permittance.*

Hill snorted perfectly audibly this time and looked at me in exasperation. "You think my *family* are going to visit me? They can't wait for me to fall off my perch. But I make it my business to disappoint them. Don't be fooled by my wheelchair."

He nodded to where it had been parked out of the way in the window bay—well out of his reach. "I just don't have the energy to get around under my own steam, what with my heart and everything. But a little recuperation and I'll be up and about again, and *they'll* just have to go on waiting. I bet they wrote the eulogy years ago. Too bad." He snorted again, *very* derisively.

The fact that he still had time eased a tight ball of anxiety inside me, but...what he said about his family, was it true? All priests had heard those dark thoughts reported in confession—in situations where family relationships had gone very wrong indeed or financial troubles were becoming overwhelming—but those were just unbidden thoughts that flitted through people's minds, causing them to recoil in horror—and take it to confession. I'd only met a handful of people who hated a parent enough to truly wish their death and some great horror had been behind the sentiment in every case.

But then...how many people had a parent like Reginald Hill? Yet his children were no paragons of virtue. They'd shown little interest in politics, but their lifestyles were toxic and selfish. From what I'd read in the press—who knew if it was true?

"What about your grandchildren? You have several, don't you?"

"You're behind the times, Kyle. Like my children in their day, my grandchildren made great props in photographs—a role my *great*-grandchildren now fill—but were otherwise of little interest to me."

"Do you not...love them? At all?"

Another snort. "I felt some wisp of emotion when my children were born, I suppose. But they wore it out years ago. I mean, first they drool and throw up, but that at least is the nanny's problem. Then they start talking and they whine and follow you around asking stupid questions. Then they get sullen and rebellious. Then they go out with unsuitable partners and misbehave and get incriminating photos plastered over the media. *Then* they start popping out more drooling specimens of humanity."

Hill glanced at the window as a large African songbird flitted past. "No, I do not love them anymore, whatever that word really means. So long as they behave themselves sufficiently and smile in photographs at important occasions—and above all, pose no threat to me—then I will favour my family above other human beings and see to their comfort and advancement, since I wish the continuation of my own genes—for what that's worth. I have long since concluded that there really is no other purpose behind registering and breeding, whatever all that foolish talk of love."

A cold, quiet horror gripped me at his loveless words. If he was unable to love even his *own family*, his situation was even graver than I'd realised.

My legs and stomach were aching much more fiercely. Okay, I was feeling the drop in morphine, this time. No matter. I must concentrate on Hill. "No threat to you? Is that why none of them followed your footsteps into politics? Did you actually discourage them?"

"Of course." Hill's flat stare suggested that *I* asked childishly stupid questions. "They carry my genes, and naturally I chose a registered partner with top genes as well—including intelligence. It would be highly imprudent to allow them to compete with me. How many kings throughout history have been toppled by their own sons?"

"Or daughters," I murmured, since Hill had two.

"Historically, usually sons. Granted, my daughters are the more likely threat in my case. My son is an imbecile. Or acts like one. But then, perhaps he just likes being alive."

I frowned. "I don't see the connection."

Hill stared at me. "Are you serious?"

I stared back, equally puzzled. "Yes."

Hill's brow crinkled. "I've seen your IQ scores, so it can't be stupidity," he muttered at last.

"What can't?"

"Anyone"—Hill's voice grew very harsh—"*anyone* who threatens me—or disobeys me—I eliminate. Do I need to make the connection any plainer?"

Cold goose bumps broke out up my arms. "You would kill your own child?"

"If necessary, yes."

"Could you truly do such a thing? Do you feel *nothing* for them?"

"They are *my* children, Kyle. *Mine.* I had to dispose of two previously—one before birth, a contraception failure—the other just after, for imperfection. If I had to dispose of another now, tell me: exactly what is the difference?"

I closed my eyes and huddled close to the Lord, so distressed that nausea actually built in my stomach. What was wrong with me? His words seemed to sear my soul...yet I'd heard similar crimes confessed before. But...never from someone I truly *loved*...

*Lord... Lord...please reach him. Please break in. Please...*

When I thought I could open my eyes and move again without retching, I reached out an aching hand and knocked another five bars off the morphine.

Hill's needs far exceeded mine.


## *MARGO*

Wrapping my hands around the fat earthenware mug, I breathed in the nice coffee steam, trying to settle my surging emotions. The bright geometric pattern painted on the mug was cheerful but hardly matched how I felt. If only Bane was here. Or that Georg could sit down and chat for a few minutes. No chance of that. He never let his guard down when on duty. One reason Eduardo sent him, no doubt. That and his undimmed eagerness to throw himself between me and any deadly threat.

But Unicorn was busy with security and my other bodyguard—currently off-duty—was a younger woman not in my circle of close friends, so I would have to sit here and stew by myself.

*How* could Kyle just lie there looking at me with his placid green eyes and insist I forgive Hill instantly, completely, like it was the easiest thing in the world? I knew what Hill had done to him.

And it wasn't just the physical suffering. Hill had been out to *damn* Kyle, not just kill him. The emotional-spiritual-psychological anguish Kyle must've gone through! The terror he must've felt, at the thought of falling. Hard to even imagine how deeply my devoted brother must have suffered.

Yet... I frowned at the wall, which I'd automatically sat facing so I could at least pretend no one was staring at me. Yet the accomplices had also sworn blind that the whole torture-murder had, by the time of Bane's arrival, descended into pure farce, with Kyle singing, laughing, humming and assuring them how much God—and he—loved them. No wonder the hospital staff hovered over Kyle as breathless as though caring for the incorrupt body of a saint.

Or for a living saint.

I rubbed my wrinkled brow. Was my big brother now...a saint? Bane had said Kyle seemed in a pretty strange state of mind when he'd arrived. *Calm and joyful,* those were the words he'd used. *Vibrating on a higher plane—you know I always make that joke. Well, it's no joke now. Just overflowing with love.*

Was Kyle still overflowing with love to such a degree that even Reginald Hill got the benefit of it?

- *Can you love Hill right now?*
- *Yes.*

*Well, I can't, Kyle. I know I should forgive immediately,*

*and I suppose I do want to. So the intent to forgive is there. But I can't love him. Not yet. Maybe not ever. I just can't.*

The very thought of what he'd done...it made me cold all over. Oh, Hill didn't believe in *actual* damnation, but he knew *Kyle* did. It wasn't the action of a bad man or a nasty man, it was pure evil. How could I love pure evil? How could Kyle? Like loving the devil.

But...did God love the devil? Strange thought. He must do. God loved everyone and everything. Kyle was only doing as He did.

To truly forgive, one had to love. Had I ever forgiven Hill, really? Had I patted myself on the back for forgiving Lucas so fully, felt that I'd got this forgiveness thing sorted, and simply mouthed the words about Hill? Maybe one never had forgiveness sorted; maybe each time was just as hard and gruelling as the first time. But I hadn't worked at it. Not with Hill.

So how had Kyle, once almost torn apart by his inability to forgive, managed it so effortlessly? A shiver of awe ran down my spine.

Exactly what *had* happened to my brother on that gurney?


## KYLE

"Kyle? Are you awake?"

I opened sleepy eyes. Margo and a vaguely familiar-looking Sister sat beside the bed. Doctor Fathiya, read her name tag, her white teeth matching her white habit and contrasting with her dark skin as she smiled at me. Probably in her early sixties, her air of calm competence might have reminded me of Croft—but for the kindness in her eyes.

I smiled back, then directed a look around the room. The sun struck effortlessly through the thick red curtains—now closed for shade—casting a half-circle of intense brightness that extended from the window bay, but reached neither bed. Even with the drapes, it threw the rest of the room into shadow, relieved by the electric lights. I'd been asleep for several hours. Hill still lay opposite, sleeping or ignoring everyone. Someone had turned the morphine back up. Bother.

Wait until they'd gone? But I couldn't shake a feeling of...of urgency. I had to get it down at least a bit. I raised a hand and lowered it five notches.

"Father Kyle, please don't touch that..." Doctor Fathiya reached towards it.

I fended her awkwardly away with my three-fingered hand. "Please, Doctor, it really is set too high, I assure you."

She studied me thoughtfully, but, thank God, withdrew her hand. "Perhaps you have a very high sensitivity. But if you are in pain you must raise it again. Or click this and it will deliver a top-up dose if it is safe."

I smiled meekly, and she seemed satisfied.

"Now, Father Kyle, how do you feel? Your sister tells me you were awake earlier and very with it."

I shrugged. "I couldn't honestly say I'm at my sharpest, but I feel fine. Things ache a little, nothing more. Thank you for putting me back together."

She waved my thanks away. "You've our head surgeon to thank for the knee operation. We've fitted a good knee brace around your joint, which should allow your torso the sort of movement needed to prevent bed sores, but it's still very important that you don't move the leg around at all. The skin was straightforward. The hands..."

She drew rather a deep breath, her fingers checking the fastening of the upside down lapel watch she wore pinned to her habit in an automatic gesture. Clearly she was here to talk about my hands. "Well, we did what we could for them, closing up the wounds as neatly as possible. But I expect you're wondering why we weren't able to replace the missing digits?"

I blinked. "Actually...I just...assumed they were gone and that was that."

Doctor Fathiya winced. "Well...unfortunately that does seem to be the case. I believe you've been on this continent long enough to know that the window for preserving transplant-compatibility in nerves is considerably shorter than in the cold climate of Europe?"

I saw Margo's lip quirk involuntarily at that—she found the summer heat of Rome oppressive, especially when pregnant—but I nodded.

The doctor hardly needed to expand, but she did anyway. "Well, when you reached the hospital, the nerve damage was already extremely severe."

"They brought you absolutely as fast as they could," Margo put in. "Eduardo did look for a helicopter, but they're just too expensive and rare. By the time the closest one had reached you, stopping to refuel en route, Bane could have driven you to the hospital twice over! So they simply put their foot down. But...it wasn't quite enough."

Doctor Fathiya nodded. "When you arrived, an immediate attempt might actually have been possible, *if* the donor material had been to hand and the patient fit to undergo immediate surgery. Alas, neither was the case. Once it was safe to operate on you, even with our efforts to retard the decay, the nerves had gone completely past viability. I'm so very, *very* sorry, Father Kyle."

"Why are you apologising?" I tried to keep the exasperation from my voice. "You did everything you could, I'm certain."

"Yes... I'm just...sure you must be so very disappointed."

"Oh, I'm content to keep the hand I was dealt."

Margo winced, clearly too emotional to cope with such humour, but the doctor's lip twitched. Hill, just sipping from a glass of water, choked and began to cough and laugh alternately.

"Are you alright, Mr Hill?" I asked, when the choking threatened to outweigh the laughing.

Lips thin with disapproval, Doctor Fathiya whisked over to his bed, sat him up and had him merely laughing again in no time.

"You are quite insane; you know that, Kyle Verrall?" For all his chuckles, Hill's eyes were narrowed; malicious.

There wasn't much I could say to that, so I simply shrugged. Sleep dragged at my eyelids, for all I'd not been awake long. Doctor Fathiya noticed, and brisk fingers checked my readings and tucked me firmly in. Obediently, I closed my eyes...

\* \* \*

Beeping. Aches and pains. Rather more pronounced. Had they left the morphine alone? Good. Even if it didn't feel good.

From the waist down, I was one big ache. My chest twinged. My hands throbbed. I'd only knocked five bars off, though.

I opened my eyes. The sunlight caressed Hill's bed now, soft and golden-red, but still glinting off the tubular metal frame. Evening. No Margo. Dinner time, no doubt. No nurses in sight either. Just guards in the doorway, and Hill. I quickly lowered the machine five more bars. How often did they check it? Ah well. I was doing what I could.

Hill gazed grimly out the window—the heavy red curtains had been drawn aside again. They framed the crucifix hanging above the window bay very nicely, in fact.

I opened my mouth...then shut it again.

Oops. I'd almost asked if he'd learned whether he had any chance of getting a transplant here—but I knew the answer to that. Children and mothers were top of the transplant list, older individuals last and strictly in order of health—and thus likely transplant success. Hill had a weak heart, making him a poor candidate of his age for transplant—even leaving aside the minor issue of him being a mass murderer/torturer/minion of the devil. No, Hill would've had little chance of qualifying for an organ even if he'd had the good fortune to be of a tissue type common in Africa. To even mention the subject would be cruel.

"I hope you are being looked after, Mr Hill."

He turned a disapproving look on me. "I can't say that I've ever been all that enamoured of African cuisine." But after a moment, he shrugged. "All things considered, I can't complain."

"I should think not," I couldn't help muttering.

He just smirked—rather wearily.

"I can't help wondering, Mr Hill, why you're so happy to remain here."

"Did I say I was happy?"

"Well, you're not asking to be released."

"I've always had an aversion to wasting my breath."

"Then don't you think you'd better let them treat you?"

"I don't need anything other than a bed and some R and R. I dare say everything will resolve itself soon enough."

Resolve itself... Belatedly, the cent dropped. Or *a* cent. Of course Hill didn't want to be *released*. What had Margo said, that the EuroGov would only want him back so they could stage a nice, showy, face-saving execution? Hill must be downright desperate *not* to be released! Just playing it cool.

"You can relax, Mr Hill. The Underground has a long-standing policy of not releasing prisoners back to blocs that may use capital punishment on them. As you should be perfectly well aware."

Hill's lip curled. "I will admit to a certain curiosity as to whether you sanctimonious prigs decide to make an exception in my case."

"I'm quite certain that no exception will be on the table. If it were, I would oppose it." As the injured party, my plea would carry considerable weight, not that the issue would arise. But to reassure Hill further, I added, "And—of even more weight in any such discussion—so would my sister."

Hill's eyebrow rose. "Would she?"

"Yes," I said very firmly. "Without question."

"Your faith in her is touching. And from the looks she's been directing my way, possibly misplaced."

Had Margo been glowering at him? My heart sank. But how could I possibly raise the subject with her again after being so big-footed before? "Doing the right thing has more to do with *will* than emotions. Or it should do."

Hill gave a faint snort. "Strange to say, I would agree with that. Emotion should not enter into any important decision-making process. Only reason."

"Yes," I agreed, "though one can take that to extremes, you know. *You* do."

Hill raised an eyebrow again. "A tad judgmental there, aren't we, *Father* Verrall?"

I thought about everything he'd told me so far. "Just factual, Mr Hill."

Hill...cackled. "Your sister's behaviour is perfectly explicable. You, however, make conversation with me—admittedly, conversation varying from moronic to rude—as though I am a newly discovered uncle. I cannot make you out."

I nodded. "Umm. Newly discovered uncle. That's much how it feels."

Hill frowned, his whole face crinkling up. "Aren't you…the slightest bit *cross* with me?"

"I'm far, far too worried about you, dear uncle, to be cross."

Hill swore in disgust and turned his face away.

"Which do you object to, the 'dear' or the 'uncle'?"

He glanced at me, brow creasing as though startled I'd not taken the hint and abandoned the conversation. "Both give me rather high temperature feelings, but not of the warm, fuzzy kind. I am not your 'dear' anything, and as you pointed out yourself, we are not even remotely related."

"But you *are* dear to me, Mr Hill, and you have only yourself to blame for that."

"*What?*"

"If you didn't want me to care, you shouldn't have forced me to spend so much time with you. And in the Vatican, any older individual one cares about becomes an honorary 'uncle'. As you must know, having spent your life studying us, the better to train your spies and anticipate our every move."

"I'm not having much luck anticipating *you*," was Hill's frank retort. "But then, I'm coming to the conclusion that you're insane. Or it's the fastest case of Stockholm Syndrome in the history of the human race. No, the torture clearly addled your mind. That happens, sometimes."

"It merely *focussed* my mind, Mr Hill. You have no idea how much it focussed it and how grateful I am for that."

"I give up on this conversation." Hill turned his head away again. "You don't make any sense, Kyle Verrall."

Obligingly, I stayed silent for a few minutes, passing the time comfortably by saying my confraternity prayers and then resting a while in that still discernible sense of the Lord's presence. *Please stay with me, Lord. Give me the right words to open a path for you.*

Okay, Hill was probably getting bored by now. Time to try again.

"If you don't mind me asking, Mr Hill, I'm very curious

about what motivates you."

Hill gave a long, put upon sigh, but turned his head to look at me. "*Motivates* me?"

"Yes. You've spent your whole life fighting to get to the top and then stay there. Why? What could be worth that constant, brutal, all-consuming struggle?"

Hill once again eyed me as though *he* couldn't figure out what made *me* tick. "Isn't it obvious?"

"Not to me."

"Power, Kyle. Power. And money, but only because money is power."

"Umm." I tilted my head in acknowledgement. "I thought you'd say something like that. But *why?*"

"Why?"

"Why is power worth all that work?"

"Why? Because the only security in life is through power. The only satisfaction. The only freedom."

I thought about that list. Security. Satisfaction. Freedom.

"Power makes you secure?"

"Of course."

"Most people have no power beyond that of their vote, yet they sleep peacefully in their beds. You, with all your power? Do you really sleep secure? I'm quite sure the thought of being attacked, politically or even physically, and pulled from your position—or your very life—is a constant worry, sapping all peace from your life. How are you better off than the almost powerless citizen?"

Hill jerked his head impatiently. "If I *am* threatened, I have the power to defend myself. When peril comes to the ordinary man, it simply leaves him crushed in its wake."

"But your power makes you a target. Without your power, the chances of that peril coming your way would be so vastly reduced as to be scarcely worth worrying about. You cannot claim that power is security."

"It is to me."

"Well...look at me. I've lived safe and secure for years with ever so little in the way of worldly power."

Hill gave a huge snort. "*You?* Safe and secure? Have you looked at your hands recently?"

"Ah, yes." I lifted one and waved it at him. "But that just

proves my point. Trouble came my way because of my sister's *power*, not because of *my* powerlessness. Power draws more trouble than it wards off, *that* is my point."

"That is your *opinion*."

"No, I'm pretty sure that is a fact, actually. Any statistics would surely—" A movement from the doorway drew my eye—just in time to see the hem of a skirt disappearing from sight behind a guard's knee. Margo? *Margo! Oh, no, no, no!*

"Margo?" I called frantically. "Hey, little sis, aren't you coming in to visit me?"

The faint footsteps paused. After a moment, Margo appeared in-between the two guards, a strained smile on her face. She'd heard me. She had. Oh *rats*. I didn't mean it like...like that...not *blaming* her.

"Have you been at dinner, Margo?" My voice sounded too bright, too cheerful. "Was it something nice?"

"The Sisters kindly invited me to eat with them, and the food was certainly different." She approached the bed, still smiling in that horrible, fixed way. "Have you had anything?"

"No. Maybe they came while I was asleep. They'll be back. Mr Hill, have you eaten yet?"

Hill eyed me, then Margo. "No. I imagine they will only feed me when they feed you. So we can carry on discussing how your sister is responsible for everything that's happened to you for a bit longer."

Margo's lips compressed; her face twisted. She was trying not to cry. *Oh Lord, help me... Help us...*

"Margo, ignore him. Mr Hill is tired and hungry and...well, mean. He's talking nonsense."

"Nonsense?" Hill's eyebrow rose. "I'm merely repeating what you just said, Kyle, am I not?"

"You are *twisting* what I said."

"No, I'm really not."

I shot another look at Margo. "Would you please *be quiet?*"

"But you keep engaging me in conversation, Father Kyle. I am merely obliging you. So do tell me more about how your sister caused the loss of so many of your body parts..."

"Shut up," snapped Margo.

"Just ignore him, Margo. He's old and sour and...well, let's face it, rather evil..."

"Rather hungry, too. If you really don't want to discuss what Margaret's policies have done to your strong young body, then perhaps you would press your call button and get us some food? There's a good boy. We can continue our conversation later, since you clearly don't want to discuss how you feel about your sister's part in all this while she's here."

Margo whirled towards him. "Just shut up you evil, lying—"

"Temper, temper, little girl," tutted Hill.

Margo grabbed an empty bedpan from the bedside unit and hurled it at Hill. Fortunately, it was only cardboard, but it made him jerk in momentary, startled fright. When it bounced harmlessly off his chest, he relaxed, giving vent to such a mocking laugh that Margo's hand slipped inside her waistband...

"*Margo, no!*"

Hill stopped laughing so abruptly he clearly knew what she reached for. But her hand had paused, the nonLee undrawn.

Friedrich appeared at her shoulder, quivering with eagerness. "Would you like me to shoot him for you? How many times?"

Margo took several deep breaths. Then took her hand away from her gun. "No, thank you, Georg. He's just a nasty, mean-spirited, evil old man who's going to hell. Nothing we can do to him can match the fate he's choosing for himself. I'm a fool to let him get to me." She waved Friedrich back to the doorway, turned the chair beside the bed so the back pointed towards Hill and sat in it, then reached out briskly and pressed my call button. "Let's get you some dinner, Kyle."

My stomach was rumbling a little, though her words had brought that deep anxiety about Hill—and her—boiling up more fiercely than ever. "That would be nice. Would you... er...do something for me?"

She eyed me warily. "What?"

"Pray a rosary while I eat."

"For what?"

"Well...if you think through what you just said, you may see a really serious need somewhere. Right?"

Margo's lips thinned. But eventually her nostrils flared and she nodded. And sure enough, when some kind nurses had brought my dinner—soup and bread—she took out her rosary and set to work, breaking off only occasionally to field escaping bread or help me recapture the fat straw they'd provided for the soup. These half-hands were going to take some getting used to. Opposable thumbs were highly under-appreciated things. Still, at least with this meal, I could feed myself. More or less.

Despite the earlier gurgles from my stomach, I couldn't finish it all. Tiredness hung over me, weighting my eyelids and slowing my thoughts. And I'd been asleep almost all day! Margo and I made slightly forced conversation about the children for a while—Hill, thank the Lord, had gone back to ignoring us—then Margo excused herself under what was probably, alas, the mere pretext of needing to call Bane. Lord grant she wasn't just going off to cry her eyes out. Or maybe she needed to cry down the phone to him.

All these years of marriage and they were still best friends. Not that they didn't have some rotten arguments sometimes—two very strong wills in one relationship—but they were good at forgiving and making up. I knew about *that* more from Bane than from Margo, loyal as ever to her spouse. But Bane made a point of confessing to me when I visited, claiming that knowing he would have to bare his soul to his wife's brother helped him to be a better husband.

I wanted to ask her if she'd at least heard enough context to understand what I'd really meant, but I couldn't bring myself to raise the subject. Hill might start at her again, despite his earlier near miss with her nonLee. But the mere fact she'd almost drawn on him told me how deeply he'd—or I'd?—touched a nerve.

I stared at Hill. How far would he go for revenge? If he could provoke Margo into shooting him with her nonLee, triggering a fatal heart attack, it would utterly destroy her reputation. Little Miss Forgiveness, as some tabloids still referred to her, killing her oldest, most loudly-forgiven enemy. Her influence on the world stage would be catastrophically reduced.

But to achieve it, he would have to sacrifice however many months—or even years—remained of his life. From the speed with which he'd shut up, he wasn't ready to make that trade. He wanted to be alive when things 'resolved themselves' in the hope of somehow gaining his liberty and being able to buy a new liver on the black market. Then he could live for decades. No, Hill would not die for revenge. He was far, far too cold and calculating. And, I was beginning to suspect, far too afraid of death.

Despite sleeping most of the day, I possibly felt more tired now than when I'd first woken. Ridiculous. It must be shock or the delayed result of all my accumulated injuries. Everything hurt. Really *hurt*, since taking off the extra five bars, my chest not least of all, though why *that* should hurt was beyond me.

Still, despite that crushing tiredness, I really didn't want to sleep again yet. I knocked a couple more bars off the morphine. Maybe the pain would keep me awake, while also helping Hill.

Hill, who'd gone back to staring out of the window.

"You're *really* not a nice person, are you?" I couldn't keep the sadness out of my voice. Considering he'd done all this to get at Margo, the way he'd treated her shouldn't surprise me, but it still did. When had I last met someone who'd acted so cruelly?

Indeed, he looked at me in disgust—and derision—and spoke mockingly. "Stop press, Reginald Hill is not a nice person! Stop the presses!" He—surprise, surprise—snorted. "*Nice?* What value is there in *nice?* Nice just gets you...lying in a hospital bed with only six digits waiting to... And moping over a busted knee. Should I break my heart over not being *nice?*"

"If you hadn't informed me of your need for a new one, I might wonder if you have a heart at all, Mr Hill."

"*Boo-hoo.*"

"I know; you don't care. Well, we established that power doesn't really bring security, so what about satisfaction?"

"*You* established."

"Whichever. Satisfaction. How do you even measure

that? And mere 'satisfaction'? Pretty feeble compared to 'joy' or 'happiness', let alone 'beatific vision'. Well, I imagine you did feel satisfaction when you finally clawed your way onto the High Committee itself. Or *back* on, after one of your little eclipses. But did it last?"

"Every time I reflect on the fact that I am one of the most powerful men in the world, I can assure you I feel *immense* satisfaction." Hill was terse.

"But you're *not*, now. You are more thoroughly in the dog house than my sister has ever managed to send you and you put *yourself* there. If you go back, they'll execute you. Your power has evaporated like a morning mist."

To my surprise, Hill smiled. A slow, cold, bleak smile, but a smile nonetheless. "You think I didn't know it could end like this? An unofficial mission with unreliable muscle? How stupid do you think I am?"

"I don't think you're stupid at all, though the reasoning behind some of your recent decisions still eludes me. Like why you didn't just buy an organ on the black market, rather than throwing everything away like this."

"No one in their right mind would think I could have got to the top of a transplant list legitimately, what with my heart, and the public don't stand for that sort of thing anymore, thanks to your sister. I'd have been finished."

"So you could have bought the organ and retired quietly. To another bloc if necessary. Whereas now... Well, you know once they've got you back on your feet—or at least into your wheelchair—you'll be off to the rehabilitation farm, right? Light duties only, I'm sure, but that's where you're going, and no chance of a transplant."

Hill smiled sourly. "Perhaps I figured if it was retirement either way, I'd rather hit Margaret where it hurts—while I still had the power to do so."

I stared at him. Something still didn't add up. I just couldn't believe that this cold, rational man had really chosen to swap a long, comfortable, luxurious retirement in a location of his choice for a short, tedious one peeling potatoes in a convict kitchen, attending endless catechesis lessons and psychological examinations.

There was definitely a missing piece here somewhere.

But exhaustion fogged my mind. I would have to sleep soon.

"Freedom... Yes, that leads rather nicely into the subject of freedom," I managed. "At the absolute height of your power, Mr Hill, can you honestly tell me you were free?"

"Of course I was." Hill's irritated tone made it clear he was fed up with the conversation, but I ploughed on anyway.

"But the requirements of keeping your power—let alone the responsibilities of your job—were a prison around you. The workload. The constant machinations. You were never truly free to go where you wanted and do what you wanted and say what you wanted. Your position imprisoned you just as surely as poverty or ill health or prison bars imprison the most powerless person in the world.

"Now your bad health and your crimes are imprisoning you as well. But like every man, woman, and child on this planet, you have *always* been in prison, you just subscribed to the common illusion that you were free because—at least up until now—no physical walls actually held you in. But true freedom exists only in choosing to follow God's will. In following the path of selfless *love*, not selfishness. *Only* in that."

Hill yawned widely. "Goodnight, crazy boy. Have a nice sleep. I'm sure you need it by now." With that, he turned stiffly onto his side and pulled a sheet almost up over his head.

I wasn't getting any further with him tonight, clearly. I turned my weary head and eyed the bedside unit, but no Office book presented itself to my gaze. Bother. Should I press the call button and ask for one?

But why trouble them? A nurse would bustle back in here soon enough. I could simply wait a few minutes and...and...


*MARGO*
"He said it, Bane. He said it was my fault." My voice almost choked off and I hugged the phone to my ear, curling up still more tightly in the guest room's armchair. I'd barely managed to get myself sufficiently under control to phone

Bane at all.

"Margo, I really do find that very hard to believe. Kyle wouldn't think like—"

"I *heard* him! He said 'Trouble came my way because of my sister's power'." Those words...it felt like a knife had sliced open my chest and yanked my heart out.

"Well, that's not the same as, 'Margo, this was your fault,' is it? Trouble did come his way because of your power. But it was Reginald Hill's decision to attack you on those grounds, so it's Hill's *fault*. Not yours. And I've absolutely no doubt Kyle thinks so."

I knew that, of course. In my head. But I needed to hear Bane say it. Because a nasty sly voice kept whispering that this *was* all my fault. And however many times I slapped it away, called it a lying demon, it kept coming back.

"Why did he even say that to you?" demanded Bane.

"Well, he didn't say it *to* me. He was talking to Hill. I overheard."

"There we are, then! I'm quite sure he didn't mean that he blamed you. And if you insist on doubting that, then for pity's sake just go and ask him straight out!"

"I can't. I can't even talk about it. I get so upset. And not with *Hill* there! I get so *angry!* I almost drew my nonLee and shot him, Bane. I was this close!"

Bane helpfully proceeded to laugh his head off.

"Bane! It's not funny! Not with his weak heart. I haven't got that angry with anyone since...since...well, since I pointed the thing at Kyle all those years ago."

The reference to *that* brought Bane's laughter to such an instantaneous end I wished I hadn't mentioned it.

"Well, you didn't shoot him, right?" Bane's voice was utterly sober.

"No, I never *actually* even drew it."

"Well, then. No harm done."

"I'm not so sure. I wanted to *kill* him. I feel...filthy just having the residue of that anger on my soul. I think I should go to confession."

"I'm sure Kyle will oblige."

"You know I never confess to my brother, Bane. It just feels too weird, to me."

"Sounds like your big bad sin wouldn't exactly be news. And if he's still vibrating on a higher plane the way he was last time I saw him, it could be a pretty awesome experience. But anyway. You're in an Underground-run hospital in an Underground-governed Free Town. Somehow I don't think it will be too hard to find another priest."

"I know, I know. Well...you're sure the children are okay?"

"Absolutely fine, Margo. Joey's asleep in my lap, the others are round at U's and Jane's, playing."

"Okay, I'd better go. I really miss you all."

"I miss you even more." He sighed wistfully—then it sounded like he smiled. "I wonder if Unicorn can pull up a security photo of Hill's face when you reached for your weapon."

"I threw a bedpan at him first," I admitted, mostly to make up for my thoughtless remark before. "Hit him, too. It *was* empty, though."

Bane laughed so hard this time that Joey gave a sleepy gurgle. "I'll definitely get onto U about a photo!"

"Good night, Bane. I love you."

"Love you too. Oh, I'm so calling U!"

I sighed and was about to hang up when the dim pounding of feet entered my ear from the receiver along with an urgent, "Wait, Daddy!"

"Is that Luc?"

"Yeah... Yes, yes, you can speak to Mummy. Here..."

The phone clearly changed hands. "Mummy?"

"Hi, Luc. I thought you were at Aunty Jane's?"

"Aunty Jane told me you were on the phone, so I ran all the way home!"

"Well, I'm very glad you did. Not that your Aunty Jane's setting a very good example of switchboard confidentiality, there."

"You don't *really* mind, do you?"

"No, Luc. Just saying. Are you all okay?"

"We're fine. Are you coming home?"

"Not yet, Luc. Uncle Kyle's still quite poorly, though the doctor says he should be well on the mend soon."

"Oww." A tragic sigh. "Well, I s'pose if Uncle Kyle needs you."

"He does, Luc. I'd be home at once if he didn't."

"I know." Luc still sounded gloomy. He needed something to do, knowing him.

Hmm. Maybe... "Luc? Do you think you could pray for Mr Hill? Reginald Hill?"

A short pause. "Isn't he the man who hurt Uncle Kyle?"

"Yes, he is. He needs a *lot* of prayers. He's not in great health, either. It would make Uncle Kyle very happy if you would pray for him."

"Okay, Mummy." No more hesitation. Was my son as special as I often felt, or was I just a jaded, unforgiving grown-up? That bright, precious young voice rushed on, "He must be a horrible man if he could hurt Uncle Kyle, but it would be awful if he went to *hell*, wouldn't it? I'll make sure we all pray for him. In fact, I'll get everyone together tonight to do a rosary."

Oh, Bane was going to *love* that. "Thanks, Luc. You're such a good boy."

"You can't call me a good boy just for saying I'll *pray for someone*. It's not like I just saved a toddler from falling off the Vatican wall!"

"You are a good boy, but you don't know how to take a compliment," I teased.

"Huh."

"Well, I'd better go. Or are the others there, now?"

"No, they were busy dressing Javi up as a warrior angel and s'pose they weren't paying attention to Aunty Jane."

"Okay, well, give them a kiss from me."

"Polly won't let me kiss her, mum! Ew!"

"A mutual disinclination, clearly. Just give her my love, then. Daddy can kiss her."

"Okay, I can do *that*."

"Bye, Luc. Love you."

"Love you, Mummy."

Putting the phone down felt physically painful, as though the action yanked on my heart strings. I sighed. There were reasons why I'd enjoyed travel a lot less since becoming a mother.

Although it was several hours earlier back home, I felt ready for bed. But first I really did want to find a priest.

Humiliating that my eleven-year-old was more willing to forgive Hill than I was!

**KYLE**

Cheeping birds. Beeping monitors. Gentle morning rays. A breeze played on my cheeks and I drew in a deep breath, hoping to savour the cool dawn air.

Ow.

My chest *really* hurt this morning. Especially when I breathed in. The aches and pains in the rest of my body...were less. Was I healing or...I opened my eyes and peeked at the morphine machine. Yes, someone had put it back up to the dosage I'd agreed with the head doctor. After a quick look around—no Margo, no nurses—I knocked it down by another ten bars. I'd been managing with it eight bars lower yesterday, after all. Hopefully Doctor Fathiya wouldn't find out immediately.

But if the morphine had been turned up and my chest still hurt this much... *What* was going on with that? Hill hadn't even touched my chest. It must be some side-effect of the serum.

I looked across at Hill, but he still slept. Obvious enough why he didn't want to be released—though it'd taken me long enough to work it out, in my less than A-one condition—but why was he so happy to stay in a room with me? My attempts at conversation usually seemed to exasperate him. Maybe he just enjoyed watching Margo hovering all sad and strained over my battered body. Likely and logical enough.

So why did I still feel like I was missing something?

The arrival of the hospital chaplain, Father Omwancha, middle-aged and solid—in every respect—to feed me Holy Communion in bed, put such thoughts from my mind. Followed, at an appropriate interval, by breakfast—and that barely cleared away when a whole bunch of my parishioners were crowding around, talking nineteen to the dozen and pressing a variety of bundles on me, containing everything from carrots and fresh-laid eggs to—oh so happily!—my Office book and Bible.

I couldn't get much of a word in edgeways but was far too tired to mind. When the nurse at last came to chase them away, I thanked them with deep and genuine gratitude, touched not only by the provision of my books, but also that they'd bothered to make a twelve-hour journey to visit me. They just laughed, assured me the distance was nothing, a mere day trip—true enough, in this vast continent, but still hard for me to grasp even after all these years—and set off home again.

With a happy sigh, I opened my Office book, laboriously working my way past the lost days to find my place.

I kept dozing off, but at long last I closed the book and tried to move it to the bedside unit—an attempt I quickly abandoned when it became clear that both my strength and my painful half-hands were insufficient for the task. Well, it wasn't doing any harm on the bed.

Right. Now I could give Hill my attention. Other than a mere, "Good morning, Uncle Reginald,"—which had provoked nothing but an explosive snort—and a few words of explanation about our breakfast dish, we'd not interacted much today.

I looked across to find him watching me. He'd been watching me all morning. Like I was...a play that wasn't finished yet. Or maybe he was just bored stiff.

"And how are you feeling this morning, Uncle Reginald? I trust you are recovering after your eventful weekend."

Hill smiled coldly. He'd clearly decided to ignore his new title. "Oh, no need to fret your crazy young head about me, Kyle. Rather more to the point, how are *you* feeling this morning?"

Since when did he care about that? I eyed him, puzzled, but simply said, "I'm fine, thank you for asking."

Hill...smirked. "Got some more insane questions for me, no doubt?"

Yes, he really was bored, wasn't he? The Religious Sisters who ran the hospital had shown no inclination to give him books or other forms of entertainment, clearly feeling he should be left free to contemplate his misdeeds without distraction. Even annoying conversations with me began to seem preferable to more hours lying staring out at not a lot. The gap between the beds and the window ensured that such of the sleepy town's outskirts as we could glimpse were too distant for much detail to be made out. The savannah beyond lay even further away.

"Well, something else I am curious about. What, in your view, is the point of life?"

Hill snorted. "Quite frankly, I'm far from convinced there is one. I suspect everything may just be one great cosmic accident. You, me, humanity, the planet, the universe. Pure, blind chance. We humans were simply unlucky enough to evolve to a level at which we could grasp that awful truth. Well, those of us who don't prefer to believe in fairy tales."

"I've felt God, Uncle Reginald. He's filled me, consumed me, overwhelmed me. For most of the billions of years of life on earth, His existence has been an accepted fact. It is *you* who believe the fairy tale—one of very recent invention indeed, conceived by those so obsessed with their own self-determination that they simply cannot stand the thought that the only path to true freedom is total surrender."

"Total surrender gets you where you are. Lying in a hospital bed." Hill bit off further words and smiled smugly.

"Yet here you are, lying in a hospital bed just the same as me."

Hill's smile soured slightly. "I've had considerably more of life than you, foolish boy. And I haven't wasted my life on the promise of another one. One life is all we get and it's worth fighting for. Perhaps I wasn't quite honest with you yesterday—I do still feel something for my children, not much, but *something*—but if it was them or me, I'd choose me. Every time. Because my life is the *only* thing of true value I have. And I will do anything, kill anyone, to keep it. There, are you going to cry again?"

I gave him a reproving look. "I didn't *cry*."

"Looked like you wanted to."

"Well, I did—want to. I *do*. What you just said is ghastly. What you *did* is awful. Everything about it is unspeakably tragic. Everything about *you* is unspeakably tragic." My throat burned, just thinking about it. The things he'd done. The things he believed...

He understood that life was precious, yet he was happy to take the lives of others. Over and over, for years. To torture and kill. His own children, his political opponents, thousands of priests, sisters, laypeople, reAssignees, not even to mention Resistance fighters and other criminals. His selfishness was of catastrophic proportions. And surely culpable? He *understood* the incredible value of life yet *chose* to kill. Not in self-defence, but merely for *gain*. For advantage, to gain power and comfort in life. Oh, surely, he was culpable?

And if he carried on shutting God out, I knew exactly what would become of him. I swallowed and cleared my throat, but to no avail. I had to brush a tear from the corner of my eye.

"Oh, you have got to be joking."

I stared at the blankets, trying to get a grip on myself, but the dual pains—emotional and physical—had combined to overwhelm me. Scrabbling my rosary from the bedside unit, I tried to pray, but it was so hard to 'thumb' the beads...

"Kyle?"

My sister's concerned voice broke in on my limping prayers and I glanced up, startled, my damp cheeks heating.

"Kyle, are you okay? What's the matter?" She bent over the bed, staring at my wet face, gripping my wrists anxiously, either out of reluctance to touch my maimed hands or fear of hurting me by doing so.

"I'm fine." I freed an arm and struggled to grip the taut, too well tucked-in sheet, to press it into service as a hanky, but to no avail. I made do with wiping my cheeks on the bandages that covered what was left of my hand, instead.

"This is way lower than yesterday." Margo looked up from peering at the morphine machine. "No wonder you're—"

I caught her reaching hand. "No, no. It's not that, Margo. Mr Hill was simply... Well, our conversation took a distressing turn, nothing more. I'm...I'm clearly feeling rather...fragile after...after everything." Oh no, I shouldn't have said that.

Yep, from the glare she turned on Hill, she now blamed him. "What on earth did you say to him, you evil old—"

"*Margo*. Please. He was *honest*, that's no bad thing." Okay, so I was pretty sure he'd brought things back onto the subject of his children, living and dead, in a deliberate attempt to hurt me, but still. Margo didn't need more reasons to hate him.

Hill eyed her coldly, no doubt trying to decide whether he could safely needle her today.

"Don't start on her!" I said hastily. "Or...or I won't speak to you again for ages."

"That's your notion of a *threat?*" But Hill gave a couple of almost convincing yawns and shut his eyes.

Smothering a sigh of relief, I took a deep breath and tried to raise myself slightly with my hands, tired of looking up Margo's nose—but the wave of pain from my chest so swamped the ache from my hands and elsewhere that I abandoned the effort at once and flopped against the pillows, breathing in cautious, shallow gasps.

"Kyle!" Margo scolded. "Don't try to *move*. You're not *allowed!* You'll hurt your knee! You'll hurt everything."

"I'm alright," I managed.

"How are you this morning?" She carefully turned the chair around to put the back to Hill and seated herself, then turned a bright, hopeful look on me. "Doctor Fathiya thought you should be starting to feel much better. Was she right?"

For some reason, I couldn't help glancing at Hill—yep, watching me again. Our eyes met before he looked away quickly. "I'm, uh...still rather tired, to be honest."

"Aw, of course you are." Margo fussed ineffectually with the sheet and blanket—which needed nothing doing to them—then sat back again, her nurturing energies apparently satisfied by that meagre outlet.

*I'm fine.*
*I'm alright.*
*I'm rather tired.*

Did I need to go to confession? I didn't feel fine or all right. I wasn't *rather tired*, I was *exhausted*. I felt like Saint Margaret Clitherow being crushed under her martyring load of rocks.

I drew a cautious, deeper breath. *Ow.*

*Why* was my chest hurting like that?

"U's got a team trying to isolate the serum from your blood and analyse it," Margo was telling me cheerfully.

"More as a general information gathering exercise than anything—the hospital is satisfied its effects have worn off now. But they're making slow work of it, apparently."

I tried to attend to what she was saying. "Why don't they just analyse the residue from the syringe?"

"They couldn't find one. There was an incinerator in one of the basement rooms; they eventually concluded the syringe was thrown in there in an attempt to keep the formula secret in the event of...well, this."

Did I have a vague memory of hearing the room door opening and shutting, shortly after I'd been injected? Probably. Hill was clever enough to know that recreating something from a blood sample was far more difficult than analysing the original. One of the minions must have taken the syringe out.

No, the *syringes.*

I stared at Hill. He stared back, still that smug smirk on his cruel face.

*My little insurance policy.*

Yes, and what had he said yesterday? *Do you think I didn't know how this could end?*

"Margo— Oh, sorry!" I'd interrupted her, though I'd not taken in a word she'd been saying. "Oh, well...ah, I'd quite like a word with Unicorn, actually. Do you think he could...?"

"I'm sure he'll come at once." Margo smiled. "He's been in, you know, quite a few times, but you've always been asleep."

I smiled back, but unease curled in my belly. How much longer would my poor sister be smiling?

Agent Jack Willmott, more commonly known to his friends as Unicorn or simply 'U', stood beside my bed within five minutes, his incredibly blue eyes smiling at me along with his mouth. "How are you, Father Gecko?" He used my old code name from the Liberation missions, the way a lot of mates from that time did, his very upper-class British voice warm.

I elected to ignore the question this time. "U, I just wondered if you'd been able to work out what was in the blue syringe."

Unicorn's eyes narrowed. "The *blue* syringe? According

to everything I've seen or heard, the serum was grey."

"Yes, the *serum* was." Everything he'd seen... Wait a moment, there was a video in existence of...of *everything*, wasn't there? Margo mustn't see it! Please, God, she hadn't already! But...I couldn't ask U to promise never to show it to her with her sitting right there. "Uh... Oh, yes, the *first* injection they gave me was blue. What was it?"

U's face went very still. "*What* first injection? I was aware of only one."

"Did you, uh..." I shot Margo a quick glance. "Did you watch the video?"

"Of course." U's mouth took on an even grimmer line.

"*No, he didn't let me watch it.*" Margo spoke under her breath, clearly in reassurance to me and protest to U.

"And the video," went on U, "only shows one injection."

It did? I forced my mind back to that horrible time before Our Lord's presence made everything wonderful. *Oh*. Was that when Jonas had started doing what I'd taken to be mere arty shots of the instruments, designed to torment the viewers?

"Before they gave me the serum, they injected me with something blue. I think they were videoing the instrument trays at the time. Hill told me it was his 'little insurance policy'. I thought the soft-soft voice was for dramatic effect, but now I'm wondering..."

U's lips went very tight indeed. So did his brow. I could see him adding it up in his mind. Four days, that blue stuff had been inside me, doing...who knew what. Four days in which they could have been searching for an antidote. But Hill had made jolly sure they didn't even know about it. Had he even primed that supposedly-helpful minion—who'd clearly divulged nothing about this?

U stared at me, worry clear on his face, and spoke very softly himself. "How are you feeling, Kyle?"

"Not...great. Most of me feels...as one would expect, but... I'm getting more tired, not less, and I've got this nasty pain when I breathe."

"I'm getting the medical team in here. Dash it all, if there are *two* concoctions in that blood, not *one*, no wonder..."

He hurried off, efficiency in motion, and I finally, reluctantly, looked at Margo. Yep, the bright hope was gone from her face, leaving it grey and strained.

I reached out and managed to curl my three fingers around her hand. "Everything will be alright, Margo."

Hill...sniggered. Yes, definitely a snigger. I was doomed, wasn't I?

"Everything will be fine, Margo," I told her again. "*Whatever happens.*"

My heartbeat accelerated, a fey, tingling excitement creeping through my veins. Was I not doomed to a long lonely earth-bound exile after all? *Lord, will I be with you soon?*

Was I supposed to be sorry? I didn't feel sorry. I felt...excited. Happy. Relieved. And...yes, sad. Sad for Margo and my family. My *family*...

"Where are Mum and Dad?" How hadn't I thought about them before? I suppose between worrying about Hill and Margo and the pain...

Margo swallowed and when she spoke her voice sounded thick. She'd drawn the same conclusions from Hill's snigger and it made her as miserable as it made me joyful. "We tried to contact them but they're right under Storm Huraro at the moment. We haven't managed to get a message through yet. U considered sending someone, but it didn't seem worth the risk."

The storm. Of course. It would be leaving a trail of disrupted communications and damaged transport networks behind it.

"We...we didn't think it was so very, *very* urgent, of course." Margo's voice trembled. "But...well, maybe U will send someone, now."

How long would it take someone to travel into the storm-hit Free State? And how long would it take my rather older parents to make it back out again and all the way to *here*—clear across the continent? How deadly the travelling conditions would be.

"No, he mustn't. It's too risky." My other thought—that it would surely be too late—I kept to myself. I wasn't a doctor, anyway. I might have longer than I thought. I'd already survived this stuff for four days.

"They would want to—"

"*No*. It's too dangerous! You can keep trying to get through on the phone, right?"

Margo sighed, but Doctor Fathiya's arrival stopped her replying. The religious sister seemed grimmer than before and trailed a whole array of competent and professional looking sisters behind her.

She no-nonsensely took the seat Margo vacated and leaned forward to stare at me. "So, your chest's hurting?"

I nodded and she subjected me to a brisk barrage of medical questions, seeking to pinpoint exactly how I felt and when it hurt and where, then she had me wheeled off.

I spent the rest of the morning being put through scanners and poked and prodded and having my blood drawn. They even stuck a camera inside me, quite my least favourite bit of it all, but eventually I must've fallen asleep because I woke up back in my little quiet ward, with a tearfully smiley nurse-sister laying out a meal on the lap table in front of me. Lunch time.

"Good grief, that was exhausting," I couldn't help murmuring—once the nice sister had left. Had they...yes. I dropped the morphine ten bars.

"*Utter* waste of time as well." Hill smiled smugly, lifted a spoonful of soup to his lips with one tremulous old hand and sipped. Pulled a face and turned to the bread instead.

I thought of Margo, presumably off forcing some food down her anxious throat. Hmm. I ought to try. "I don't suppose you'd care to trade the antidote for...well, I'm sure we could think of something you'd like."

Hill barked a laugh. "You're well behind the times, Kyle. Your Agent Willmott has already offered me a comfortable, private retirement apartment—guarded, since apparently there is some moral objection to letting me go entirely—if I should hand over said item, or even the formula. Since, I quote, *it's not like you'll be good for much at the farm anyway.*"

"I'd have thought that would sound quite good to you, right now."

"Indeed. But I'm not one to let my own weakness get in the way of completing something I've decided upon. Remember what we were saying about emotion and decision making?"

I frowned. "I would have thought, in your situation, such a trade would have been motivated by logic, not *emotion*."

"It would be motivated by mere fear of discomfort, surely? Fear is emotion. I made very sure I could not succumb to it."

When I still raised an eyebrow inquiringly, he added, "I'm *saying*, I chose a drug with no antidote, you silly boy."

Finally, his circuitous words made sense.

No antidote.

I waited to feel fear or dismay...but still it didn't come. If anything, the Lord's presence grew stronger, enfolding me. Calling me...

*I'm sorry, Margo. Mum, Dad... Everyone... This just sucks for you all, so badly.*

To Hill, I said, "Care to tell me what the blue stuff does? Other than kill me, I mean?"

Hill smirked. "Oh, you'll find out soon enough."

I shrugged. "Ah, well, then. Enjoy your meal, Uncle Reginald." I bowed my head, said grace, and started sucking my soup through my straw.

Hill shook his head in disgust and peevishly went back to nibbling bread.

If he hoped to see me get all teary about *this*, he was out of luck. But...a sudden dread struck me, a previously unforeseen ramification unfolding itself before my horrified mind. If I was the only one who really cared if Hill made it to heaven, and I would soon be dead... *Oh Lord, help me! Please help me to find the words!* How long did I have? Reckoning on how long *Hill* might have, I'd figured I had months to work on him, maybe even a year or two. Now? Days? Mere hours? *Oh Lord, what do I do?*

Would Margo carry on trying? Especially if I asked her to? But she was struggling with this, and if ever anyone needed to feel real love, it was Hill. And...and somehow, it just felt like he was my responsibility. Like the Lord had given him to me—or me to him. But *how? Now?*

Panicking, I reached out and knocked five more bars off the morphine.

"Trust me," Hill put down his half-eaten bread and shoved his plate away, "you really don't need to worry about getting addicted to that stuff."

"Nice to know." My mind still raced, seeking a secret door, a pickaxe, a ladder, something that would enable me to break into his heart. Nothing. I couldn't think of anything.

I pushed my own food away. Fear closed my throat, almost choking me. I couldn't eat another bite.

*Uncle Reginald, what will become of you?*

"Kyle?"

Once again, my sister's voice drew me from sleep. Pain struck like hammer blows from my legs, my knee, my hands—and my chest *seared* with each breath. Aaah, those five bars had made some difference, too right.

*Good.* That was...good. Struggling to keep my pain hidden, I opened my eyes. Margo. Sitting by my bed again, ashen-faced, her eyes pinched.

Doctor Fathiya sat beside her in a second chair, and U hovered behind them. Both equally grim-faced.

"I'm awake." I smiled obligingly.

Their answering smiles were tense and short-lived.

"Did you find out what's going on with me? Um..." Yes, I ought to make sure they knew. "Mr Hill...says that there's no antidote, I'm afraid."

"So he claimed." Unicorn gave Hill a beady look from his blue eyes. "But you'll forgive me if I don't take anything he says as Gospel truth. We'll keep trying to find one, you can be sure. We almost have the two drugs sorted out now. Well, we think so. Knowing there are two, and what they each do, is a big help."

"See, they'll find something," said Margo firmly. "So don't you worry, Kyle."

"Wasn't planning to."

That won me a frustrated look from my sister, then her gaze shot sideways to Doctor Fathiya and her face tightened still more.

Ah... "So you do know what the stuff does?"

Doctor Fathiya nodded. "It's a nasty little toxin that almost exclusively attacks the lungs."

"Makes sense," put in U. "He'd hardly inject you with something that would damage the organs he wanted to steal."

Yes, that did make sense.

"It causes gradual cellular deterioration, with increasing pain and eventually loss of lung functionality. The process is slow to begin, but gathers momentum, the destruction proceeding faster and faster until it—well, one could call it a cascade. Blood vessels in the lungs will burst at an ever-escalating rate. Within half an hour of this cascade beginning..." She paused. Checked the fastening of her watch. Drew a breath. "Well, your lungs will fill up beyond the point of viability and...you'll suffocate."

I stared at the cross hanging over the window; at the limbs drawn in agony. Oh...they were all waiting for some response from me. "Well...at least it will be quick."

Doctor Fathiya frowned, as though unsure if I was joking. But I meant it, all right. Compared to what Our Lord had suffered... And after those hours on that gurney...well, *anything* seemed quick, let alone a mere few minutes of suffocation.

U gave me a sad—and rather apologetic—smile. He'd a bad habit of blaming himself for anything that got past the VSS's protective efforts. Margo put a hand to her mouth, trying to swallow a sob.

Doctor Fathiya continued uncertainly, "Fortunately, effective palliative care is easy enough. Once the cascade is imminent, you can, well, make your goodbyes—then we will place you under deep sedation. You won't feel a thing."

Margo smiled encouragingly in support of this, her eyes swimming. I looked across at Hill, who made no attempt to conceal his satisfaction as he watched my sister's anguish. My eyes were drawn inexorably back to the cross. There were worse things than a little physical pain and my Uncle Reginald would suffer them all. Forever. Unless I succeeded as God's cat burglar and allowed Him to break in.

"It's good to know what's what," I told Doctor Fathiya. "But I don't wish to be sedated."

Her hand rose slightly towards her mouth. "You don't... Perhaps I didn't put it very clearly, Father Kyle. You will *drown.* In your own blood. It's a slow, horrible way to die."

I smiled at her. "Oh, it's really not that slow or horrible. Please don't trouble yourself about me. I shall be fine."

Doctor Fathiya shot Margo a look of appeal. I met my sister's eyes firmly.

Margo's expression passed from dismay to despair, as though she recognised I'd made my mind up. "Kyle, surely it would be much better—"

"Margo, I don't want it. Please don't make a big thing about this. It's really not that huge a deal."

"Not that huge a deal? Kyle!"

"It's *not.*"

"*It is!*"

Since we were clearly in danger of regressing to the youngest days of our childhood, I forbore to reply *isn't* and just smiled. Margo huffed slightly—but then she got up and rushed out of the room. I'd made her cry. Again. Blast. Bane would be coming back over here to have words with me if this went on.

"I really hope you will reconsider, Father Kyle." Doctor Fathiya sounded strained.

"I'll be sure to let you know if I do. Thank you for looking after me so well, Doctor Fathiya."

She got up and hurried out, unhappy lines still rucking up her brow.

That just left U, his brow deeply creased as well. "What are you doing, Father Gecko?"

"I'm within my rights to refuse the treatment option."

"Of course you're within your rights, but *why?* I mean, have you stopped to consider how ghastly this will be for Margo?"

I'd rather not think about that. "Maybe we can contrive to ensure she's not around when it happens."

"Oh, so she can spend the rest of her life torturing herself with the thought of you going through that without her there to hold your...ah...hand? That's another terrible idea and I'm not helping you with it. If you care about her feelings, just take the sedation. They won't do it until the last minute."

I shook my head.

"Well, I hope you think better of it, I really do." U turned to go.

"Uh, U? I'd...really like to see Father Omwancha, or any priest, as soon as possible. If you could..."

U nodded silently and strode away, clearly no happier than anyone else.

I sighed, shifting cautiously in a doomed attempt to make myself comfortable. Pain flared in my chest. Ouch. That'd just made it worse. Well, back to work. I looked across at Hill.

His eyes examined me as though I was an insect pinned to a card, but he didn't speak.

"I'm sorry I haven't been around much today, Uncle Reginald. I've been having a lovely pre-mortis autopsy—or that's what it felt like."

Hill laughed and for once it sounded genuine. "Oh, hospital tests are such fun, aren't they?"

Huh, something we agreed on. Pain and exhaustion sucked at me and I struggled to think of what I wanted to say to him. Bother, I'd never asked how *long* before this deadly cascade occurred. A day? A few hours? A week?

Well, not a few hours. Or Margo wouldn't have rushed off, however upset she was.

"I should probably just subcontract out the task of upsetting Margaret to you. You're doing an awfully good job of it, crazy boy."

I sighed. "Unintended, I assure you. And it hurts me almost as much as it hurts her."

"Hence why I feel so fortunate not to love anyone." Hill at his smuggest.

Huh... "Okay, Uncle Reginald, tell me, what do you think love is?"

He raised an eyebrow. "What is it? It's that warm fuzzy emotion that makes people do incredibly irrational and sometimes life-threatening things."

"No, it's not. That's a good description of an emotion that is commonly *referred to* as love, but which could more accurately be termed *passion*. It exists in various kinds: erotic, familial, amiable, platonic, etc. But it's not actually love, in the truest sense of the word."

Hill raised his eyebrow again, a trace of genuine curiosity on his face. "And what do you say love really is, crazy boy?"

"Actual love is not an emotion at all, though it's commonly *accompanied* by the emotion. Actual love is an act of the will, to will the good of the other, of the one loved, and yes, to will it up to the point of sacrificing everything, even life itself."

Hill took a moment to think about this. He looked amused, but more engaged than I'd yet seen him. This really must be something new for him.

"So," he said at last—yes, definitely amused, "when you protest so adamantly that you—and your invisible friend—love me, you're merely saying you will my good? You don't actually have any warm fuzzy feelings for me at all? It makes a little more sense how you do it, in that case."

"Sorry to explode your new theory, but it so happens that I do have some very warm familial feelings for you, Uncle Reginald. But you are correct that I don't *need* to have them, in order to love you. All I have to do is will your good. It's just hard for human beings to genuinely will good towards someone for very long without becoming emotionally engaged as well."

Hill remained silent, clearly turning this over in his mind.

"So," I ventured, at last, "thinking that you do not love your family because you simply don't feel an emotion is incorrect. If you do not love your family, it is because *you* choose not to."

Hill shrugged. "Is that supposed to bother me? Because—especially in light of what you said about the icky, troublesome emotion close following the act of will—it really doesn't."

"I'm just pointing out that even a grumpy mean old man like you can love his family—you simply have to decide to do so."

Hill snorted. "Well, I certainly choose not to."

"Shame. You must be so lonely."

"Lonely?" Hill threw a pointed look around the room and at me. "Right now, a chance of being lonely would be bliss!"

I smiled, not believing him. He'd be bored stiff in a room on his own, and we both knew it.

O Lord, protect me, my chest hurt. I closed my eyes for a moment, trying to breathe shallowly. *More* shallowly. Exhaustion pressed on me. *O Lord, stay close.* But he was. Nothing like so strongly as when back on that gurney, but he cradled me, and it was impossible for anything to seem too bad, not even the pain or the horrible quick death that awaited me.

"Good grief, are you going to sleep *again?*"

I caught Hill's grumble but couldn't respond. Blackness sucked me down...

*MARGO*
"Bane?" My voice wobbled unstoppably. I clutched the phone as tightly as I wanted to clutch him. Tears swam in my eyes, blurring the little hospital guest room where I was staying.

"Margo? Are you alright? What's wrong?"

"He's dying, Bane!"

"What... *Who?*"

"Kyle."

"Kyle...no! But they'd got him stabilised...he can't be!"

"Hill gave him something else, some poison, to make sure he'd die even if rescued, and we never found out until this morning and it's *too late*..." I bit off my words and swallowed hard, fighting for control. "No. No." My voice sounded desperate, even to me. "It's *not*. U's team are looking for an antidote. They'll find something. They will."

"Is that what U says?" Bane sounded subdued.

"He...he says..." I couldn't lie. "He says they'll keep on trying, so long as...so long as..." *so long as Kyle's still alive.*

"How's poor Kyle?"

"How's..." I choked off a sob. "How's poor *Kyle?* He didn't turn a hair when they told him, you'd think he hadn't understood but he *had!* He's *fine*. I'm the one who's...who's *upset.*"

"I'm coming over there!"

"Bane..."

"I'm coming and I'm bringing the kids. They should see their uncle if he's...if he might not make it."

"You'll never get here in time, Bane. This thing's galloping faster and faster—"

"I'm *coming*. I'll call again as soon as I can. I love you."

"I love you too."

He hung up. I swapped the knobbly handset for a cushion, hugging it close. The thought of him on his way—of them all on their way—soothed my aching heart slightly. But they would never be in time. Conceiving, arranging and executing a plan to safely—oh yes, above all, *safely*—smuggle five children across the EuroBloc onto a ship was a totally different kettle of fish than simply activating familiar deployment plans for an experienced strike team.

But that would never stop Bane trying.

And I didn't really want it to.


*KYLE*

"You know, I want to ask *you* a question," said Uncle Reginald at dinner time, after playing with his bread and ignoring another bowl of flavoursome African soup.

"Go ahead." Any excuse to put aside my straw. I just had no appetite, and pain gnawed at my chest. Not that the sly note in his voice boded all that well for the coming query. "And yes, I am a virgin, if that's the tired old question you have in mind."

Hill sniggered. "Fascinating. But no. I already know you're insane. I was thinking more about what you told me—so very confidently—about having *felt* your God. Tell me, has it seriously never occurred to you that these feelings are just the product of your human brain? Of your imagination and your subconscious?"

Snug in my Lord's presence at that very moment and all squeaky clean spiritually after the chaplain's visit—what did the pain matter in comparison?—I merely smiled at him. "I'm quite sure my sense of God does come to me at least partly *through* the activity of my brain. Is not the spiritual, by definition, intangible to physical beings? Of course there must be some earthly mediation between a spiritual experience and this physical human body through which I perceive the world while alive. But I do not accept that the experience *originates* in my brain, even if it is impossible—by definition—to track back to the intangible source through scientific means."

"So you admit that you don't have a scrap of scientific proof?"

"Hmm, not the kind you're thinking of. But doesn't one more commonly measure a thing by its effects?"

"You're suggesting measuring God by the delusions of your crazy brain?"

"I'm suggesting measuring God by how much he changes us, changes us in ways that make no evolutionary sense, that make us, as you mentioned earlier, even do things that run counter to our survival instincts. That's not what you'd expect from something with its source in the natural order, is it?" Agh, all this talking made my chest feel... Never mind. *Ignore it, Kyle.*

"That's probably why it's called insanity, you know."

"You keep *calling* me insane, Uncle Reginald, but do you really believe that? I don't think you do. Just because we don't agree on everything doesn't make me insane and you're far too clever to think so."

"Cheeky boy. What else am I supposed to consider someone who is prepared to die for an invisible friend and who claims to love his own murderer?"

"You accept that you are a murderer, then?"

"In this case? Yes. I don't recall signing your death warrant. That would have been a bit difficult, what with us being in Africa."

"It doesn't bother you?"

"What, you really think every single person I've had killed in my lifetime was under legal sentence of death?"

I sighed—then winced. When the extra surge of pain eased, I said sadly, "No, I imagine that would be too much to hope for. Do you...not feel the slightest bit sorry about the things you've done?"

Hill snorted. "Sorry? Why should I? Survival of the fittest, boy, that's what life's about. Do you see a wolf wringing its paws after defeating its father and taking over leadership of the pack?"

"Human beings aren't *wolves.*"

"Humans are animals. Do you dispute that?"

"Of course humans are animals, but we are far more than that. Human beings are the only animals with an immortal soul."

Hill made a rude noise.

"Why does the idea of a soul scare you so much?"

"Scare me?" His brow darkened. "It doesn't *scare* me, stupid boy! The whole concept is simply pure lunacy!"

"Really?" I said reflectively. "Well, *I* know precisely why it scares you so much. Because if you have a soul, I'm right and you're wrong. And if I'm right and you're wrong, you're not some big alpha wolf, you're just a cruel selfish murderer who's going to hell. Yes, if I were you, I'd be pretty terrified of having a soul, too. With good reason."

"Oh, are you *ever* going to *shut up*, you dribbling *imbecile!*" Hill grabbed a bedpan with one frail hand and hefted it in my direction. It fell short, so with a disgusted snort he turned on his side and fixed his eyes on the crimson curtains—drawn for the night—sending me to Coventry.

The two guards who'd bounded into the room, nonLees drawn, gave me inquiring looks. I shook my head at them, smiled and wiggled my fingers in the direction of the doorway. One smirking—no doubt at Hill's pathetic throw—the other scowling—at the fact he'd tried it at all—they withdrew.

I eyed Uncle Reginald. No, I really had better give him some time to cool off. Still, his reaction took me aback.

Actually, his failure to simply laugh in my face...gave me just a tiny glimmer of hope. Because somewhere inside him, however deep down, however tiny, however close to going out, there must smoulder a tiny ember of doubt. Or he wouldn't have got angry.

A fresh wave of determination swept me—closely followed by all too familiar worry.

How on earth could I fan that ember to a blaze? Especially in the time left to me?

*Lord, please. Is there anything more I can do? Anything more I can offer?*

I considered the morphine machine for a moment. But if I dropped it much more, would I be up to rational conversation at all? Or was that just the devil's whisper? No harm in trying. My heart thumping in unenthusiastic anticipation, I knocked off five more bars. What was I, twenty bars under the agreed level, now; thirty under the original? As soon as they spotted it, they were going to put it back up, no question.

"Uncle Reginald?" I ventured.

He ignored me.

"Uncle Reginald, surely you don't expect me to apologise for being honest?"

"I don't care what you do, so long as I don't have to listen to any more of your inane chatter."

"I was only giving my opinion, was I not?"

"Oh, just hurry up and die!" And he refused to say another word.

Pain lay over my body like a heat haze. A whimper crawled up my throat, but just in time I choked it back. Clearly no one had spotted the morphine level yet. Opening my eyes, I looked around, trying to distract myself from the agony. Evening. No Margo. She must feel like every time she popped out to eat or use the loo I woke up, poor thing.

Uncle Reginald now lay on his back, staring at the ceiling. Maybe a neutral question...

"Do you know what time it is?"

No answer.

Panic tightened my burning chest. How long would he keep this up? I had so little time.

*Lord, please. What else can I do? Is there anything else I can give? I'm begging you, if there is, let me know.*

*...you won't like it...*

*I don't have to like it. Whatever it takes, Lord. Please?*

So He told me. Showed me. Understanding entered my mind, anyway...

I recoiled mentally, my head pushing back into the pillows.

*No! No, not that!*

*...you don't have to. Never have to...*

*Please, there must be something else...*

*...what else is there left, dear child?...*

His message was so clear it was almost words. I had my answer. There was one more thing I could give. It was not *asked* of me. It was not *expected* of me. But it was *possible* for me.

I looked across at my Uncle Reginald, who now lay staring out of the window with a petulant, angry frown creasing his brow. *No, no, no, I can't give this, I* can't!

But the memory of what awaited that precious soul filled my mind.

I shuddered.

I closed my eyes.

*Yes, Lord. If it will help him, yes. Take it back. Take it all.*
The sense of many words filled me...

*...beloved...brave...child...loved...precious...beautiful...joy...*

The sense of my Lord's presence deepened, intensified, like...like a divine hug.

And faded.

And

was

gone.

Aaah, the aching emptiness He left behind. An agony far worse than anything my body threw at me. Tears spilled from my eyes as lonely anguish swallowed me. Four whole days—five days?—I'd nestled, snug and safe, in His presence. No longer. And even when I prayed, I would feel nothing. Not even that precious sense of cherishing I used to so often feel. Nothing.

Well, maybe not nothing at all. Some far more mundane, less supernatural sense of peace and calm, perhaps. Such as Margo might feel. Such as most people might feel.

*Yes, Kyle. Most people never feel what you've felt, above once or twice in their life—if ever. So stop crying. Okay, you had to give it up. Just be grateful that you've been so exceptionally blessed for so long—and that you had something more to give.*

But I couldn't. I couldn't stop crying. I'd never felt so bereft, abandoned, alone, in my entire life. I knew I wasn't alone. I was no more alone than I'd been a moment before. He was right there with me, I just couldn't feel Him.

But the knowledge couldn't change how I felt, nor could

it stop the tears of desolation streaming down my face. This wouldn't do. Uncle Reginald watched me now—covert and sidelong, so as not to invite conversation, but he watched. I picked up my Office book—fumbled and dropped it before I could open it and had to pick it up again. The effort made me pant and that made me hurt.

Finally, I had it open to evening prayer. Tuesday. Only one day out. Did I have the energy to change it?

Actually...my eyes fell on the first psalm. Well, if Uncle Reginald wouldn't talk, he still couldn't help *listening*. Latin, but he'd understand. I propped the book up as well as I could and began to read aloud. Raising my voice didn't feel good, but my physical discomfort was the least of my worries.

"Hear this, all nations, pay attention all who live on earth, important people, ordinary people, rich and poor alike!"

Uncle Reginald groaned and turned on his side, doing his best to put his back to me. I kept going.

"...But man could never redeem himself or pay his ransom to God; it costs so much to redeem his life, it is beyond him; how then could he live on forever and never see the Pit—when all the time he sees that wise men die, that foolish and stupid perish both alike, and leave their fortunes to others.

"Their tombs are their eternal home, their lasting residence, though they owned estates that bore their names.

"Man when he prospers forfeits intelligence: he is one with the cattle doomed to slaughter."

"Oh, *shut up!*"

"Are you speaking to me again, then?"

Uncle Reginald clamped his lips together.

I took up the psalm once more. "So on they go in their self-assurance, with men to run after them when they raise their voice.

"Like sheep to be penned in Sheol, Death will herd them to pasture and the upright will have the better of them.

"Dawn will come and then the show they made will disappear, Sheol the home for them! But God will redeem my life from the grasp of Sheol, and will receive me."

"This surely counts as torture!"

"Clearly we have very different ideas about what that word means, Uncle Reginald."

No response. Fine.

"...when he dies he can take nothing with him, his glory cannot follow him down..."

Tears still oozed onto my cheeks and the agony in my heart and soul dwarfed that of my failing body, but at least the words might help Uncle Reginald. When I'd finished the forty-ninth psalm, I flicked on, trusting in the Holy Spirit and reading whatever my eyes fell upon.

Uncle Reginald's occasional protests dwindled into a sullen silence and eventually he turned onto his back once again and simply glowered up at the ceiling.

"Listen to this hymn, Uncle Reginald. It must be one of the most beautiful ever written:

"Alone with none but Thee, my God, I journey on my way; what need I fear, when Thou art near, O King of night and day? More safe am I within Thy hand, than if a host did round me stand."

Oh, Margo had appeared by the bed...but I couldn't stop. If I stopped, I'd start sobbing full out.

"My destined time is fixed by Thee, and Death doth know his hour. Did warriors strong around me throng, they could not stay his power; no walls of stone can man defend when Thou Thy messenger dost send."

"Kyle?"

I tried to smile at her just as though there weren't little streams running down my cheeks and hurried on. "My life I yield to Thy decree and bow to Thy control. In peaceful calm, for from Thine arm no power can wrest my soul. Could earthly omens e'er appal a man that heeds the heavenly call!"

"Kyle, are you alright?" Margo sat in the chair beside the bed and leant very close, peering at my face.

"Fine, Margo. Just reading to Uncle Reginald." Quickly, I ploughed on, "The child of God can fear no ill, his chosen dread no foe; we leave our fate with Thee and wait Thy bidding when to go."

"I hope *you* can stop him," Uncle Reginald said over the top of me. "I can't and he's been going on like that for—well, it certainly *feels* like hours. The crying *and* the recitation."

From the quirk of Margo's lips, the fact that Hill wanted me silenced made her *less* keen to stop me, not more. She sat back in the chair with a bemused look. But I'd almost reached the end of the hymn.

"'Tis not from chance our comfort springs, Thou art our trust, O King of kings. Beautiful, isn't it, Uncle Reginald? Well, perhaps you don't think so. Do you like that hymn, Margo? What's next..." I tried to leaf forward. "Any suggestions, Margo?"

"Kyle, enough." Margo drew the book from my very un-grippy hands and put it to one side. "What's the matter? Why are you crying?"

"I'm just tired and in pain. Pain makes one's eyes run, you know. Seems I can't do anything about it right now, but I really am quite alright."

"Quite alright? Kyle!"

"I am! The Lord is with me. What could possibly be wrong?"

"*Kyle!*" Her anguish stabbed at my heart. "You don't have to *pretend—*"

"I'm *fine*, Margo. I'm the one who should be feeling sorry for *you*, right? You have to stay here, while I get to go and be with Him. Just who is getting the better deal here?"

This won a tense smile, but a smile nonetheless.

"I really can't help it that my eyes are leaking, Margo. I'm only sorry it's upsetting you."

"So long as you are...alright."

"*Never better* would be physically inaccurate, but I am fine." Not a lie, not really. I wasn't suddenly feeling all scared and depressed about my impending end—just lonesome for God. If anything, I now longed to be in the Lord's presence even more keenly than before. I would never feel Him again any other way.

Darkness reigned outside. How long *had* I been reading to Uncle Reginald? Okay, *at* him.

"What time is it, Margo?"

"It's almost ten, Kyle. I'm sorry I was gone for so long. I was triaging my emails. I did it absolutely as fast as I could."

"No need to apologise, Margo. The world doesn't revolve

around me and it certainly won't be so helpful as to pause while I shuffle off this mortal coil."

Margo gave a pained grimace but didn't argue with this irrefutable fact. She opened her mouth, then glanced across at Uncle Reginald—a rather measuring glance.

"Ah, yes, he does seem to have rather good ears, for someone his age," I told her.

A scowl replaced the measuring look. "That's because they're not his. Twenty years ago he stole a set of lungs from some poor reAssignee and a year before the Abolition of Sorting he added the theft of a complete set of hearing organs."

Right. So Uncle Reginald seemed to have the hearing of a far younger individual because...he did.

"Stole them, did I?" Uncle Reginald smirked across at Margo. "Well, *I* could say the same about what happened to my original lungs. Ruined by forced exposure to dodgy toxins when I was much lower down the pecking order." His tone—though would-be light—sounded bitter to me. "Not that I worried about it much back then, when it promised such rapid advancement—after all, who could conceive of new organs not being freely available?"

He directed a black look at Margo, but then he smirked again. "*Such* a good thing I didn't put off the auditory transplant any longer, now isn't it?"

The self-congratulatory remark was clearly aimed to needle Margo, but thankfully she just shifted a little further around in her chair, ignoring him, and leant close to me.

"Bane and the children are on their way." She spoke very softly.

Scarcely likely that Uncle Reginald could find someone here who would pass messages along for him and even less so, in his current state of disgrace, that they would be acted on, but I still understood why Margo kept this information from him.

I couldn't help frowning, though. "How long do the doctors think I have, Margo? I forgot to ask."

Margo swallowed. "A day. Or perhaps two. If you're...very lucky or they manage to delay things a bit."

Hardly surprising, but my heart sank. *So* little time to

help Uncle Reginald. On the other hand, not long to lie around feeling miserably lonely, either. This empty feeling chilled me to the core—in fact, it rather freaked me out.

I spoke very softly. "They can't possibly get here in time, can they?" Just maybe, with the longer estimate. No chance, with the shorter.

Margo grimaced. "They're giving it their best shot, so you do your best too."

Ah. She didn't really think I would see them, she merely told me for...motivational purposes. My dear stubborn sister.

The tears had finally trailed off a bit, a black blanket of exhaustion replacing them. It would've been nice if it cloaked the other feelings, but instead it just seemed to combine badly with them. Bleakly. Maybe I would fall asleep soon.

Oh... "Margo, I haven't actually done evening prayer yet, not properly. Could you read it to me?" My voice rasped, my chest burning worse than ever. I'd overdone the talking.

"Kyle, you're not well. You don't have to do it."

"I want to. Please?"

Margo sighed and picked up the Office book from where she'd deposited it out of my reach.

"Oh no, here we go a-blooming-gain," muttered Uncle Reginald. "I suppose there's no chance of a pair of earplugs?"

"You suppose rightly." Coolly, Margo opened the book, found the place and began to read, never looking at him—but she kept her voice loud enough to be clearly audible all over the room.

I tried to listen, to concentrate, to pray, but that exhaustion gnawed all around the edges of my consciousness and I just wasn't sure how long I could stay...

*I knelt in Saint Peter's, trying to pray, trying desperately to pray. If only I could quiet my thoughts. They buzzed like wasps, loud and aggressive, drowning out everything.*

*Especially that still, small voice in my soul.*

*Okay, if I couldn't pray, I would try and reason through everything. Surely this time it would help.*

*Bane... No. No, I couldn't even start on that one. Just the thought of it and that angry buzzing in my head intensified,* rage gripping my brain like a vice. If I so much as tried to think, 'Bane's been going through a tough time,' something would explode. Probably my head.

Margo, then. My little sis. Who'd pointed a gun at me and thrown me out of her home. Told me she never wanted to see me, ever again.

Okay, so she'd taken that back, the other day up in the hospital.

And I, I'd said to her...I'd said some harsh things. Things I didn't mean, things I shouldn't have said... I should apologise. I should.

But...but she shouldn't *have done what she did. Risked all our lives, risked the future of every Believer and reAssignee in the whole Bloc. For a murderer. Snakey's murderer.*

*Of* course, forgiveness was important, but she could have just sat there and forgiven Georg Friedrich verbally. *There was too much at stake to try to forgive so...so completely hands on,* and *for someone who didn't even* deserve *it...*

...oh? So *you* deserve it, do you, Kyle?...

I just about caught the soft whisper over that incessant buzz of anger and...hate?

So easy to pretend I hadn't.

Someone had propped a photo of Snakey at the foot of the little side altar in front of which I was failing to pray. Hard to believe he wouldn't push aside the curtain and walk in with a cheerful grin and a jest: "Praying again, Deacon Gecko? You are without doubt the most devout lizard I've ever met, si?"

I'd laugh and tease him back: "How many of your lizard-friends are in seminary, O slithery one?"

That would cause another grin. "Good point, Deacon Gecko, good point..."

The imagining faded. I was alone in the chapel and would remain alone in the chapel, because Snakey was dead, as dead as J...

I jerked my mind from my little brother, from that grief overload.

I *did* believe *in forgiveness. I did! If Margo could have saved Georg Friedrich with no risk to anyone, then great. I'd have been behind her. I* would. But how could she risk us

110

all? Didn't she care about us? Not even her own family?
   ...he who does the will of the one who sent me is my mother, and sister, and brother...
   No! *I pushed the words away as they tried to whisper through my mind. What about one's duty to the innocent? The safety of the many* had *to come before the fate of one stray.*
   ...what man who has a hundred sheep...
   "It's not the same!" *Only when I heard my own tortured voice did I realise that I'd whispered it to the night silence.*
   *I wasn't getting anywhere. My mind ran in circles.*
   ...that's because you're not listening...
   I am listening, but none of it makes sense! *I had, had, had to make sense of all this...*
   ...why not just forgive?...
   It's not that *simple*!
   ...why isn't it?...
   I can't...I can't work out how I feel about any of this. I can't make sense of any of it!
   ...does forgiveness have to make sense?...
   Yes, it does! *Everything* has to make sense!
   ...does it?...
   *I* could *go to my sister and...and say sorry. Forgive what she'd said and done to me. But that...that would be like saying that what Georg Friedrich did to Snakey didn't matter! Wouldn't it? Which was like saying that what the EuroGov did to Joe didn't* matter*! Like what Bane did didn't...*
   *The buzzing filled my head again, deafening me. I found myself on my feet. I wanted to punch Bane until his face turned purple and* bled...
   "God, help me..." *I whispered.*
   *But I could hear nothing but* rage.
   *I wrapped my arms around my head, shaking. I wanted to let the hate go. Wanted it so much. It was like acid searing my soul. But if I let it go, there'd be nothing to mask the grief.*
   *And that agony hurt even worse.*

   My eyes flew open and I tried to sit up. Bad mistake. Needles of pain impaled my legs, my stomach, my hands—

and my chest outdid them all. Gingerly, I relaxed back against the pillows. My heart pounded like a herd of stampeding wildebeest and cold sweat coated my forehead. I gasped for breath, whether from the nightmarish memories of that time—more than a decade ago now—when Margo and I had been so horribly at odds over Bane's behaviour and her risky rescue of Georg Friedrich or because of my dissolving lungs, I'd no idea.

"Awake, are you?" A cold voice penetrated my ears. "Finally. Perhaps you can stop all that moaning and let an old man get his sleep."

With effort, I focussed my gaze on the person in the bed opposite. *Wait, had someone...*

Yes, the morphine machine showed the agreed level. The acute pain had only come from my foolhardy attempt at moving. I reached for the button but could barely lift my hand. So weak, now. I used my three fingers to walk my arm across the sheets, then managed to claw my way high enough to reach the button. Knocking a full twenty bars off, I let my hand flop back onto the bed and looked at Uncle Reginald again.

Somehow, I spoke composedly. "Have I been disturbing you, Uncle Reginald? I'm very sorry. I had something of a nightmare."

"Oh?" Hill snorted. "Twenty eager naked young women chasing you, was it?"

I didn't answer. My body shook, clammy and chill. Twenty naked women—or even a hundred—and I could've whispered a prayer of thanks to God for the beauty of his creation, a rather longer prayer for chastity, and gone back to sleep. This nightmare—this *memory*—left me flayed.

Yes, this explained why the feeling of God's absence freaked me out so much. The last time I'd lost my sense of the Lord so completely...it had been the blackest time in my entire life. My fault, too. Like the psalm...

*When my soul was embittered, when I was pricked in heart, I was stupid and ignorant; I was like a brute beast toward you.*

But what was the next verse?

*Nevertheless I am continually with you; you hold my*

*right hand.*

Yes. I tried to drag my thoughts out of the dark past—all that was over, done, long resolved—but they stuck there, as though caught in quicksand. *How* had I made such a mess of things? Even as I'd been rampaging around, going from bad to worse, getting everything wrong, deep down I'd known what I needed to do. That one, single, simple thing.

Love.

Specifically: forgive. But I'd failed...no, I'd *refused*...for far too long. Shame enveloped me, just thinking about it. And sorrow. Had I ever really apologised properly to Margo? Was it even possible to apologise properly for something like that?

I groped feebly—but urgently—for the call button and pressed it. What if this poison took me before I could speak to her?

In bare moments an unfamiliar nurse stood beside the bed, looking down anxiously. "Father Kyle? Are you alright?"

"Oh, I'm fine. I'm so sorry to trouble you, but I'd really like to speak to my sister."

Relief covered the kind face under the veil—but still some surprise. "Of course. I will get someone to fetch her at once. Are you sure you don't require any medical assistance, Father Kyle?"

"No, really, it's just...just a personal matter."

Only when she turned to go did the reason for her surprise occur to me.

"Wait! What time is it?"

"It's ten past two, Father Kyle."

My eyes went to the dark, curtained windows. Ten past two in the *morning*. Oops. "I'm sorry, Sister, I didn't realise it was so late...early... Please don't wake her. I can speak to her in the morning, Lord willing. I'm sorry to disturb you."

"That's what I'm here for, Father Kyle." Smiling, she went on her way.

I lay still—not that I could do anything else—trying to slow my breathing and calm down. If only it wasn't the middle of the night. My need to speak to Margo made my chest ache. An emotional pain to match the physical and spiritual ones. But I couldn't wake her. Not when she'd believed me asleep for the night and gone to catch a few winks herself. She still got so tired after those complications following Georgie's birth.

I tried to concentrate on how lovely it would be to see little Georgie again—to meet him properly—struggling to take my mind off my stomach-churning emotions.

Deep, steady almost-snores from opposite—Uncle Reginald had settled off again. He might grumble when I fell asleep on him, but he could nap for the EuroBloc himself.

However hard I tried to calm myself, my breathing remained rough and catchy. Hmm. Not the dream, then. The poison making itself felt. But Margo had said a day, minimum, so surely I'd still be around in the morning to speak to her?

I did so desperately want to speak to her. But I couldn't bear to wake her. Not with everything she had to deal with at the moment, I just couldn't...

"Kyle?"

I struggled free from the drowsy state of hag-ridden half-sleep into which I'd sunk, just in time to make a supreme effort and catch Margo's hand as she reached for the morphine machine. Was it morning? A glance at the curtains showed otherwise. "Margo? What time is it?"

"Twenty past two." With a sigh, she withdrew her hand. "Are you alright?"

"Twenty past..." She wore a dressing gown... "But I said not to wake you! I'm so sorry, Margo! I thought the nurse understood that I'd changed my mind."

"She did. She guessed—correctly—that I'd like to be woken anyway. What's wrong? Do you need Doctor Fathiya?"

Uncle Reginald slept on. Ten minutes' silence had left him deeply enough asleep that our soft voices didn't disturb him. No question all humans were hard-wired to react more to sounds of distress. Even Reginald Hill.

"No, I don't need a doctor. I need to apologise. To you..." I managed to grip her hand again, tightly, irrationally afraid she might get away before I'd finished.

"To me? For *what?*"

"How I treated you. You and Bane and...and Georg. I

totally failed you. I said such hateful things to you. I hated Georg. Wanted him dead. Wasn't there for you, for Bane..."

Margo's eyes widened, her lips parting. "Kyle—"

"I'm sorry. I'm *so* sorry. I have to tell you..."

"Kyle! You *did* tell me. We apologised to *each other*, remember? And we put it behind us and moved on. At least, I thought we did. It was so long ago, Kyle. I was pregnant with *Luc*. He's *eleven* now. Where on earth has this come from?"

Her bemusement confused me, drying up my flow of words. My heart, barely slowed after the dream, pounded uncomfortably. I felt so...rattled. Sick at heart. Filled with horror at my past sins. With that Absence, everything felt so like *then*. "I...I dreamt...of that time..."

Margo ran a cloth over my damp forehead; her fingers brushed my hair into place. "Shhh, Kyle. Calm down. Everything's fine between us. It's been fine for a long, long time. And with Bane. And with Georg. You come to dinner along with Georg at least once every visit, right? We're all great friends now."

That...that was true. I relaxed against the pillows as she mopped the cold sweat from my neck. Had I got a touch...hysterical from the dream? I was on morphine, after all...

That time *was* past and gone. But its shadow loomed over me in the night darkness. "Will you stay?" I whispered. Immediately, guilt pricked me. "No, you should go back to bed. I'm perfectly alright. I think maybe the morphine scrambled me up a little."

Margo snorted. "Well, maybe. Though goodness knows your dosage is low enough. I'm staying, anyway. If I'd known you'd wake up in the night, I wouldn't have left."

"You need to sleep, Margo."

"I'm fine. Look, I'll grab this extra pillow, put it like this, and sit up here—if it doesn't hurt you. I can doze very comfortably like this." Suiting action to word, Margo positioned an extra pillow against the headboard of my bed and squeezed herself into the space beside my pillows.

The slight movements of the mattress *did* hurt, but I offered it up with all my other pains and betrayed no sign of it. Fine once she was settled, anyway.

"Rest, Kyle." She stroked my hair. "Get some rest."

Uncle Reginald was out like a light; I might as well get some shut-eye too. Margo might sleep, then, as well...


*MARGO*

Kyle's pain-tense face smoothed as sleep took him. As soon as he was well out of it, I slowly, carefully, leant forward and put the morphine back up to a sensible level. Why was he being so funny about it?

Impossible to be angry with him, at the moment.

Almost as impossible to believe that in less than a day, my kind, brave, infuriating big brother would be dead.

Except...remembering how weakly he'd gripped my hand just now, even when clinging as tight as he could, it wasn't quite so impossible. He was weakening fast.

*Lord, why do you have to take him?* I stroked my brother's sleeping head gently, tidying his short hair, so much darker brown than mine. *Won't you* please *let us keep him? Even just for a very little while longer? Please? Just* a little while *longer?*


My neck ached fiercely. I opened my eyes, remembering just in time not to move and hurt Kyle. He still slept, his face relaxed and pain-free. I shot a glance over at Hill. Awake and watching me. I looked away quickly. If the Lord granted me life, Hill would get his forgiveness, but—God forgive me—I really could only cope with one emotionally excruciating business at a time.

Surely I hadn't jolted the mattress at all? But Kyle was stirring, his face tightening, his eyelids fluttering for a few moments before opening all the way.

He promptly smiled at me, of course. "Good morning, Margo." His voice was a feeble rasp.

Somehow, I managed to smile back. "Good morning, Kyle."

His eyes moved across to Hill and, switching to English with scrupulous politeness, he struggled to raise his voice, a flicker of pain crossing his face. "Good morning, Uncle

Reginald."

I tried not to scowl at the affectionate title. Maybe Kyle really was a saint.

Reginald Hill gave a tiny nod. "Crazy boy." But he spoke to Kyle more coldly than usual.

What was wrong with *him*? Why *had* Kyle been reading at him like that last night, anyway?

Hill's cool response seemed to make Kyle awfully happy, though. His grin would've gone ear to ear, had he not tamped it down.

"Would you like me to read morning prayer, Kyle?" He'd try to do it himself, otherwise.

Kyle's smile went up a notch again. "That would be lovely, Margo. Though, first..." He struggled to raise his hand, to reach that dratted morphine machine.

"Leave it, Kyle!"

He ignored me. Down went the level. Flop went his exhausted arm onto the bed. On came his smile. His tired smile, for all he'd just woken up. "Morning prayer?" he suggested brightly.

I complied.

Kyle dozed off briefly in the middle of one psalm but didn't seem to realise, so I simply kept going. When I finished he stirred enough to smile and thank me. But once I'd put the book to one side, his eyes opened again and his hand twitched as though to detain me.

"Margo, I've been meaning to ask. Could you find me a new cord?"

"Cord?"

His fingers moved towards his waist.

"Oh, a confraternity cord? Did you lose yours?"

He nodded. "It's not *urgent*, but...well, I did always expect to be buried in it, you see."

I swallowed hard, my heart clenching, my eyes pricking. "I'll get one for you, Kyle." It wouldn't be hard. Practically everyone I knew had one, including Bane and myself. If a new one wasn't to be found, any guy with the right sized waist would be happy to donate theirs, no doubt.

"Thank you." He spoke so weakly yet seemed so calm.

"Kyle..."

"Umm?"

The question forced its way out at last. "Are you...scared?"

He met my gaze, and for a moment I feared he would give the maddening big brotherly—or priestly?—response: *Of what?*

Instead, his eyes serene as a still pool, he just said, "No."

With a lump in my throat, shame in my heart and awe in my mind, I looked away.

Hill still watched us.

## KYLE

Uncle Reginald was speaking to me again. Probably just to avoid another Assault of the Psalms, but no matter why. It was a good morning.

My last morning?

Probably. That agonising rasp to my breathing was far more pronounced now. I wasn't sure how I'd managed to reach that morphine button. I'd almost no strength left.

*Lord, let me manage even one more conversation with him.*

Could that be enough? *How* could that be enough? But what more could I do?

Father Omwancha brought me Holy Communion again, wonderful man, singing much of the brief bedside liturgy in his strong booming voice. After a time of thanksgiving—and an inadvertent nap—Margo helped me eat my breakfast. Okay, she fed me most of it. When she'd stuffed as much down me as I could bring myself to swallow—not a lot—she slipped off to dress and freshen up.

With some relief, I turned my attention to the other bed. I didn't dare try to engage Uncle Reginald in conversation while she was there—he would have no thought of anything other than getting at her.

"I've got a question for you, Uncle Reginald." Agh, raising my voice even a little was exhausting. *Excruciatingly* exhausting.

"Oh, what a surprise." His tone remained cool and unencouraging.

"What do you *really* think love is?"

Uncle Reginald snorted. "I told you, the other day."

"The warm woolly emotion? Alright, then. What makes a person worthy of being loved?"

"Worthy?" Uncle Reginald stayed silent for some time. At last he said, "I'm not sure anyone's worthy of the sort of love *you* define."

Interesting.

"Do you still think love is merely an emotion?" Because he'd just answered the question according to *my* definition, not *his*.

"I don't know which definition is correct, boy, and I don't particularly care. I want no part of either of them."

"Again, I can only say, how utterly lonely."

"I am perfectly happy with my life, boy."

"No, you're not. Happy people don't seek revenge. Especially not at such a high cost to themselves. Such is the action of deeply unhappy people only."

"You're starting to irritate me again." Hill's voice was glacial, his tone one of warning.

I tried to think of a response, but all this speaking up was making my head swim. As though I couldn't get enough air. Maybe I couldn't. I closed my eyes and stayed quiet and still, hoping it would go off.

It did. A little. But my chest felt clogged. Bubbly. Was it blood? Well, I wouldn't ring the call button. If the cascade was starting, maybe I could get it all done with before Margo came back...

## MARGO

Kyle was so pale when I returned—well, more greyish with his heavy tan—and his breathing so rough that I ignored his protestations of alrightness and fetched Doctor Fathiya at once. She questioned him on his symptoms, listened to his chest and diagnosed fluid in his lungs—not, she hastened to reassure us, blood. Not yet. The cells in his lungs were over-producing mucus as they fought their futile battle with the poison.

She adjusted Kyle's bed to put his chest in a more upright position and leave most of his lungs clear, gave him some medicine and hooked an oxygen tube under his nose to give his partially waterlogged lungs a little extra help.

When she'd finished, he still looked very wan. He tried to address me at a normal volume, but winced, grew greyer again and switched to using a very soft voice. And soon dozed off.

When I returned from a quick visit to the little room, I found the curtains drawn around the bed. I hurried forward in alarm, pausing as I heard Georg's voice. Oh. Good. I'd mentioned to Georg that I thought Kyle might appreciate a visit, since he was off-duty. Prove to him that the past really was past and all that. He'd been so distressed last night...

"But you see," Georg was saying earnestly, "whenever I picture *Herr* Hill burning in hell, the first thing that pops into my head is *marshmallows*. And sausages. And some forks. And maybe some bananas. You know how to make Bonfire Bananas? You cut a slit in the skin, stuff them with chocolate, then wrap them in silver foil and bake them in the embers... *Ja, ja,* I'm digressing. I'm finding it hard to forgive the *schwein*, anyway. I mean, for *this*. I put the rest behind me. Like to think so, anyway. Erm...well, for these and any other sins I cannot now remember, I am truly sorry..."

I stopped in mid step and skipped backwards a few paces, my cheeks heating. Georg was making his *confession*, that must've been why he'd drawn the curtains. Oops.

Hill watched me curiously. *Oh, Lord, don't let him speak!* Panicking, I turned and bolted—my unexpected exit must've taken him by surprise, because I was through the door and clean away. Phew.

Now I just had to forget what I'd overheard. Easier said than done. The image of Georg toasting marshmallows over Hill's flaming soul was...memorable. To put it mildly.

And recipes aside, all too relatable.

*Lord, help me?*

I hid out in the hospital chapel for twenty minutes before venturing back to Kyle's room. I met Georg in the corridor outside carrying a tea tray. He gave me a pained smile, drew a deep breath, squared his shoulders as though entering mortal combat and finally marched into the room. And approached *Hill's* bed. I stopped in the doorway to watch.

"I thought you might like a cup of tea, *Herr* Hill." Georg's voice was tense, but civil.

Hill eyed him measuringly. "One dash of bleach or two, I imagine?"

"Not the cup of tea that you *deserve*, *Herr* Hill." Georg's tone grew cooler. "Just a nice, normal, healthy cup of tea. I'm sure Father Kyle would enjoy a cup too."

"Hmm." Hill couldn't hide his keen interest in the contents of the teapot. "Yes, then."

Georg set down the tray and poured two cups, handing one carefully to Mr Hill and placing the other on Kyle's bedside table with a glance in my direction. No, Kyle certainly couldn't drink it without help.

"I hope you enjoy the tea, *Herr* Hill." With that, Georg picked up the tray and trod out of the room again.

He paused in the corridor, rolled his shoulders as though to relax them, then pulled a face and sighed deeply. "Margo, your brother gives *cruel* penances."

Since even telling him I'd overheard something would break the Seal of Confession, I simply said, "He told you to make Mr Hill a cup of tea?"

"*Do something nice for*, actually, 'cause honestly, right now I kind of hate the guy. So I thought for a Brit, several days in here with strange African beverages and he was probably ready to kill for a cup. Well, not that it takes much to make *Herr* Hill ready to kill, but you know what I mean."

Knowing Kyle, there had been an additional clause to the penance, something like: Do something nice for Mr Hill and *do it with love*, but it was entirely up to Georg what he disclosed.

"My sympathy," I said. "Forgiveness is never easy. And this time it's..." I couldn't finish.

Georg's eyes widened. "Haven't *you* forgiven him yet? I thought...you know...*Little Miss Forgiveness*, that's what the papers still call you occasionally. I thought you were *good* at it."

My cheeks warmed up like gel heat cubes. "It's always

hard, Georg," I said, rather lamely. "I swear, I *am* going to forgive him properly, but...it's going to take time. A terminal diagnosis or a load of news crews showing up is about the only thing that could speed *this one* up."

Georg grinned—very widely. "*Do not* say that in your brother's hearing. Or he'll whistle up some media before you can say *Bless me, Father!*"

*KYLE*
Lord help me, the pain devoured everything. My head still swam on and off, every breath pure torture. I tried to breathe more shallowly, but the more shallowly I breathed, the more breaths I had to take.

The angle of the bed left me more sitting up than lying down, but speaking to Uncle Reginald was impossible. The *effort* it had taken to attend to Georg's confession; to give him appropriate words of advice. Thank God I hadn't passed out in the middle and left him riddled with guilt. The last thing I'd want, when I felt so pleased he'd asked me. After all, I was a priest to death and beyond; it was good to be useful. I'd made it through to the Absolution, then slept, and woken feeling worse than ever.

Well, I wasn't likely to improve now. Not unless the doctors came up with something clever. I'd overheard Doctor Fathiya telling Margo about other treatment options—things like *vacuuming the fluid from my lungs*, God forbid!—but that they would gain so little time and were so invasive that short of the lab being on the verge of a breakthrough—they weren't even close—she judged them not in my best interests. Thank the Lord for that. My lungs hurt enough already. If someone came towards me with a medical vacuum right now, I'd probably scream like a baby!

But there were so many things I should've talked to Uncle Reginald about and now I couldn't. I'd never even brought up heaven—or hell. I hadn't even mentioned God's love! Surely, I should've started with that? Well, I suppose I did start with that, back on the gurney, but how could I not have followed up on it? And now it was too late.

*O Holy Spirit, I am only your mouthpiece. I just pray,*

*pray, pray that I have relayed what you wanted and not lost anything in the translation. And that it's enough.*

I wanted to believe it was enough, but how could it be? Those few little conversations...

*Lord, what can I do for Uncle Reginald?*

I tried to pray, the simplest prayer of all, the rosary, that appeal to our spiritual mother to pray with us and for us, but I'd grown too weak to manage the beads at all now, and I kept losing track with my fingers. Three hands plus one extra finger per decade. It just didn't make for easy reckoning and pain fogged my mind...

*Oh Lord, I wish I could feel you again!*

*No, no, I'm not taking it back. Not sure I can, but I'm not. Uncle Reginald needs it all. Just wishing.* But even the thought brought tears to my cheeks. This long, lingering descent into death was so much harder to face without His Blessed Presence enveloping me.

Lingering? No. Dismantling was *lingering*. This was quick, clean and comfortable by comparison. It was. I must stop whining and count my blessings. I could still think and therefore I could still pray.

I pushed away the little voice pointing out that dismantling would be *all over* by now and once again struggled to pick up the thread of my sputtering rosary.

"Kyle?"

Margo. I tried to smile at her, but my smile wobbled, along with my state of consciousness. A haze of pain enveloped everything.

"Kyle, this is absurd! I'm putting the morphine back up!"

"No, leave it!" My voice came out a mere rasp. "I don't think I can reach it anymore."

"Good! Maybe we can keep it at the right level, now."

"Margo!" I tried to reach for her hand...no, I couldn't. Desperation engulfed me. "Margo, please! Leave it! I *need* you to leave it!"

"I'm just supposed to sit here and watch you suffering? Why don't you want it up?"

"I *do*, but...I *can't!* It's the *only* thing I can *do*, now, *the only thing. Please* don't take this away from me." My voice wobbled, a sob crowding up my throat. "*Please*, Margo..."

## MARGO

Kyle seemed on the point of tears. He was *begging* me. His distress struck like an unseen hand slapping my face. A hot wash of shame followed. How could I try to override him like this? He was my *brother*, not my child. An adult. Entitled to make his own decisions, even if they seemed crazy.

Actually...his pain-glazed gaze clung to Hill as he spoke. So. *That* was what it was all about. The morphine. The sedation. Or lack of. My brother; not crazy, just saintly. A saintly over-ambitious optimist who would never say damned. And far too humble, far too set on not letting the left hand know what the right hand was doing, to simply tell me.

Reaching out, I dropped the morphine back to his preferred level. "There. Of course it's up to you. I'm really sorry. I just hate...I hate seeing you in pain."

Kyle smiled weakly. "It's mutual. I'm so sorry to hurt you like this. Really. I am. But...I just *have to*."

"It's alright, Kyle." Okay, it still hurt, but now I'd seen how desperately it mattered to him, now I'd realised *why*, at least I understood.

Kyle sunk back into his increasingly out-of-it state of pain and exhaustion. I sat, helplessly, watching his remaining fingers twitch in a slow sequence. Praying, even now?

Or especially now?

I should be praying too, shouldn't I? I reached in my pocket for my rosary. Nothing. Don't tell me I'd left it in my room? Yes, I had. With a sigh, I got to my feet—and accidentally made eye contact with Hill.

With immense effort, I mustered a small, polite smile and turned to go.

"What's his issue with the morphine?" The cool voice was also pretty polite, as that voice went. "How on earth can he still be worried about addiction?"

Taking a deep breath—*Lord, please guard my tongue*—I turned around again. "He's not worried about addiction, Mr Hill."

"Then why won't he accept an effective dose? Is he a masochist?"

"Of course not."

"Then why does he choose to lie there in agony? Ah,

correct me if I'm wrong? He *is* in agony?"

Responses flashed through my mind, angry, sarcastic, bitter, outright lies...but what fell out of my mouth was the truth. "He's doing it for *you.*"

Hill frowned, total bafflement on his face. "For me? What do you mean, *he's doing it for me?*"

"For your soul." With enormous effort, I bit back, *if you actually have one.* Hill had one, all right, and ignored it at his peril.

"I thought you people were adamant that only your imaginary friend can save anyone."

"Of course God is the only one who can actually *save* anyone, Mr Hill."

Hill's bewilderment hadn't eased. "So how can lying there in agony be *for me?* What possible benefit can it bring me?"

I took another deep breath, struggling for the words to explain. "Mr Hill, which demonstrates more love on my part: if I do something for my children that I enjoy, something pleasant, or if I do something that involves a sacrifice, or a discomfort, on my part?"

"The second. *Obviously.*"

"Obviously? Well, you grasp that, which is something."

Hill stared at me, eyes narrowed.

Glancing around, my eyes fell on the crucifix over the window, on that tortured figure hanging in agony on the cross. I pointed to it, my throat tight. "*There*, Mr Hill. *That* is how much *God* loves you."

I swung round and pointed to Kyle, so still and quiet, barely conscious, forehead pain-drenched, still struggling to pray. My voice broke. "And *that* is how much my *brother* loves you. Though *God knows you don't deserve him!*"

Tears escaped from my eyes—I turned and ran for it.

## KYLE

"Crazy boy?" That cold, precious voice sliced through the haze of pain gripping me. "I've just had a curious conversation with that pesky sister of yours."

I dragged my eyes open at last and focussed on Uncle Reginald, trying to smile. Yes...I'd heard the conversation.

Rather like overhearing a distant radio, but I'd heard it.

"Do I correctly deduce from her hysterical ravings that you have some foolish superstitious goal of...what is the expression? *Saving my soul?*"

Still smiling at him, I managed a slight nod. I hadn't meant Margo to find out, but he, he could know.

Uncle Reginald shook his head disgustedly. "Well, you'd be better forgetting that nonsense, crazy boy. I *have* no soul. You may as well take the morphine, for all the good it's doing *me.*"

Could I speak? That loudly? But the words burned in me, demanding to be united with his stolen ears. I could muster only Latin, but he'd understand. "You...do have...a...soul... Uncle...Reginald... And it...is...precious...and beautiful...in the Lord's...eyes...and...He wants it...with Him..." I fell silent, panting, head spinning with pain.

"Deranged," muttered Uncle Reginald. "The whole lot of you."

If only I could *reply*, but it took all I had just to stay...to stay consciou...

"Kyle? Kyle?" Margo's dear gentle voice this time, drawing me out of myself.

I got my eyes open.

She stood there, smiling a bitter-sweet smile and proffering a phone. "It's Bane. Here..." Carefully, she tucked the handset between my ear and shoulder.

"Bane?" Even little more than a whisper made me feel light-headed.

"Hi, bro. I hear you're feeling poorly."

"Umm... A little... Where are you?"

"Can Hill hear me?"

"No."

"We're on the ship. Making port in an hour or two. Then it's about twelve to fourteen hours on the bullet train."

Twelve to fourteen *hours?* "I think...you're going to be late by...quite a few hours."

"I know." Bane's voice was soft. Yes, hence why he was calling. Even he'd accepted that they weren't going to make it. "I'm sorry, Kyle. I did my best."

"Bane, I'm amazed...you've got this far...in the time. Don't apologise."

Wind and waves and children's voices murmured in the background. My heart stretched, trying to reach down the phone and hug them all.

Were they enjoying being on a ship? What an adventure for them! Children's attention spans were too short for the reason for their trip to spoil it for them. Luc, that little bit older, might be feeling it more. How many questions he always had for me when I visited. Most about the priesthood, or seminary, but also about Africa...

*"Can you tell us the story about the lions, Uncle Kyle?"* asked Javi.

*"No, the one about the hyenas!"* Polly grabbed my arm insistently.

*"Let's hear the one about the miraculous pool!"* Luc sat forward eagerly on the sofa. *"Can we have that one, Uncle Kyle? Please?"*

"Sorry, Bane, he's fallen asleep." A soft voice spoke nearby. "Speaking exhausts him."

I dragged my eyes open again as Margo started to move away, the phone to her ear. "Wait..." I wheezed. *Wait, I haven't...haven't said goodbye...*

"Oh, he's woken up. Here you are." Margo restored the handset to its place under my ear.

"Bane?"

"Hi, bro."

Now I had him back on the line, I struggled for words. "I'll give...your love...to Georgie..."

When Bane replied his voice was thick and low. "Thanks. Don't forget Blessed Peter and Father Mark. Or Snakey. Or Lucas. Or...well, there's a bit of a list, isn't there? Say hi to them all from us."

"I...will. Tell...children I love them."

"Of course. You've...you've been an awesome brother, Kyle." Bane's voice wobbled slightly, and I pictured him standing at the ship's rail, staring out over the ocean in the hope that the tears on his cheeks would be ascribed to the sea breeze blowing in his eyes. "And I don't just mean in comparison to Eliot!"

"You've...been a...great brother...too...Bane. I know you'll... carry right on...looking...after Margo and..."

"'Course I will."

"Daddy? *Daddy?* Polly's climbing over the lifeboat and she's probably going to fall *overboard,* but she won't listen to *me.*"

Luc's plaintive voice came faintly to my ears.

"Uh, Kyle, mate, I've got to go."

I sensed myself plummet down Bane's scale of priorities and smiled. "Bye, Bane."

"You'll...uh...you'll see me someday, okay?"

"I'd *better.*"

That won a wry snort from Bane, then he took the phone away from his mouth and the sounds grew faint. "Where is she, Luc? How many times have I told her..." Clanging footsteps, then Bane cut the call.

I dimly felt Margo easing the handset out, then blackness swum up around me.

*If a man takes your cloak, give him your shirt also.*

The words were lodged in my head as I woke. Blearily, I played around with them, trying them for size, turning them this way and that as though they were a garment themselves. Why were they echoing in my mind?

A clink of a glass being put down and a familiar voice. "If a man presses you to go a mile with him, go two..."

Oh, Margo was reading to me. I'd a vague recollection, now, of her offering, when I'd sort of woken up a few...minutes?...ago. She'd asked me what I'd like to hear, and I'd muttered a Bible citation at random rather than disappoint her, too fog-brained to have any idea what I'd asked for.

*If a man takes your cloak, give him your shirt also...*

I drew in a breath so suddenly I choked. Margo's frantic attempts to help caused pain but no relief, and soon Doctor Fathiya perched at my bedside, encouraging my body to behave itself.

Once she'd got me breathing normally again, she stood up to go. "Can I help you with anything else, Father Kyle?"

"Actually," I whispered, "you can."

## MARGO

Sobs tore unstoppably from me as I turned away from Kyle's curtained off bed and moved towards Reginald Hill's. Ugh, I had to get hold of myself. I couldn't speak to the man in this state.

I made it to the monster's bedside, but still I couldn't stem the sobs. This last straw had caused my heart to swell and break, or so it felt.

Hill looked up at me unemotionally. "So he's dead, then? That was quieter than I expected."

I still couldn't speak. Putting my back to him, I wrestled with my misbehaving body. Finally, I could breathe normally—a little quiveringly, but normally *enough*—and I turned around again.

Hill stared over at Kyle's bed, or at its drawn curtains, an unreadable expression on his cold face.

"No, Mr Hill." My voice still trembled infuriatingly. "He's not dead. Not *yet*." It wouldn't be long, though. He'd fallen asleep twice while talking to Doctor Fathiya and the surgeon and could only just be considered conscious now.

"Then why are you trying to flood the room? Is it a cunning plan to drown me and make it look like an accident?"

I gritted my teeth, fighting to ignore the needling. "Mr Hill, my brother asked me to come over here and tell you something."

"Otherwise you wouldn't be speaking to me, eh, Little Miss Forgiveness?"

Blast, Hill knew I didn't forgive him, didn't he? I felt such a naked hypocrite, standing here talking to him.

*Just say it, Margo.*

"Mr Hill, my brother wishes you to know that he is donating you his liver and heart."

Hill stared at me, now, his face oddly...frozen.

"He has arranged for a transplant team to be ready, so when...when his heart stops..." somehow, somehow I didn't break down again, "the organs can be transferred straight into revival boxes for evaluation and then transplanted without any need for freezing."

No need to explain to *Hill* that organ freezing and revival—although possible for decades and vastly increasing both the ethics of organ donation and the quantity of organs available—took some years off the life of the frozen organ. He knew that, well enough.

My turn to stare at Hill. Who said absolutely *nothing*. Good grief, cold old cuss or not, this took the biscuit. *Kyle* had insisted on closing the bed curtains—to stop Hill lip-reading—and having a top secret whispered conference with the medical staff rather than risk raising Hill's hopes prematurely if they judged his relevant organs unlikely to be viable, and here was *Hill*, unable to muster so much as a reply, let alone a *Thank you.*

When the silence went on and on, I said, as politely as I could, "Did you understand what I just told you, Mr Hill?"

His eyes snapped to me at last. "I'm not senile, girl!" A hesitation, and he added, "I was just…thinking about the medicine I'll require. For the operation. I need to make a phone call and order it."

"You, make a phone call?" I snorted. "Dream on!"

"The transplant will be a waste of time without it. I suffer from a variety of complicated conditions. A healthy young thing like yourself wouldn't understand."

Fuming, I raised my wristCell and opened U's channel. "U? Mr Hill needs to make a phone call. To order medicine for the transplant op, he says."

"Isn't it anything the hospital has?" U's cultured voice issued tinnily from my wrist.

I raised an eyebrow at Hill.

He rolled his eyes. "Why on earth would I order it if it were? That's a no. It's very rare. And expensive."

"Did you catch that, U?"

"Yep. Give him your wristCell. I'll monitor."

I unfastened the device and handed it to Hill, who ignored U's unseen presence and dialled calmly.

"Hello?" A startled voice, speaking Esperanto. Was the wristCell showing an African number or a Vatican one?

"This is Hill. Reginald Hill."

A long silence. Then the voice came again, low and breathless. "I can't speak to you, *Senor* Hill. You've no idea how… I can't!"

"Listen up. One of my out-of-Bloc bank accounts has a

balance of six hundred thousand eurons. Six and five zeros, did you catch that? I want five vials of the E4367 sent to the Kenyan Free State, and I want them here within two hours. Pull rank—or bribe someone if you have to—get them on a fast jet, get them here, and you will receive access details in a few days for that very bank account. Can you speak to me *now?*"

Another long silence. The voice spoke again, nervous, but also eager. "Sir, two hours just isn't possible. But I can do it in three..."

"A minute over, and it won't be a *PIN number* you receive. Understand?"

"Yes, sir. I might even do it in two and a half. Just not in two. Sir."

"Then you'd better get on with it. Agent Willmott, would you be so kind as to give the good doctor an address?"

"Very well, Mr Hill." The wristCell went silent as U cut Hill from the call.

Hill held the device out to me. My disgust at the way he'd spoken to his subordinate—former subordinate—must've shown on my face, because he smirked. "Well, after all the, ah, present stresses the organs are undergoing, I wouldn't want them to deteriorate the *slightest* bit further, now, would I?"

Unbelievable!

And still, not a word of thanks.

Strapping my wristCell back on, I stormed out of the room, by some miracle holding back a tirade in which 'ungrateful rat' would have been the mildest phrase. And threatening to kill the doctor—some sort of military poison-developing doctor barely worthy of the title—for running *a minute* over time!

Okay, so organs couldn't be held indefinitely in an artificial revival box without suffering some slow deterioration, but Hill, at his age, even with Kyle's organs, could scarcely expect to live long enough for an extra hour to make any difference! Hill terrorised people out of sheer reflex, didn't he? The utter swine!

Oh dear! With a supreme effort I reined in my unloving, unforgiving thoughts. And turned my steps towards the chapel. I'd better take a quick break and try to calm down. The events of the last half hour had been so heart wrenching. Kyle's generosity had stunned me. Though I'd not been able to help protesting, "But does the world really need *Reginald Hill* around for another few decades, Kyle?"

Kyle had smiled tolerantly at me. "Just keep him...locked up...until you've...saved his...soul."

He spoke as though the saving of Reginald Hill's soul were some simple, easy little matter. But he had a point. We wouldn't be letting Hill go, so what did it matter if he lived a bit longer? Maybe he'd be healthy enough to make himself useful on the farm, after all. But the thought of Kyle's heart, the part of him that symbolised all his love and kindness and warmth, in *Hill's* chest; the thought of my brother being buried without it...it hurt more than I could have imagined possible.

But the worst moment had been after the organ donation was arranged and I mentioned to Doctor Fathiya that it must be time for Kyle's lunch, since it was nearly one o'clock? And she'd given me a compassionate look and said that right now, food would only cause his body undue stress.

And I, with stubborn determined optimism, had said well, he could always make up for it at dinnertime.

And then she'd looked at me even more compassionately—her fingers checking her watch remained in place—and said very gently that the question of dinner really wasn't going to arise.

Before six o'clock, Kyle would be dead.


*KYLE*
Drip. Drip. Drip.
*Ah, the pain was so bad.*
Could I *really* hear a dripping?
*Every breath, searing my lungs...*
The sound of the morphine, trickling from its bag?
*Morphine...*
I'd never heard the noise before. My imagination? The devil?

Margo had put a stop to nurses turning the morphine up. The thought of what she'd deduced from my unguarded words made my cheeks warm. I hadn't meant the right hand to know what the left hand...

And then she'd told Doctor Fathiya? My face burned at the thought.

But they'd stopped adjusting it.

Thank God. If someone turned it up now, could I even muster the strength to ask them to turn it back down?

*Yes, you could, Kyle. Because it's not about your strength. The* Lord *has the strength...*

Two candles burned by the bed, on either side of a crucifix. Such a familiar sight...I'd just never been the one in the bed before. Welcome, though. The crucifix over the window was hard to focus on, but I could see this one easily. I'd a vague memory of the chaplain saying the litanies of the dying with Margo and some of the nurses after putting it there. I'd tried to mouth the responses but...fallen asleep?

Father—oh, what was his name, was my brain going?—he'd gone off to minister to some of the other patients, assuring Margo he would return before the end. Yes, I didn't want him spending time on me, when others needed him more. I'd received all the Sacraments of the Dying, Margo was here, and I didn't need comforting, anyway. I was as big a sinner as anyone, but God's mercy was bigger.

Blackness nibbled my mind again...a familiar stab of fear pricked me...the next time I woke, would I be drowning? Suffocating?

If so...then I would be very close. To being with Him. No reason for fear, then.

I was fighting, fighting to surrender to Him. Fighting *so hard.* But how could I tell if I succeeded, without even my old awareness of Him?

*Mother Mary, pray for me. Guardian Angel, protect me.*

Drip. Drip. Drip.

The morphine hung right there, by the bed. A word from me and...no more agony. A pain-free passage could be mine.

*I have no soul.* That's what Uncle Reginald said. That's what he believed. How wrong he was.

*Save him, Lord. Please, save him. Use the extra time he's getting and save him.*

Would it really matter if I turned the morphine up? Even just a few bars? He *had* all that extra time now, after all...

I pictured a full team of hefty African football players bearing down on that temptation as though it were a deflating football.

And for good measure, myself, from the sidelines, bellowing: *Get thee behind me, Satan!*


## MARGO

I returned to Kyle after only a short time and sat by his bed, quietly reciting the prayers for the dying from the booklet Father Omwancha had left me. Kyle rarely became fully conscious, his breathing bubbly and pain-racked. No sign of any blood, yet.

Doctor Fathiya predicted that he would fall almost entirely unconscious soon and that although he would—unfortunately—return to a significant level of awareness once the cascade started, it would be far too late for communication. Had I missed my chance to say goodbye? *Please, no...*

Thank God, not long before three o'clock he finally seemed to grow a little more aware of his surroundings.

"Kyle?"

His eyes focussed on my face for the first time in an hour.

I took his half hand, very gently. I always feared it must hurt him terribly to have it held, yet I sensed he preferred it. Maybe when I took his wrist instead, it felt like a rejection, somehow.

His lips curved in a slight smile.

I leant closer. "Kyle, I love you, and I'm so glad you've been my big brother. You know that, right?"

He smiled that weak smile again. His mouth opened and after a couple of attempts he managed, "Ditto...little sis... Love...you."

I kissed his cheek. How I longed to hug him—but I'd only cause him more pain.

"Mum...? Dad...?" he whispered.

I shook my head, my heart aching. "I'm sorry, Kyle. We still can't get through. The storm's barely moving away yet, and the communications are all down."

Our poor parents. They would emerge after the storm, intent on evaluating the damage and getting things straight, but when, to great joy, communications were restored, they would get the worst news any parent could ever receive. *Mum, Dad, Kyle is dead because I riled up Reginald Hill once too often...*

*No, stop it, Margo! This isn't your fault.*

Kyle still focussed on me. I rubbed the back of his bandaged hand gently with my thumb, in preference to squeezing it.

"Let me...hear you...say it..."

I frowned. "Say what?"

"One thing I want...hear you say...make me...very happy..." He looked like he'd pass out from the effort of so many words, but his eyes strayed from me to Hill...

Oh.

He looked at me again, his green eyes daring me to refuse his last request. "Just...to...me?"

*Oh Lord, give me strength. Give me...willingness.*

I put my mouth very close to Kyle's ear, and somehow, somehow I whispered, "I forgive Reginald Hill."

Kyle came as close to beaming as his condition allowed.

"That was low and sneaky," I grumbled.

His eyes twinkled with an irritating depth of amusement. "Be as...gentle as..."

"...doves and as cunning as serpents," I finished, before he could exhaust himself further, though I felt a familiar desire to slap him. Apparently, even being on his deathbed couldn't stop my brother from being annoying!

"Promise...look after...Uncle Regi...?"

I couldn't help glaring at him for this audacious request, but his pleading eyes were irresistible. "I'll do my best," I muttered.

He attempted to beam again, clearly delighted by my reply.

Oh no. Doing my *best* must be the highest commitment I

could've made! Why hadn't I gone for something nice and vague like 'I'll try.' Too late now. Maybe Angel Margaret and Angel Kyle colluded to make me speak without thinking.

I looked at Kyle, at his pain-glazed eyes and pallid face, and my heart tried to turn itself inside out.

He must've seen my anguish, because he smiled again, mustering a few more words. "Not long...I...with *Him*..."

The eager joy in his eyes filled me with awe—but did soothe my aching heart slightly.

Kyle murmured another word. "Hug?"

"It'll hurt you..."

The faintest of snorts was his only response to that, so very carefully, making sure I didn't knock that oxygen tube from his face, I slipped my arms around him.

"I'll be...praying...you all..." I only caught the words because he breathed them right in my ear.

I went on holding him until he slipped unconscious again, only a few moments later.

I stayed beside him as the minutes ticked on, the blessed candles slowly burned and the hand of the clock inched its way to half past three. He didn't wake again. Part of me wanted Father Omwancha's towering, uplifting presence, but most of me dreaded his return, because the nurses would have told him it was...time.

Finally, I simply had to go to the little room. I ran all the way, terrified Kyle might be embarking on that horrible death, alone. He wouldn't really be alone, of course. The nurses would rush to comfort him, to fetch the chaplain. But it wouldn't be the same.

Nature mollified, I raced back towards Kyle's room, coming face to face with U in the stairwell.

Only his quick reactions averted a collision. "Margo! Excellent. I can give you this and get back to the lab."

My heart lurched in fearful hope. "Have they...?"

U's face fell. "No, Margo, I'm sorry. I didn't mean to raise your hopes. Progress is...dreadfully slow. The lead doctor says that on current evidence, Mr Hill may well have been telling the truth, but that they're certainly not going to stop trying. I just...I feel more useful *there*, you know?"

I needed to be by Kyle's side and Unicorn needed to be overseeing the hunt for the cure that probably didn't exist. I understood that well enough. "That's alright, U. I'm grateful you're working so hard."

U shrugged this away and handed me a packet. "Mr Hill's medicine. If you wouldn't mind giving it to him. He'll need to give instructions to the doctors for what to do with it."

I drew a plastic vial out of the little packet, feeling more rolling inside. At my shoulder, Georg, now back on duty, tensed.

"Relax, Friedrich," said U. "We ran it through a basic security screening and it's not toxic, flammable, explosive, or obviously dangerous in any way. Seems to be what it's supposed to be: medicine. All the same, if Hill shows any sign of chucking it at Margo or trying any funny business, plug him. Just the once, mind."

Georg relaxed again. "Yes, sir."

U hurried off before I could think of a reason for him to give it to Hill himself, so reluctantly I resumed my canter down the hospital corridors.

*Well, Margo, you promised you'd 'do your best', so you're going to have to somehow get used to interacting with the old buzzard, aren't you?*

Suffice to say, this sage advice did nothing to make it any easier walking up to Hill's bed.

"Mr Hill? Your medicine arrived." I held out the package and he took it quickly, his eyes flying to the clock.

"Less than two and a half hours, not bad going, *Senor* Doctor."

His self-satisfied tone did nothing to soothe my temper, but I held back any comment and simply moved to return to Kyle's bedside.

"Wait." Hill's sharp voice paused me.

I turned back to him, even more irritated at his bossy manner, but somehow kept my voice level and polite. "What is it, Mr Hill?"

He took a vial from the packet, turning it meditatively in his hands.

"*Mr Hill?*" I wanted to get back to Kyle, blast him!

As though reading my mind, Hill glanced across at Kyle's

unconscious form, cocking an ear as though listening to his wheezing breathing, clearly audible even from across the room. The heart monitor made a mournful—but reassuring—counterpoint to the heart-wrenching sound. Hill had got the nurses to mute his, claiming it gave him a headache.

A tiny beep from the morphine machine—warning that the far too slowly emptying bag would need changing before long—seemed to draw Hill out of his abstraction. Decisively, he slid the vial back into the packet—and held it out. "The medicine's not for me. It's for him." He nodded towards Kyle.

My mind gummed up and shuddered to a standstill as it attempted to understand what Hill had just said. "Wh...wh... Do you mean it...?"

"*Yes*, it *is* the *antidote*," said Hill, as slowly and clearly as if speaking to a toddler.

I snatched the packet back, desperate hope now bursting insuppressibly in my heart, though I hardly dared believe... "But...you said there *wasn't one.*"

Hill rolled his eyes mockingly. "Now, little girl, I hate to break it to you, but there is such a thing as *lying*. But then, you're quite good at that already, aren't you—*Little Miss Forgiveness?*"

I peered into the packet, at those vials, my mind reeling, hope and joy and fear struggling in my chest. The antidote? *Really?* "How do we administer it?"

"One vial in his IV drip every two hours. Three is the normal dosage, but at his advanced stage, I'd give him four. The fifth vial is for your security guys to have fun with."

My eyes went back to Kyle. Barely alive...

Hill clearly saw the doubt on my face. "It's actually an *exceptionally* good antidote, if I say it myself—*I* commissioned the drug, after all—and it will work at any time up until the cascade starts. *However*, it will *not* work afterwards, so if you do want to save him, I don't think you've got a moment to waste."

*If* I *did* want to save him! Ugh, that man! But he was right! Why was I standing around wasting time?

I grabbed Hill's call button and pressed it—wait, would people respond quickly to *his*?—I raced over to Kyle's bed and *held* his button down.

A dozen nurses spilled into the room like ants from a kicked anthill, followed by Doctor Fathiya, closely followed by U, pinged by Georg, no doubt. The medical staff converged on Kyle and almost immediately began to assure me that his condition hadn't greatly deteriorated.

But U's eyes locked onto the packet I clutched to my chest. "Margo?"

"This is the antidote...Mr Hill says."

"The antidote! To think I *tested* it and..." Beet red, U didn't stop to dwell on his embarrassment. "Do you believe him?"

*Did* I believe Hill? *Why* would Hill give Kyle the antidote? Give up the organs he needed so much? Yet...if it was a cruel trick, it was an exceptionally expensive one. Six hundred thousand eurons, just to turn the knife in my back one more time? Surely, once Hill had his new organs he would hope to escape and make use of that off-shore money? But if it *was* the antidote, he'd never *get* the organs... It just didn't make *sense*.

I glanced at Hill, but he watched, his expression detached, with only the barest hint of amusement for our suspicion. We'd no time to plumb the murky depths of Hill's twisted psyche and figure out *why*. And what did we have to lose? "I think we might as well try it. I mean, even Mr Hill would have trouble coming up with something *more* unpleasant for Kyle, right? And if it does nothing, it does nothing."

Or *could* the drug actually cause Kyle even worse pain? Hard to imagine, considering what he suffered already. But if it did...if it did, well, we could fix it by raising his morphine, right?

"Let's do it," I said. "Come on! Mr Hill said it only works *before* the cascade." I held a vial out to Doctor Fathiya. "One of these in his drip, every two hours, up to a total of four. One is for analysis." I handed a second vial to U.

"Only works before the cascade begins?" echoed Doctor Fathiya, her free hand moving towards her watch, then dropping to the rosary hanging from her belt.

I nodded.

"There's no time for analysis, then. The cascade could

start at any moment."

I glanced at U.

He frowned—allowing Kyle to receive an unknown drug went against his professional instincts—but he nodded firmly. Intellect over instinct.

"Do it," I said.

Doctor Fathiya moved briskly to Kyle's drip and in moments the pale blue liquid from the vial was diffusing into the bag. And was gone.

Now we could only wait.

And pray.

"Mr Hill? Your dinner."

I opened my eyes as a soft voice spoke on the other side of the room. I must've dozed off beside Kyle's bed. My rosary had fallen to the ground...

Wait...*dinnertime!* My gaze flew to Kyle...

I couldn't hear his strained breathing—panic gripped me—then the gentle beep of his heart monitor reached my ears. He lived. Dinnertime and he still lived! And...I leaned closer, listening. Yes, a breathy wheeze still rattled his breathing, but far less pronounced than earlier. Could he...could he actually be improving?

Still being alive was hard proof of that, surely?

But would he really recover? My heart thudded even more painfully as my hope grew more and more swollen and raw.

*Live, Kyle. Come on, live... Please, Lord?*

"Doctor Fathiya reviewed your meal records at lunch time," the nurse was saying to Hill, "and wasn't at all happy with the amount you're eating. So she asked the chef to make something a bit more European for you. This is called, ah, Sheep's Pie, I think."

I caught Hill's eye roll at this mangling of the dish's title, and he greeted its arrival in front of him with his usual lack of enthusiasm. What a picky eater and no mistake. Okay, so the chances of it tasting exactly like Shepherd's Pie were probably slim, but the hospital had made a real effort. In fact, it sounded like this had got underway even before Hill had—apparently—shown mercy to Kyle.

Well, I'd learned better than to expect gratitude from Reginald Hill.

Except... If it *was* the antidote... Okay, so he hadn't *said* thank you, but you couldn't get a bigger thank you than that, right?

But *why*? When Kyle *living* would cost him far, far more than a mere six hundred thousand eurons?

Maybe...maybe he thought we'd be grateful enough to *let him go*. Somewhere outside of the EuroBloc. Then he could go off and use another out-of-bloc bank account to buy himself his new organs. Surely Hill had our measure better than that—he remained far too grave a threat to the safety of innocents to be released—yet...that *must* be it. He thought this way he could win his freedom *and* get his transplants. But in that case...why hadn't he *bargained* for it?

Hill's head turned slightly in my direction as he scrutinised his meal, and I looked away quickly before our gazes could cross. I wasn't thanking him until certain Kyle would really live, and I'd no idea what to say to him until then.

"Margo..." U appeared in the doorway.

I shot to my feet. "What's the result?"

"Oh, they haven't finished the analysis yet. Certainly, no sign yet of it being harmful. Results so far are very promising, in fact. But it's not that. We've got your parents on the line."

"Oh, good grief!" The *timing!* Okay, so I didn't now have to tell them Kyle was definitely dying—or dead—but what if I held out hope he would be okay and then... Ugh, bad timing, without question. "Okay, I'm coming."

I paused to kiss Kyle's cheek and whisper a rather fierce "Live, Kyle!" in his ear. I'd be as quick as I could and get back to him, but I didn't fancy carrying on this emotional conversation with Hill listening in.

*KYLE*

Birds sang in the dawn quiet. I lay still, enjoying the sound. God's little feathered friends had such beautiful voices. Actually, some of those splitting the dawn with their calls were rather *big* feathered friends. I knew that, though I couldn't actually see them.

That ghastly, searing pain in my chest had eased so much. Bliss...

*Wait a sec.* No, *not* good. Someone must've raised the morphine.

I opened my eyes and checked the readout. Huh. Odd. The level was *correct.* I lifted my half-hands slightly, one at a time, checking my wrists in case they'd connected a second morphine line—nothing.

*Hang on a minute...* How was I able to even slightly raise my hands?

Looking a little further afield, I saw Margo dozing in a chair beside the bed. Uncle Reginald lay in his bed opposite, asleep. Why wasn't I choking to death on my own blood? Why was I so...well, pain-free wasn't quite accurate, though compared to what it had been, it almost felt like it. And I felt so much stronger. I'd actually managed to move my hands.

*Lord, am I...getting better? Did they* find an antidote in time?

The inescapable conclusion had the same effect on my heart that cutting the cables has on an elevator. It plummeted down my skinned legs into my big-toeless foot, landing with a dull, wind-ing thud.

I would *live?*

My horrified mind reviewed the 'terms'—if one could call it that—of my greatest and most painful offering on Uncle Reginald's behalf.

*Lord, does this mean I could live to be a hundred and twenty and never feel you ever again?*

Probably. It hadn't crossed my mind when I gave my *yes* that I might *live.* Would I still have given it, if I'd known?

Uncle Reginald's sleeping form drew my eyes again. Yes. I *hoped.* But it would've been even *harder.*

"Kyle!" Margo's delighted cry cut off my anguished thoughts. "Kyle, you're awake! How do you feel?"

"Astonishingly well." Her arms went around me, gently. I managed to turn my hands upwards and clasp her slightly in return.

"Whatever's been happening while I was asleep?" I asked, as she sat down again. I could talk almost normally.

"Hill gave you the antidote."

I stared at her, gobsmacked. "*Mr Hill* gave it to me?"

"Yes. He got it from Europe from some doctor he knows. On a fast jet. He had to pay the fellow *six hundred thousand* eurons."

A *jet?* Six hundred *thousand*... That would have built an orphanage and funded it for about ten *years*. "But..."

Margo spread her arms, looking frustrated. "No one can figure out *why*, Kyle. It makes no sense, but he did it."

"Did anyone try asking him?"

Margo's cheeks grew red. "Well, I haven't really spoken to him. I was...you know, waiting to see how you were. It's been night-time, anyway."

"Oh. Yes." It'd been...what, mid-afternoon...the last I remembered. I'd been out of it for a long time. Despite that, sleep dragged at my eyelids again already.

By the time Doctor Fathiya had examined me, a nap more than beckoned. I shot another look across at Uncle Reginald, but he still slept—or pretended to. Waking him to thank him—and interrogate him!—would be a poor show of gratitude.

*MARGO*

My heart felt like it had grown lips and a voice box, so it could sing away lustily in my chest. They'd completed analysis of the antidote: one hundred percent beneficial and harmless. It completely undid the effects of Mr Hill's nasty 'Insurance Policy'.

Doctor Fathiya's assessment of Kyle confirmed it. Significantly improved already, Kyle should make a full recovery. Well, from the lung poison. It wouldn't grow his missing parts back.

I could still scarcely dare to believe it. Since Kyle had gone to sleep again, I hurried to the chapel to catch the early Mass and prayed for a while afterwards, trying to somehow express the profound thanksgiving in my heart. Then I went to the hospital canteen for a quick bite of breakfast before hastening back to my brother.

I needn't have worried, he still slept.

Hill sat up in bed, though, eyes open. *Blast.*

I couldn't put it off any longer, could I?

With a quick prayer to Angel Margaret and the Holy Spirit, I approached his bed. "Mr Hill?"

"Ah, good. I need your wristCell again."

"You do, *do* you?" What a *bossy-boots.*

"Your brother's medicine is not yet paid for, little girl. Would you like *Senor* Doctor, so angry and disappointed—and *very* out of pocket—to send some rather less health-inducing packets? Not that *I* care, so I'll keep the money if you prefer anthrax to honesty."

Of course, Hill hadn't actually *made* the payment yet, and clearly he wanted to honour his bargain, though he pretended indifference. An obscene amount of blood money being transferred from one evil specimen of humanity to another... I scarcely liked to be involved, even so slightly. Still, we hadn't gainsaid Hill when he promised payment... and Lord knows what the doctor *did* have access to, if he felt inclined to act as Hill predicted.

I called U and relayed Hill's request. U's hesitation suggested that he shared my distaste for the transaction, but he agreed to the loan of the communication device and no doubt monitored the text messages Hill quickly typed out and sent.

Hill handed back my wristCell—without thanks—and I returned it to my wrist, then took a deep breath. "Actually, I'd like to thank you—"

Hill's mouth twisted in a malevolent sneer and he cut me off at once. "*You* do not owe me any thanks, Margaret Verrall, nor do I wish to hear any. I did not do this for you. I would never do this for *you.* The fact that this brought any benefit to *you* is in my eyes no more than an irritating—but unavoidable—side-effect of my desired outcome."

His desired outcome...Kyle not dying? *He* poisoned Kyle in the first place.

"If my thanks are going to cause you such discomfort, then since, like it or not, I am grateful to you, I will withhold them. But I have to ask, Mr Hill, in the circumstances, all things being as they are...why did you do it?"

His eyes ran over me, balefully. "I don't like you, Margaret

Verrall. If I believed in the devil, then as far as I'm concerned you'd be the devil's daughter, hell-cat that you are. But your brother...he's a nice young man. Totally insane, of course. But a nice young man, all the same."

A hint of a frown crossed Hill's brow. "But then, I place no value on *nice*, so that's not why. No, in the end, I suppose it just seemed...such a waste."

"A *waste*? Although you got two new organs out of it and would've made me cry, to boot?"

A supremely nasty smile curved Hill's lips. "But I've made you cry before, Margaret. Nothing new there. Is there?"

His expression drew my mind straight back to blood-splashed paving slabs...Lucas; to Bane lying there, blind and in agony; to Father Mark, ready to die rather than commit the evil Hill had tried to make him do; to Dominique, to Snakey, to Hyena, to *myself*, lying on that gurney...

No, not the slightest point denying what Hill said. He'd made me cry, all right. Many, many times.

"And what about the organs?"

"If I really needed your brother's organs so badly as that, do you truly think he'd still be breathing? I'd have had them out of him at once, the moment we kidnapped him. No, this was never anything but a self-indulgent little game of mine."

So Kyle's organs would only ever have been a...a what? A perk? A little bonus? This really had been all about revenge and his need for a transplant was nowhere near so urgent as he'd led Kyle to believe. Had he told Kyle otherwise just to...to try to make him feel bad?

"You are a very twisted man, Mr Hill," I said. "But thank you for sparing him, anyway."

"I didn't hear that!" Hill spat the words, turning to stare at the window.

He really didn't want me thanking him, did he? Too late.

Kyle's eyes were still closed. I glanced at the clock and headed briskly for my room.

Our parents would be up. I could give them an update.

*KYLE*

By the time I opened my eyes, Margo had left. She must've thought me asleep. I'd woken when she first spoke but felt it tactful to keep a low profile.

I looked across at Uncle Reginald. I needed to thank him too. Even though I felt little joy, personally, at finding myself recovering, thankfulness filled me on Margo's account. On all my family's account. It made me especially happy that Uncle Reginald had allowed himself to perform a good action.

"Uncle Reginald?"

He shot a glance my way and spoke—grumpily. "I thought you were awake."

"Will you accept a thank you from me?"

"If you must."

"Thank you, then."

He shrugged.

"Why, though? Why did you do it?"

"You heard what I just told Margaret."

"Yes. And I don't believe it. Well, I believe the first part. But you were in a wheelchair when we met. You haven't got out of that bed since you arrived. You barely eat, picking at your food. You sleep...well, less than I've been sleeping, but *a lot*. You expect me to believe that you don't need that transplant and maybe need it more badly than you've been letting on? So *why*?"

Uncle Reginald stared out of the window, chewing his lips. Finally, he let out a long breath and began to speak. "A couple of years ago, my doctor told me I now needed a liver transplant. A somewhat less surprising diagnosis after the passing of those extra two decades, though probably also due to that nasty toxin they made me work with...

"But with Sorting no more, this was—at my age—a far more serious matter. My heart had been a bit temperamental for a while—but not bad enough to be worth the risk of a transplant, either above-board or black market. But it *was* bad enough to make me ineligible for a legitimate liver—and it was getting worse.

"Well, you know the public mood about black market organs, nowadays. *But*, my doctor gave the opinion that I had time—time to start a campaign."

"You really thought you could...?"

"Ah, no, I wasn't delusional. I had no expectation of bringing back Sorting. But I thought I might shift public opinion just enough—even for a short time—that an appropriately discreet black-market transplant—or even two—wouldn't end my political career.

"But as a result of my campaign—or rather, your sister's counter-campaign—public opinion did shift, as I'm sure you recall. The wrong way. Retirement—and the black market—became my only option."

"So why didn't you?"

"Because my doctor had made a miscalculation. A transplant was no longer a viable treatment and, like that cascade you are so lucky to have avoided, other health problems were...snowballing.

"So yes, crazy boy. I needed your organs. Two years ago. But they're no good to me now." He still stared out of the window, avoiding my eyes. "Well, I can't hide it for much longer. I'd say I now have...a couple of days to live." A grimace crossed his face. "Less...maybe.

"So," he looked at me at last, his face pale, "tell me exactly what good Margaret's tears—or my six hundred thousand eurons, for that matter—will do me now? Tell me that? Why should I not keep your heart beating, if that takes my fancy more?"

I looked back at him, my mind buzzing with dismay. A couple of *days*? No, he clearly believed he had even less time than *that* and modern diagnoses, especially with some conditions, were very accurate. Oh, no, no, no. If *I'd* died...others could have kept trying to get through to him. But once *he* died... Game over.

*Oh Lord, help me! Help* him.

Uncle Reginald managed a strained, ironic smile. "Father Kyle Verrall, lost for words? Well, this is a first. If I'd known telling the truth would silence you, I'd have done it a day or two back and saved myself some inane chatter."

"I'm just...I'm really sorry. I had no idea things were that bad. Why on earth haven't you accepted treatment from the doctors here?"

"Because I've exhausted all treatment options already, and I prefer not to have my condition public knowledge."

"This is bad. This is very, very bad..." I tried to get my thoughts together, to plan.

"It's good for *you*, crazy boy. It just saved your life."

"I know, but...so little time for...for you to realise. About God."

Uncle Reginald snorted. "Oh, here we go again. See how fast you can make me regret saving you, why don't you?"

"It's important, Uncle Reginald." I spoke very, very intently. "It is the most important decision you will make in your entire life. The very most important. And so far, you have consistently chosen wrong and you clearly have no idea how awful the consequences of that are going to be in just a few short days—"

"Listen to me, Kyle Verrall!" Uncle Reginald's tone grew equally intense. "I don't expect to see anything after my heart stops beating. I don't expect to sense anything or experience anything. I will be gone as though I'd never been. But I assure you, if, contrary to my expectations, I see God, I will believe in His existence. *When* I see Him. Understand?"

I shook my head, opening my mouth, but Margo walked back into the room before I could speak. Nothing about Margo's and Uncle Reginald's earlier exchange suggested three-way conversations had suddenly become a good idea, so I bit my tongue.

*Lord, please keep Uncle Reginald alive as long as possible?*

"I told Mum and Dad how much better you are." Beaming, Margo sat in the chair beside my bed. "They're so relieved. Oh, you won't know—they called last night..."

The happy warmth in her voice as she recounted our parents' joy made me glad to be alive. Though tiredness tugged at me again. Not that utter, life-sapping tiredness of before, just a deep, healthier tiredness, like after over-doing it an awful lot on the football pitch.

Okay, I wasn't thinking about football. Nope.

I tried to listen to Margo instead, but her cheerful voice soon faded to background noise...

\* \* \*

Chattering, giggling, shuffling...

"*Shhhh*... Uncle Kyle's sleeping. You can see him, but you've got to be *quiet.*"

A high-pitched squeal. "There he is!"

"Polly! *Shhh!*"

A younger voice piped up, "*Where's* Uncle Kyle, Mummy?"

"In the bed there. *Shhh.*"

"Oh, good grief." The cold—horrified—mutter came from across the room. "It's an *infestation.*"

"Hang on, hang on," Margo was saying. "Before we go in, you need to listen to me for a moment. Are you all listening? You see that other bed and that old man in it?"

"Yes, Mummy." A deafening chorus.

"Well, picture a line down the middle of the room from the window to the door. Can you picture it?"

"Yes, Mummy."

"You are all to stay on Uncle Kyle's side of that line, is that clear? Because that old man is very evil and he wants to hurt you. You are not to speak to him. If he offers you something, he is lying. He doesn't have sweets or chocolate or...or *ponies*, or whatever he says. It's all lies. You stay on Uncle Kyle's side of the line. Is that absolutely clear?"

"Yes, Mummy."

"Alright, we can go in and see Uncle Kyle. But you must be quiet because he's asleep."

"You were just talking *really loud* about the old man, Mummy..."

"*Shhhh!*"

Smiling, I opened my eyes. Like Margo or Bane would allow any of the children to be in this room unsupervised!

Still, sensible warnings. The fact that Uncle Reginald no longer wanted *me* dead hadn't changed his feelings about Margo one iota. Nor Bane, no doubt. And much as I'd like to believe he wouldn't hurt children, I wasn't *that* naive. Okay, so even from the earliest days of his political career he'd always paid others to do his dirty work for him. But one didn't need to be a martial arts expert to harm an unsuspecting child.

"It's alright," I said, as they approached with, well, a *suggestion* of quietness. "I'm awake."

"See, you woke him up, Mummy." But Polly hung back beside her mother, staring at my half-hands.

"*You* woke him up, shrieking like that!" Luc was also looking, his eyes wide and his face tight. He'd understand better than any of them what my loss meant to me.

Javi came right up to the bed and peered solemnly at my poor hands. "Do they hurt, Uncle Kyle?"

"Not much. No need to worry about them."

Lizzie climbed up onto the chair beside the bed and took hold of my closest half-hand in her tiny ones, examining it with four-year-old straight-forwardness.

"Lizzie! You'll hurt him," protested Margo, but I waved her back with my other hand. Much better the children touch my strange hands and not be afraid of them.

Finally, Lizzie looked up at me, her eyes very big. "Are they really *gone*, Uncle Kyle?"

"Ummm, I'm afraid so."

"But if we all kiss them better, won't they grow back?"

"Um..." A lump formed in my throat at this innocent offer. "Well, they won't actually *grow back*, but I'm sure it would make them feel much better."

Very seriously, Lizzie placed a kiss on both my bandaged hands. Javi reached out and did the same, unprompted.

"Come on, Polly!" Lizzie urged. "You've got to kiss Uncle Kyle better!"

"I don't want to!"

"She doesn't have to, Lizzie," I said quickly. "It's fine. You and Javi have done them a lot of good."

Lizzie jumped down off the chair and stuck her hands on her little hips. "But Polly could do them MORE good!"

"I don't want to!" yelled Polly.

"You don't have to..." But my voice went unheard as Polly, Javi, and Lizzie all talked over one another. Sighing, I finally had time to look for Bane. He stood behind Margo, Joey in his arms, looking tired. But a broad smile lightened his face when I met his eyes, which I returned.

Luc, still incredibly sombre, ignored the argument and approached the bed at last. He took my hands, one by one, and placed a kiss on them. Not on the injured edge, but on what remained of my anointed palms.

He looked at me, tears swimming in his eyes. "Can you...can you still...?" He stopped, biting his lip.

"Can I say Mass?" Somehow, I kept my voice steady. "No. I'd drop Him, wouldn't I? Plenty I can do, though." I managed to speak cheerfully. "I heard a confession just the other day, you know. Plenty of work for me still; don't fret. And..." A cheering thought pushed its way through the black clouds surrounding this subject. "And I bet I can still con-celebrate. With other priests. And you never know. Maybe if I practise a lot."

Deep down, I doubted I'd ever want to risk desecrating my Lord and God, however accidentally, but no point worrying about it right now.

Bane deposited his sleeping armful on the bed beside me. As Joey nestled drowsily to my chest and went right on sleeping, I raised a hand and stroked a wisp of soft two-year-old hair into place, my heart full.

I'd thought I'd never see them again. Not like this.

*Thank you, Lord.*

Once Margo—who considered Bane deserved a break from childcare—had firmly led away younger, fractious darlings for a nap, I said a belated morning prayer with Luc and Bane. Then—since I wasn't dying after all—I encouraged them to go out and explore the town. This first ever foreign trip might as well be re-categorised as a holiday.

And I needed the time to speak to Uncle Reginald.

"Aah, peace and quiet," sighed my roommate, as Luc's youthful voice faded away down the corridor.

I smiled. "You really don't like children, do you?"

"Nannies were invented for a reason. Thankfully no one ever expected me to have more than three."

"Nannies?"

He shot me an unamused look. "*Children.*"

"I know, just pulling your leg."

"Hilarious."

"Okay, well, you know what you said earlier, that you'd believe in God when you saw Him?"

"Oh, give me strength. You're like a boomerang. The harder I chuck you away, the faster you come back!"

"Because it's *important*. You're a very well-educated man, now, aren't you? You know an awful lot about espionage, national security, interrogation, plus medicine and science as well. Am I wrong?"

"Of course, you're not."

"Right. But despite studying our habits and activities in considerable detail, you're *not* actually very well up on metaphysics, theology, or philosophy. And this notion that one can see God when one dies and change one's mind, that idea commits an absolute schoolboy error when it comes to metaphysics and human nature."

"Does it really." Uncle Reginald's flat tone failed to deter me.

"The statement you just made is the statement of a temporal being, that is to say, a being that exists *within* time and cannot easily think about things any other way. But God is outside of time. Heaven is the metaphysical state of being in God's presence. Hell is the state of being cut off from God's presence. He's still there, but those in hell have rejected Him, which causes them extreme suffering.

"But the point is that both states exist *out of time*, along with God. Without meaning to talk too much in terms of souls and bodies, which are far more closely connected than a simple explanation of this tends to suggest, when you die, the spiritual part of you ceases to exist *in time* but exists *out* of time, with God. But, *without time*, you can't *change*. You become unchanging."

Uncle Reginald watched me more intently, now, as though the intellectual puzzle caught at his attention, in spite of himself.

"Do you understand the implications?" I went on. "Whatever you thought about God when you died, is what you will think about God for eternity. Because outside of time, human beings can't *change their mind*. We're temporal beings and it's just not our nature to be able to do that. So you *can't* see Him then and decide you believe in Him and love Him after all. This life, *within time*, is where our eternity is decided. After we die, that's it. It's too late.

And it's nothing about legalism or vengefulness or anything like that. It's just simple metaphysics. Do you see?"

Uncle Reginald pursed his lips slightly. "*If* there were such a thing as a timeless, all-powerful being and *if* there were such things as souls, then yes, I understand the argument you are making. But neither exist, so it's hardly something for grown men to waste their time arguing about. When I die, I'll be outside of time alright—I won't exist at all."

"Oh, you'll exist." The memory of how he would exist forced its way into my mind again, and I shuddered. "I've felt *how* you'll exist—or a mere fraction of it—and it's..." I choked, unable to continue.

"And now you're going spooky on me." Uncle Reginald sighed. "You're barking mad, no mistake. Though what that makes me for bothering to save you..."

*That makes you a lonely old man, scared to die alone.* The thought darted into my mind like a sunbeam. Yes, if Uncle Reginald seemed a little uncertain of his motive in saving me, well, he probably *was*.

Oh, I think he had come to like me a bit, according to his very underdeveloped capacity for love. And no doubt it *had* felt a waste to let me die. But was there not a third reason, one he'd perhaps not acknowledged or even fully articulated to himself? A very simple reason, namely, that he felt quite sure I would stick to him like a burr and that meant if I lived he could be sure of having company at the last?

I considered my next line of argument, then hesitated, eyeing the old man in the bed opposite. His head was nodding. He'd seemed very...deflated, today. Weary. I suppose having given up the...game...that'd been energising and motivating him, he'd nothing to look forward to but his own imminent demise. That was likely to cut the legs from under anyone.

How often had some sick or elderly parishioner, who seemed to be doing so well, attained the goal they were so eagerly looking forward to—either some milestone, feast day, or family event—only to fail and be with the Lord within days—or even hours—of reaching it. I'd better let him rest.

I kept silence, and soft snores soon drifted across the room.

"*Herr* Hill?" A German accent drew me from a post-lunch nap. Georg Friedrich stood beside Uncle Reginald's bed.

Uncle Reginald raised one eyebrow. "Yes?"

"What's your favourite meal?"

"My favourite meal?"

"*Ja.*" Friedrich's lip twitched. "I'm presuming Full English Breakfast isn't near the top of the list?"

An extremely black look crossed Uncle Reginald's face. "Not for the last decade or so," he said, *very* coldly.

"So what is?"

Uncle Reginald studied Friedrich for a moment, clearly deciding whether to answer. At last, he said, "I'll admit to being partial to minted lamb sausages, with mashed potatoes and onions in thick gravy."

"*Ja?* Well, that's nice and specific." Friedrich turned on his heel and left.

When another noisy visit from my nephews and nieces ended with all of them setting off on an afternoon sight-seeing expedition with their mum and dad, I turned my attention to Uncle Reginald.

He'd done a good job of concealing the true severity of his condition up until now, but to my eyes—either because I knew the truth or because of the crushing effect of losing his motivation to keep going—he looked desperately ill. His skin had taken on a yellowish-grey hue and dark rings encircled his eyes. For the first time, he called a nurse to help him attend to a simpler call of nature, a tremor in his hand as he reached for the call button.

*Lord, help him. Quickly! Give me the words.*

Once the nurse had drawn the curtains back again—directing a scrutinising look at him—and departed, I gave him a few minutes to recover from the exertion. Then I asked, "You know what you said earlier, Uncle Reginald?"

Before I could continue, Doctor Fathiya strode into the room, gripping her medical bag. Another examination?

Ah. The doctor bore down on *Uncle Reginald's* bed with

obvious intent, her tall, white-habited form making her look like a mountain peak shrouded in cloud. "Mr Hill, it really is past time we had a look at you."

"How many times do I have to tell you to leave me alone!" From Uncle Reginald's vehemence, I'd clearly slept through some previous arguments.

"Are you improving, left to your own devices, Mr Hill? I think not. I must examine you properly." Opening her bag and whipping out a stethoscope, Doctor Fathiya leaned towards him.

He grabbed the stethoscope and tried—unsuccessfully—to yank it from her hands. The effort made him pant alarmingly. "Stay...away from me...you holy cow!"

Doctor Fathiya straightened and glared at him, her free hand flying to her rosary. She gripped it tightly, the firm set of her jaw showing that she wasn't going to be put off this time.

Uncle Reginald glowered at her as though hoping to repel her by the force of his stare, the only defensive option he had left. Hunching away from her in his bed, he looked very sick and frail and vulnerable.

Thank God—the thought slipped into my head for the first time—thank God that out of all Uncle Reginald's many, *many* enemies, it was *our* hands into which he'd fallen.

The doctor raised the stethoscope again...

Much as I wanted Uncle Reginald to live as long as possible, if he said he'd exhausted every option, I believed him. And the sight of him struggling to defend the privacy he valued so much...

"Doctor Fathiya," I said hastily, "Surely, like anyone of sound mind, Mr Hill has the right to accept or refuse treatment?"

Doctor Fathiya's gaze drilled into mine as though she sought to read my mind. "You are, of course, correct, Father Kyle," she said at last. "But if you care about this...old...man—which I believe you do—you will persuade him to accept our help. And quickly. I suspect his condition is more serious than he realises—or perhaps chooses to let on."

*You've got that right.* But I just smiled and nodded. "I'll do what I can, Doctor Fathiya. Thank *you* for caring."

She sighed, the tension draining out of her shoulders, and smiled warmly at me. "Oh, I'm only doing my job. God bless *you*, Father Kyle. Do you need anything?"

"No, I'm very well, thank you."

She departed with her bag. Uncle Reginald carried on glowering after her for a moment, then shifted, making himself comfortable again. He offered me no thanks, but the glance he shot my way held a definite spark of gratitude.

When he seemed to be settled, I said, "So, about what you said earlier."

"*Which* thing, Boomerang Boy?" His tone held more resignation than anything.

"About Margo's tears and your money being no use to you?"

He eyed me unenthusiastically. "Yes."

"Well...don't you realise that was precisely what I was getting at the other day? You've spent your whole life chasing the things you thought would make you safe—power and money—and now you realise they don't make you safe at all. How can you find any permanent safety in something impermanent? You need to go to an eternal store for *that* product."

"For pity's sake! Will you spare me your tedious sermons and let me die in peace?"

"I'm not inclined to. Because you might die in peace—or at any rate, in quiet—but you won't be at peace afterwards."

"If you keep this up, I swear I'm going to crawl over there and strangle you with my bare hands!"

"Are you *really* at peace, Uncle Reginald? I mean, I'm asking seriously. Does your atheism give you peace?"

He smirked at me, tiredly. "Knowing that I won't be burning in hell for all my so-called misdeeds gives me great peace, thank you."

"Do you think that accepting God means you have to go to hell? If you accept God and ask His forgiveness, you'll go to *heaven*, silly."

"Fairytales, crazy boy."

"I suppose by accepting God, you also accept your own guilt. And if you're too proud to simply say, *I'm sorry, forgive me*, I can see why you feel that leads you straight to hell. Or at least strands you in a wasteland of pain and guilt—hell on one side, pride on the other. But you have to understand that hell is always *your choice*—and you're choosing hell anyway, whether you believe you are or not."

Uncle Reginald yawned pointedly but failed to conceal the irritation in his tone. "You're boring me, crazy boy."

Was the fact he was getting grumpier and less tolerant of these conversations simply a symptom of his growing frailty, or were my words making any impact on him at all? Hard to know.

"You really are at peace, then? You don't *seem* at peace."

Uncle Reginald scowled, speaking with sudden passion, as though, consciously or not, he needed to share. "When I realised it really was all up for me, I read all the major texts, educated myself on what to expect. *Apparently,* I'm supposed to be in a nice state of acceptance by now. The scientific equivalent of peace, I suppose. I'd like to shoot the authors! Acceptance, my..." He used the rudest word I'd yet heard him utter. But a jerkiness about his manner, a shake to his voice, betrayed his real state of mind. Fear.

"The Lord must be taking pity on you."

"Pity?" He spat the word.

"Yes. If you'd reached some worldly level of acceptance, you'd be even less likely to turn to Him."

"Pah. I've still got some time. I don't need fantasies to bring my acceptance. It's a normal part of a healthy dying process. I'll get there."

"There's nothing healthy about you, Uncle Reginald, body or soul. I wouldn't count on it."

He turned his attention to the window and refused to speak to me for ten minutes. Had I exhausted his patience—or hit a nerve?

At dinnertime, Georg Friedrich wheeled in a meal trolley bearing, surprise, surprise, fat juicy minted lamb sausages, mashed potato, onions, and, yes, thick gravy. Since I'd kept Uncle Reginald's confidence about his condition, it was clearly Friedrich's way of thanking him for saving me—and maybe continuing the spirit of his penance at the same time. Not that Friedrich needed much excuse to start cooking, when off-duty.

He dished up well-calculated portions—modest for Uncle Reginald, massive for me. My appetite had returned with a vengeance. I had more than enough strength to feed myself, too, and though I struggled with the fork and spoon provided, regularly dropping both, Friedrich had cannily served my food in a deep bowl so I lost none of my tasty grub. I polished off the lot, fending away the little hands that kept making lunges for my sausages.

"Stealing food from your sick uncle!" I scolded them. "Well, I'm sorry, I'm eating it all. I was almost dead yesterday, you know, and you lot get to eat your Uncle Georg's cooking regularly!"

"Awwww..."

A well-timed suggestion from Friedrich that they go and 'help' him wash up resulted in a stampede in the direction of the kitchens and a quiet conclusion to the delicious meal.

Uncle Reginald sampled everything on his plate and even smiled a few times as he did so but left most of it untouched. My appetite had abandoned me almost completely as I approached what would have been the end. How long did *he* have?

Margo removed his plate with her own hands, clearly to ensure that the remaining contents went straight into a bin and not into the stomachs of any stray children that might encounter it. I really didn't think Uncle Reginald had access to anything with which he might have tainted the food—but it wasn't worth the risk, was it?

Doctor Fathiya came in soon afterwards to make another thorough examination of me. She smiled a lot as she summarised her findings. I was recovering well from the poison, and my general recovery was also progressing rapidly—though the skin on my legs hadn't reattached properly yet, thanks to the inhibiting effects of my condition up till now. The same went for my knee, so she emphasised the importance of not moving either leg—but especially the left one—even the slightest bit.

But she also reconfirmed that so long as I kept off it long enough, there was every reason to believe I would be able to walk again, unaided. *No, not run, sorry Father Kyle. But walk* unaided, *mind you.*

That *was* a big deal. She was right. The difference between hobbling with a stick or walking on my own... I offered up a prayer of thanks to the Lord and assured her I wouldn't be moving around at all until she said I could.

Margo and Bane kept me company for a while after she'd left—the children no doubt still busy cleaning all Friedrich's dirty bowls by the simple expedient of licking them—but, full and comfortable, my eyes soon grew heavy...

"Crazy boy?" A hoarse voice.

"Uncle Reginald?" I opened my eyes. We were alone. Margo and Bane must've taken charge of the children again and retired to the guest suite. The room door remained closed.

Desperate for maximum privacy in the brief time left with Uncle Reginald, I'd asked U if we could have the door shut when it was only the two of us. After deliberating, U obviously concluded that Uncle Reginald seemed very unlikely to want to harm me and equally unlikely to be physically able to do so. Nonetheless, he used a cable tie to fasten my call button to my bed, with a wristCell beside it, so there was no possibility of me being unable to reach either, made me swear to call for help if Uncle Reginald put a foot wrong, and finally gave permission. The guard still stood outside the door, within earshot—of a shout.

I glanced at the clock—eight in the evening—then at Uncle Reginald. "Are you alright?" A sheen of sweat covered his brow, and his gaze darted around in an agitated manner.

"Fine." He clipped the word short. "*Fine.* I don't want to talk, alright? I don't want any more of your confounded lectures. I just wondered if you could lend me a book. Anything..."

A distraction. He desperately sought a distraction. What did he make of his vital signs? After a career in interrogation, being around the dead and dying through all stages of the process, he could probably read his monitors as well as any doctor, at least when it came to *this*.

"I've only one book I can lend you, and I don't think you'll want it."

"Anything." He spoke between gritted teeth. "I will take *anything.*"

"Well, if you're sure." I reached out and actually managed to lift the volume from my bedside cabinet onto the bed, pinning it between my palms, or what was left of them. The square meal had restored a lot of my strength. "Promise you won't chuck it across the room, though?"

"I'm not strong enough to chuck it *anywhere*," snarled Uncle Reginald.

"Alright, then." I pressed my call button carefully with my middle finger. My new pointing finger. I'd get used to that. I would.

A nurse was already opening the door. She came to my bed, all smiles.

"I'm very sorry to trouble you," I said to her, "but would you mind very much taking this book"—I lifted it awkwardly, still held between both half-hands—"over to Mr Hill?"

At that, the sister's lips thinned in automatic disapproval—then her eyes fell on the book in question, and her smile came back. "Of course, Father Kyle."

She bore the black, leather-bound volume carefully across the room and placed it in Uncle Reginald's eagerly—or desperately—reaching hands.

"Can I help you with anything else, Father Kyle?"

"No, Sister. Thank you very much for your help."

Out she went. Uncle Reginald got the book open to the title page...and groaned. "I should have guessed!"

"You asked for *a* book, Uncle Reginald, and I've lent you a whole library. Seriously, you might be pleasantly surprised. What would you like to read? Adventure, history, poetry... Hmm, political intrigue? Hang on, what about an espionage thriller?"

Uncle Reginald eyed me doubtfully. "Where do I find that?"

"It's called *Judith*. Check the contents page."

Uncle Reginald flicked through the pages for a while, then settled down to read, so I occupied myself with evening prayer.

After a while, Uncle Reginald muttered, "This is badly written. I'm up to chapter seven, and I still haven't met the title character."

"Fashions in literature change, Uncle Reginald," I told him. "Are you seriously going to judge a book that's well over two thousand years old by the conventions of modern literary genres that didn't even exist when it was written?"

"Are we seriously now going to argue about *literary conventions?*" retorted Uncle Reginald, keeping his nose in my Bible.

I went back to the Divine Office. When I'd finished, I wasn't drowsy yet. Huh, I really *must* be improving! If I had my Bible, I'd have opened it; instead, I picked up my rosary and practised 'thumbing' the beads with three fingers only. Praying for Uncle Reginald, of course. *Lord, I know you give very special graces to the dying. Please send them to him most powerfully in his grave need.*

I *would* have liked to talk to Uncle Reginald some more, of course, but...well, I hoped I wasn't anywhere near arrogant enough to think that anything I could say would do him more good than God's own Word!

A cackle of feeble but unrestrained laughter from the bed opposite finally interrupted our peaceful evening. "That'll teach him to underestimate a woman. I always drummed that into my agents, you know, of both sexes. *Never* underestimate a woman. Silly fool. She certainly educated *him.*"

"She did rather."

When Uncle Reginald had recovered from all that laughing—which took a while, he was so weak now—and finished the story, he looked up again. "Anything else good in here?"

"Plenty. Let's see...you might enjoy the history of King David."


*MARGO*
The children were all tucked up in bed. In bed and asleep. With a weary sigh, I settled on the sofa beside Bane and snuggled contentedly under the arm he put around me. This larger guest suite had its own little lounge.

"I can't believe you brought them all the way here, by

yourself! You must be exhausted."

Bane's cheeks reddened. "Well, I wasn't exactly by *myself,* was I, Margo? I had lots of VSS guys with me. VSS gals, even. Two of them."

"Yes, but I know who the children took every last little thing to."

Bane shrugged and tucked me closer. Then, for good measure, he turned and wrapped his other arm around me as well. "I missed you."

I hugged him back. "I missed you more! You should have seen me hugging that cushion, wishing it was you."

"What, this one?" He let go of me and grabbed it.

"Yep."

"Doesn't look much like me."

"What, square, soft, and squidgy? Close enough, surely?"

"Close enough, huh? I'll show you how squidgy *I* am..." He drew me in for a kiss.

Tiredness was—temporarily—forgotten.


KYLE

"Kyle..."

Such a nice dream...I grabbed at it, wanting to retain it, but it floated away like mist.

"*Kyle...*" A low voice. Strained. *Agonised.*

My eyes flew open. I stared across the dimly lit room. "Uncle Reginald?"

"Help me... Please?"

"Shall I call the doctors?"

"No! I don't want them. Can't...can't do *anything.* Just...*help me...*"

The desperate pleading in his voice went right to my heart. But what did he want me to *do*? I was no doctor.

"*Please...* I need...I need... Just...just *help me...*" His voice choked off.

He wasn't seeking physical help, was he? No. He sought emotional help; he *needed* spiritual help. But how could I *do* this across the gulf of this darkened room? Should I call the nurses and ask them to wheel me over there?

No, I couldn't invite someone else in, not right now. That

slender, fragile thread of trust stretched like a physical thing between me and Uncle Reginald, almost unseen on the other side of the room. Weeping, nakedly vulnerable, he'd reached out to me for help. Only to me. Get someone else in here—to, in his eyes, see his shame—and the thread would snap. And there'd be no time to spin it anew.

I had to get to him. Somehow. Just me.

I placed my hands flat on the bed and slowly, painfully, levered myself into a sitting position. The intensified pain from my legs made me gasp, though insignificant enough compared to the lung pain I'd suffered before. I looked around in the dim glow of my night-light. Was there anything fixed I could take hold of and use to drag my bed across the room?

Nope.

Anything long enough that I could use to kind of...punt... my way over?

Nope.

*This is hopeless, Lord. How do I get over there?*

Uncle Reginald had stopped speaking now, stopped begging me, but I could hear his shuddering breaths, his barely smothered sobs. I *had* to get to him!

But *how*, short of climbing off this bed and crawling over there?

*Oh, rats.*

Could I possibly do it without moving my knee? I mean, the brace would help...

*Dream on, Kyle.*

*Lord...* But my appeal petered out. I'd only one option. The sole question was whether I was prepared to do it or not. And that was up to me.

Blast it all, I wasn't losing him now! Not if I could possibly save him! *Whatever it took*, right?

First things first...deal with the heart monitor. I leant over and scrutinised the display. Yes, very like the ones they used in the hospital nearest to my own parish. I pressed a few buttons and it turned itself off, silently. Good—I shook the sensor from my finger. What next? The morphine machine was mounted to the side of the bed, and a glance at the IV in my wrist showed it far too fiddly to remove with any care. I wrapped the tube twice around my other wrist, set my teeth—yanked.

Fiery pain ripped along the path of the needle's forced exit. *Ooouch.* But I was free. No, not quite. After repeating the DIY removal procedure with the standard IV drip, I tried to shift myself to the side of the bed without moving my left knee, ignoring the sharp, searing pain that erupted over the surface of my legs and stomach with every tiny movement. I stared down at the floor below. How on earth did I get down there without half-killing myself?

Margo's chair... I manage to grab it, drag it closer, then slide my bottom off the bed... I dropped into it with a thud. The impact exploded fireworks of pain in my left knee. So much for the brace. I'd definitely jolted it. Blast, blast, blast.

I wasn't stopping to worry about it. Uncle Reginald was crying like a lonely kitten. He'd lost it entirely. The icy self-control that'd helped him succeed so much, his whole life, had surely been achieved through a great proficiency in delayed gratification. But, believing as he did, what future prize could he possibly offer himself for motivation now?

Rather than repeat my previous unsuccessful manoeuvre, I bent my right knee and lowered myself down onto it. A slipping sensation followed by excruciating pain ran right up that leg as half the skin tore completely free. I lay there gasping until the pain eased, then started crawling across the floor, trying to merely drag my left leg behind me, but every movement drew an ominous complaint from my bad knee, as though someone stabbed it with a knife.

*I'm never going to walk again without a stick.* I pushed the little voice to the back of my mind and kept going. *Whatever it takes. Whatever it takes...*

Surely, I'd been crawling in this haze of pain and rapidly increasing exhaustion for...for *years*... Where was I even going...? Why was I...? Wait! A bed loomed ahead. Uncle Reginald's bed. My head cleared. Nearly there. Thank God.

Finally, I lay staring up at the bed-shape above me. Just the minor matter of *getting up there* remained. Oh, this would be fun.

I hooked my remaining fingers around the bed frame and dragged myself into a sitting position, panting in agony.

Then I got my right leg under me and tried to push myself up. Okay, I was still weaker than I thought. Or I'd used all my recovered strength crossing the room.

*O God, I can't do it. I can't. I've put myself through this for nothing...*

No!

*Lord, help me!* I pushed with my left leg as well. Something—several things—tore searingly in my knee—but my chest came level with the bed, a little higher...I tipped myself onto the mattress just before my left knee buckled completely and somehow managed not to topple back off. Then I simply used my half-hands to help heave my wobbling legs up after me.

Finally, finally, I lay beside Uncle Reginald, my legs and hands fiery balls of pain, my chest aching fiercely. I buried my face in the pillow and gasped—sobbed—as I struggled to get control of myself.

*Okay, okay, enough, Kyle. Enough. Uncle Reginald needs your attention.*

I turned onto my side and looked at him in the glow of his night-light. Although his body shook and trembled with sobs, he was staring at me, his eyes wide and shocked, as though he still couldn't believe I'd just climbed up there beside him.

I could barely believe it myself.

Quickly, I slipped my arms around him and held him tight. "I'm here. I'm here..."

His thin frame was so rigid with tension he could've been suffering *rigor mortis* already. But the words, *it's alright*, stuck in my throat. I *didn't* believe he would be all right. I couldn't bring myself to lie to him, not even now. Especially not now.

So I just held him and held him and whispered "I'm here" over and over, until his sobs trailed off into mere tremulous breathing, and he finally sniffed, tried to speak, cleared his throat, then said with a shadow of his usual harshness, "What the blazes are you doing over here?"

"You asked me for help. I'm helping. Trying to, anyway."

"How did you even...?"

"Crawled."

"You're not supposed to be using your—"

"I don't really want to talk about my knee, Uncle Reginald. I'd rather talk about you. Are you alright?"

"Alright..." His voice trailed off into a sob. He jerked his head at his muted monitor, glowing silently in the darkness. "I'm on my way out, Kyle. Very soon. Where's my blasted acceptance? Where is it?" Smaller, softer, despairing sniffs trickled from him.

I tightened my grip again. "I'm here."

"Is that all you can say?" snapped Uncle Reginald. A hesitation and he added, "I'm...I am glad you are."

"What else *can* I say? If I tell you it will be alright, I'm lying. If you accept God, accept His forgiveness, everything will be fine. You'll be safe with the infinite Creator—to say nothing of blissfully happy. But since you refuse to accept him—and with everything you've done—well, things are going to be about as far from alright as it's possible for them to be. I'm terrified for you, Uncle Reginald. But *you're* the only one who can save yourself. I can't do it for you!"

"Do you really...believe all that?" The words straggled from him, his voice thin.

"*Do* I really believe it?" I didn't try to keep the astonishment from my own voice. "Have I done anything, anything at all, since we first met, to suggest that I don't believe it with all my heart and soul?"

Startling me, Uncle Reginald burst into full-out crying. I hugged him tighter, afraid he would sob himself to death.

When he finally quieted, he whispered, "Baptise me."

Desperate hope stiffened my body. "Did you just say...?"

"Yes."

Goodness knows I wanted to ask what had changed his mind—but that could wait. Turning agonisingly onto my back, I somehow managed to get his water glass between my palms and with enormous care, lift it over and onto the bed.

"Now," I told him, "Remember, you don't need to have any *emotional* feeling of belief. You need only desire it and assent to it with your will and intellect. Do you understand?"

He nodded, still sniffing slightly.

"Very well. Do you believe in God; the Father, Son, and

Holy Spirit?"

A frown wrinkled his brow as he considered this, but finally, he whispered, "Yes."

"Do you reject Satan and all his works?"

"What if I am Satan?" His tone was dry—but troubled. Had he finally accepted his guilt?

"You're *not* Satan," I said firmly. "One of his favoured instruments, perhaps, but you can reject him and start over. Do you?"

"Start over? I'll have to be quick. But yes." His brow creased—real distress flickered across his face. "Do I...need a new name? Only...my mother named me..."

His *mother? You fool, Kyle!* If his age hadn't blinded me, I'd have thought to probe *that* key human relationship several *days* ago.

"You don't have to," I said quickly, "though it's nicely symbolic. Or you can just add one."

"Add one. You...you choose."

"Uh—right." *Quick, a name, Lord?* Memory stirred of the very first time I'd ever performed this Sacrament. *Yes, perfect.*

With exquisite care and a big, big prayer in my heart against clumsiness, I lifted that glass between what remained of my two hands and tipped it over his forehead, just enough. Once...twice...thrice... "Reginald Joseph Hill, I baptise you in the name of the Father, and of the Son, and of the Holy Spirit."

Trying to set it down on the bed again, I dropped it at last. What remained of the water drained into the pillow as the glass rolled down against the headboard, but it didn't matter anymore. I traced a cross on Uncle Reginald's forehead with my middle finger.

Finally, I could relax—and so could he. "There. All done. No more worrying about hell, Uncle Reginald. No more worrying about *nothingness.* You're a child of God and will go straight into his arms, if you can just try not to have any nasty thoughts for the next little while and will good to everyone."

A faint laugh puffed from his lips, at that. But as I slipped my arms around him again, I felt the absence of that painful tension. Something in him had relaxed, unwound. He'd stopped struggling against death, hadn't he?

"Do you understand, then? That God loves you?"

"It's hard to imagine. But you seem very certain it's true."

"If *you're* not certain, why get baptised?"

Hill stayed silent for a long time. "Because...you were right, I *don't* really think you're mad. Yet you came over here to help me. Everything else, I've managed to explain away. But this...I can't explain this away. The way you love me, despite everything I've done to you—well, according to my understanding of reality, you're either mad or...or amnesiac or...or it's a miracle. You're not mad, and you're clearly not suffering from amnesia, so...it's something that can't exist. And that means you're right and I'm wrong. So...I accepted your version of reality."

"Just like that?" Although I'd seen the Holy Spirit's work before and shouldn't be surprised, it still took my breath away. Every time.

"What else can I do? You really think I survived this long without knowing how to recognise an indefensible position—when to cut my losses and surrender? Live to fight another day and all that. Not that that's...exactly what I've achieved here."

I couldn't help a soft snort. "Uncle Reginald, that is *exactly* what you've achieved."

His brow wrinkled up for a moment. "*Yes*... Huh."

"So you *do* believe God loves you?"

"I suppose...I'm starting to get an inkling." His eyes probed mine in the dimness. "If...He loves me the way you do."

"The way *I* do? Infinitely more, Uncle Reginald. *Infinitely* more. Do you love *Him?*"

Silence. "That could take some practise, for me."

"How about you practise now? Just will to love him and say it. The emotion will follow in time."

"I imagine I'm going to miss out on that, then." Uncle Reginald stared at the ceiling, his brow creasing again. "I don't know how to do this."

"Just will. And speak."

Uncle Reginald huffed slightly. But finally spoke tentatively. "I love...God. *I love God.* I love the Father, the Holy

Spirit, and, er, Jesus. Am I even doing it right?"

"Are you willing it?"

"I'm *trying.*"

"Then you're doing it right."

"Huh. You know, I've never really loved anyone but myself before." After a moment, he added, very softly, "And maybe you—crazy boy."

"Well, now you love me *and* the Most High. Your list of friends is growing exponentially."

"I wish…wish I'd met you…long time ago…boy…"

"Nah. You'd just have killed me. For a Being Who exists outside of time, the Lord really does have the most incredible sense of timing, you know."

He smiled faintly, but he strained to draw breath to reply. "Well…they say…it's never too late…to learn something…new."

My turn to smile. "Now you really sound like an old uncle."

His lip twisted. "I note…you don't add…wise…or *nice*…"

I gave him a gentle squeeze. "You're getting there, Uncle Reginald. You're getting there."

No reply.

I stole a look at the monitor. I wasn't as expert as he was at interpreting it, but it did not look anything like a healthy heart rhythm to me and from its soundless flashing, it agreed.

"Uncle Reginald?" No, he'd fallen unconscious.

I carried on holding him, trying to ignore the pain devouring my body. The morphine was wearing off, just to cap it all.

*Lord, thank You that he has accepted You—Your forgiveness, Your mercy. Thank You for this miracle you have wrought in his stubborn, prideful heart, that now he seeks to love and follow You…*

Eventually, Uncle Reginald's eyelids fluttered. "Am I still here?" he murmured.

"Yep. You're keeping the Lord waiting."

His lip twitched, but he seemed too weak to laugh. "Shall I…will some good…towards your sister…while I…kick my heels?"

My eyebrow shot up. "If you could, that would be

wonderful."

"Right. Tell her...no, tell Bane, more to the point...or Willmott... Don't be...complacent...because I'm gone. Be careful of...especially...of Gunvald..."

"Gunvald Anfeltson? Head of the EuroBloc Genetics Department, what's left of it?"

"Him. Hates...Margaret. Even more than...than I do. Did. Thorn in my side, your sister...but...destroyed Gunvald's whole department. He gets a chance...he'll hurt her. Any way he can... She should...be careful."

"I'll tell her. I'll tell all three of them. And Eduardo."

He gave a tiny, satisfied, nod.

"Will *you* give my love to your namesake?"

His brow creased in thought. But only for a moment. "Joe Whitelow?"

Yes, I'd thought he could figure it out. Margo had finally felt it safe—for Joe's parents, that was—to share Joe's story on her blog, which Uncle Reginald was known to read attentively. Know your (former) enemy and all that. "Joseph Verrall Whitelow, yes."

A faint smile touched the corner of his lip. "I'm..." His laboured breathing made speaking so hard, now, but he forced the word out. "...honoured."

He fell silent again, so I started to recite a psalm to him. "Out of the depths I cry to thee, O Lord! Lord, hear my voice!"

He listened quietly, until I reached the lines, "My soul longs for the Lord more than watchmen long for the morning..."

As though in sudden enlightenment, he broke in hoarsely, "If there really is...God...then there's no reason...to fight fight fight...against death...no reason to kill...torture...lie...maim... No reason..." He dragged in another breath, barely able to speak, but struggling to finish. "Say...something like... that...more eloquent...more...*useful*... *I* said it...okay? You're a...a bright boy..."

With another great effort, he went on, "But...I can't...now... I think...I'm...due at a...a very, very important meeting..."

I kissed his forehead and spoke softly in his ear. "Go in peace, Uncle Reginald. You are a child of God and all your sins are forgiven. You are a new person, clothed in a spotless white garment and fit to enter the presence of God and dwell there forever. Pray for me..."

He didn't speak—couldn't speak?—so I carried on with the psalm. Soon he lost consciousness entirely. It seemed ironic for someone who had overseen so many lingering, agonising deaths, yet so appropriate too, in light of his new birth, but he slipped away very peacefully about fifteen minutes later, without waking again.

I held him the whole time, until finally that thin, flat line appeared on the monitor, and I knew that I needed to turn my thoughts to the welfare of the living: namely, me. Not that I wanted to *do* anything. Emotionally and physically, it felt as though giants had been beating me with massive hammers and axes. I just wanted to close my eyes and sleep for a decade or two, right there beside Uncle Reginald. Or be *with* Uncle Reginald in God's loving embrace. But *that* was out of my control.

Anyway, the damp stickiness on my legs—especially around my precious left knee—suggested that I needed medical attention, and I couldn't just leave Uncle Reginald lying there all night—however much of it remained—unattended to. I had to get someone in here. Pain fogged my mind worse than ever and reaction left me cold and shaking, a few tears of pain and irrational grief oozing from my eyes.

Laboriously, I inched onto my other side, looking for Uncle Reginald's call button. I could just shout for the guard, but the thought of him rushing in, the glare of the lights coming on, the panic and overreaction...I couldn't face it. I'd just ring for a nurse, nice and calm.

But where was the...

There. It'd slipped almost off the bed, hanging down near the floor. If I leaned over, surely I could just reach it?

Almost...almost...

The blanket shifted, slid—and I was falling. The ground smacked me hard, pain exploded in my knee and black spots spun over my vision...

*Was I going to pass out? Well, that would stop the pai...*

## MARGO

Ugh, those noisy African birds.

I glanced at the guest room's bedside clock. I'd woken early again. Despite all my sleepless nights of late, I couldn't settle back off, so I left Bane sleeping soundly, pulled my clothes on and crept out.

Only a room guard stood outside the guest suite—already raising his wristCell—no doubt one of my poor bodyguards would be rousted from their bed and dispatched after me in about a minute flat. Prudently avoiding eye contact, I hurried off before the guard could suggest I wait for them.

I'd see if Kyle was awake. If he wasn't, I'd head to the chapel for a little quiet time before the children got up.

Another guard leant against the wall outside Kyle's room, equally bored and equally wide awake. He gave me a slight nod, and I smiled back at him, then opened the door quietly and slipped inside.

The sunlight spilling around the curtains clearly illuminated the room, and as I turned from closing the door I stopped, confusion morphing into horror as my eyes darted around.

Kyle's bed was *empty!* A trail of blood ran across the floor to Hill's bed...and beside it... *Kyle, oh no!* I rushed forward, drawing my nonLee automatically as my eyes flew to Hill, checking for danger the way Eduardo—and every first aid course—had drilled into me. But Hill lay so white and deathly still that it barely needed the glance I threw at the heart monitor to know that he posed no threat to anyone. Not anymore. But what had he done to *Kyle?*

Kyle lay motionless beside the bed, tangled in a gore-soaked blanket. As I crouched beside him and sucked in a breath, coppery blood smell filled my lungs, but I managed a strangled yell: "Help!"

Then I turned Kyle gently onto his back and tried to check his pulse with one hand—*O Lord, you can't have taken him from us, not now, not after everything!*—while drawing the blanket away with the other, looking for wounds.

He had a pulse. O Lord be praised, *he had a pulse!* He

wasn't dead.

The blood covered his legs, mostly, though the bandages on his hands were also soaked, so I tried shaking him, very gently. "Kyle? *Kyle?*"

He stirred feebly, opening pain-glazed eyes. Good grief, where was his... Yes, the morphine machine remained attached to his bed, nothing but a bloody wound visible in his wrist. How *long* had it been disconnected? He'd never turned if off *entirely;* what must he be *suffering?*

"Kyle, are you alright? What happened? What did Hill do to you?"

"M'fine..." he mumbled incoherently. "Fine, Margo. Just want to...just need to sleep. Tha's all... Just sleep..."

"You can't sleep. You need a doctor!"

The horrified guard leaned over my shoulder, reaching for the call button that lay on the ground nearby. He grabbed it and held it down, much as I had the other day.

Soon a bevy of nurse-sisters rushed into the room, only just beating U, who followed close on their heels, dressed in a long silk dressing gown with his nonLee holster strapped on over the top.

"Oh!" One of the sisters gasped as her eyes fell on the unexpected corpse. "Mr Hill is with God, it seems."

"I very much doubt that!" The words fell from my lips with unstoppable honesty.

Kyle's attention sharpened slightly, a joyful, though pain-addled, smile curving his lips. "Oh, but he is...*he is...*"

My gaze returned to Hill. This time I noticed the empty water glass on the bed, resting near Hill's body. "Did you...*baptise him?*"

Kyle nodded, still smiling that smile: half-joy, half-grimace.

"For pity's sake," I said to the nurses, "can you get him some morphine?"

"Of course. Sister Mwassaa." The senior nurse addressed one of her juniors as an alarmed looking Georg darted into the room. "Unfasten the machine and bring it here. We mustn't move him until the surgeon has evaluated his knee."

"I'm fine..." Kyle murmured again. "Just need to sleep. Can sleep here...right here..."

I tried to soothe him, stroking his hair, but wasn't sure he noticed. "What did Hill *do* to him?" I glared at the lifeless figure in the bed, while Georg, relaxing a little, silently took up his protective stance nearby.

U straightened from his inspection of Kyle's empty bed and trod back over to us, avoiding the bloody trail on the floor. "Margo, I've no idea what role Mr Hill played in Father Kyle's decision making, but it seems quite clear that Father Kyle did this to *himself.* Stubborn fool that he is."

Oh. I tried to look again at the scene and engage my reason. U was right. No way Reginald Hill could've got Kyle over here. Kyle had done it under his own steam—but at a devastatingly high cost.

U bent to examine Hill's bed. "O, Lord protect us," he moaned. "Father Kyle got *right up on here* beside Mr Hill! Argh..." He shook his head, as though unable to decide which thought bothered him more—the idea of the physical exertion it must've cost Kyle or the thought that Hill, had he undergone a change of mind, could have hurt him. "Margo, I swear, your brother has the self-preservation instincts of a *lemming.* Why on *earth* did I agree to closing that blasted *door?*"

"But...did you hear?" I said to U. "He baptised *Hill.* Hill's in...in *heaven.*" It seemed too incredible to be true. Too implausible. And yet...*wonderful?* Did I forgive Hill enough to believe that?

"*Aeii,* what has happened?"

Thank goodness, Doctor Fathiya and the head surgeon, whose name I kept forgetting, were now hurrying in, dressed in voluminous, all-enveloping dressing gowns and with veils askew.

Several people started explaining what we knew or thought we knew, all at once, so I kept silent. *Lord, please let Kyle be okay. Why does he have to be so* insanely *brave and good?*

But the surgeon knelt beside him and began to unfasten the blood-drenched brace from his knee, giving orders about anaesthesia and surgical equipment, and in a reassuringly short time Kyle had been transferred onto a trolley and wheeled off to the operating theatre to have his knee tended and his skin re-reattached.

A couple of other sisters prayed briefly beside Hill's body before spreading a sheet over it and wheeling it away to morgue to be cared for. Which left me and U (and on-duty-Friedrich, nominally invisible) in an empty room—into which Bane burst soon afterwards, frantic from whatever garbled rumour he'd heard.

*KYLE*

Birds were raising their voices when I woke—as usual—but more of a mid-morning demi-chorus, this time.

A memory lingered, of horrible, horrible pain, yet I felt wonderfully pain-free. I opened my eyes, peeping at the morphine machine. Yes, right up. But I felt far too drained to reach for it immediately.

Actually...Uncle Reginald was in heaven, wasn't he? All was well. I could stop hurting Margo and leave the thing alone, then. Well...I eyed the raised frame that held the covers off my legs, wondering about my knee. *Was* all well?

All that truly mattered was well. Uncle Reginald's soul rested safe in God's hands. If I walked with a stick for the rest of my life—or worse—it wasn't really very important, in comparison.

*O Lord, I really don't want to be walking with a stick for the rest of my life...* I smothered that plaintive prayer-grumble as it tried to pop to the surface.

"Kyle?" Bane sat beside the bed, leaning forward, his hands lying loosely on his knees. "Awake, huh?"

"Seem to be."

"Margo and Unicorn are quite upset with you, y'know."

"Are they? What about you?"

Bane shrugged. "I figure you did what you felt you had to do. Though I am really sorry about your knee."

My turn to shrug. "On an eternal scale, knees don't really matter—useful as they are."

"Watch out, Kyle, I think you may be levitating slightly."

"Ha ha." But heat rushed to my cheeks. Many stupid jokes like that and I'd probably spontaneously combust! How *was* my knee, though? I opened my mouth, but Bane had just picked up something from the bedside cabinet, placing it beside me. My Bible.

"This was on the floor when they found you. Looked like it had slid off the bed along with you and the blanket. Some of the pages were rather crumpled and there was blood on it. Mostly on the cover. I've cleaned it up, but a few pages are stained."

"Thanks, Bane. I really appreciate it."

"How did you even *get* that over there with you?" Bane eyed me bemusedly.

"I didn't. I'd lent it to Uncle Reginald earlier, via a nurse."

"Oh." Mystery solved, Bane leaned back in the chair, but his eyes never left my face. "How are you, Kyle?"

"Oh, fine, they seem to have glued me back together—"

"No, *how are you? Really.* 'Cause...I know what it's like to have everyone flapping joyfully around you, so delighted you're alive, so cheerful—while all the time, you're actually feeling..." He shrugged again, then said, "...plain awful. Because I'm looking at you, Kyle, and there's no smile in your eyes. Hasn't been since I got here."

I swallowed, taken aback by the depth of his perception. But I didn't want Margo to know how I felt...

"I won't tell Margo if you don't want me to." He read my mind—or maybe my expression. "I know she'd rather that—and you talk to me—than that you don't."

I wasn't sure I wanted to talk about it, really. But I probably *should.* And Bane was clearly worried. I struggled for words. "It's just...when I was on that gurney...I was...I got *so close* to God. It was...I can't possibly describe it, Bane. I just can't... It was... No, there just aren't *words.* I wanted to be with Him—completely with Him—*so much.*

"Then..." I stumbled on, "then I was rescued, and I was going to live and...and that was good for, for different reasons. And then I turned out to be poisoned, so I was going to be with Him again. And then...then that fell through. *Again.* And...*and part of me wishes it hadn't.*" The final confession squeezed out all in a rush, before I could stop it. "I just...I long for Him *so much.*"

Bane's eyes were wider than normal, his brows drawn together. What did he read on my face? "Wow. This is the first time I've felt like I need to apologise for saving someone."

Guilt stabbed me. "No! No, you *don't* need to apologise, Bane! I'm so grateful you came to get me. If I'm alive, it's because the Lord wants me alive, so I'm just...kicking against His will by feeling sorry for myself and I should stop. Don't worry about me. I'll be fine."

"But easier said than done, right?"

I looked away. My throat burned and my eyes stung, but I didn't want to cry in front of Bane. I was his confessor, for pity's sake. Now and then. And older than him, although those couple of years that had seemed so important as children barely seemed to matter these days.

But the next thing I knew, his arm settled around my shoulder. "It's okay, bro. It's okay. You can cry. You've had a hellish time. Just cry if you want to. Let it out..."

His kindness and understanding undid me. The tears broke out after all, and I sobbed and sobbed and sobbed. All the disappointment and heartache and fear and grief of the last week just poured out of me in a salty wave.

And poured out...

And poured out...

And poured...

"Kyle?"

I opened my eyes. Margo. I smiled at her. No sign of Bane. My eyes felt gummy, scratchy. I rubbed one. Ah, salt. I must've cried myself to sleep. Hopefully it looked like mere sleepy dust.

She smiled back, looking more anxious than cross. "Kyle, why did you do it?"

"I had no choice, Margo." Not really true, I suppose. I could have stayed right there in my bed and let Uncle Reginald cry himself to hell—but I don't know how I could've lived with myself afterwards.

"Kyle..." Margo's voice shook slightly. "The surgeon says you'll be lucky if you can get around on a *crutch* after this."

A crutch. One worse than a mere stick. And designed for people with opposable thumbs. Blast. "That's...a shame. But it can't be helped."

"You *must not move* from that bed. Do you understand? Not until it's healed!"

"I won't. Why would I?"

My sister glared at me, so I smiled as innocently as I could.

Her glare intensified. But after a moment, she sighed, relenting. "Oh, some good news. Pope Cornelius said you're to come home with us to the Vatican. Not just to recuperate. Permanently. He said there'll be plenty of work for you there and you'll have your family around to..." She shifted awkwardly. "Um, to help you, you know..."

*Adjust to being a cripple* she sought so delicately to say. But my heart lifted at her words. Yes, I would miss my parish, my parishioners, this vast, wild, beautiful, dangerous country. But to be able to see Margo, Bane, and the children every day... It seemed the Lord had answered my yearning in a very roundabout way.

"We're, uh, taking Hill back with us, too." Margo sounded bemused, as though she still couldn't quite make out how she felt about Reginald Hill. "His funeral Mass is to be held there. That's going to be some balancing act and no mistake."

Yes... I could see what she meant. On the one hand, we'd want to make it quite clear he'd converted, that he was one of us—massive win for us on the world stage, that it was—and that we'd totally accepted him—but on the other hand, the man's entire life, bar the last few hours, had been an unmitigated disaster, one evil act after another, and it must not, for one moment, seem like we were celebrating *that*. I wouldn't want to be the one trying to balance all those needs and choreograph the event.

"He's stuck me with the organisation," Margo added glumly.

I laughed, then tried to look apologetic. "Sorry. I was just feeling bad for the person with that job and then you said..." I grinned at her. "Well, I'd be very happy to do the homily, if that helps."

Margo smiled. "Perfect." She glanced at the clock but didn't move.

"Are you supposed to be somewhere?"

"No. There are some elephants close to the town and Bane's taking the children out to see them, with a guide. But I'm going to stay right here with you." She gave a determined nod, though her eyes slid longingly to the clock again.

I looked at her in disbelief. "Margo, you're in Africa for the first time in your life—and for all we know, the last, if Eduardo has any say in the matter—and you're passing up the chance to see *elephants*? I'm perfectly alright. Look, they've put me back together again, and I'm leaving the morphine turned up, and you've just told me that you'll be seeing me all the time in future, anyway."

From the stubborn set of her chin, she'd made up her mind that staying behind to keep me company was the *right thing to do*.

"And all I'm going to do today is sleep, you know?" I added. "In fact, I'm going to settle off again right now." No acting required to let rip a big yawn. "So if you really…" another—unplanned—yawn stretched my jaws, "want to sit and watch me snoring, instead of go ogle elephants, then be my guest. But *I'd* much, much rather you went and enjoyed yourself."

I settled my head comfortably into the pillow and closed my eyes. And kept them closed. And kept them closed. Blast, I wanted Margo to go and join the others too badly to actually doze off…

But finally, after several long minutes, a creak of floorboards marked her departure. Good.

I opened my eyes again and looked across at Uncle Reginald's empty bed, suddenly lonely, for all I'd encouraged Margo to go.

Achingly lonely. Sleep had fled far away.

It wasn't really Margo's temporary absence, of course, or Uncle Reginald's permanent one. It was The Absence. The Absence I would have to bear as long as I lived. The thing I had not mentioned to Bane, despite it being the very worst wound of all. It was just too private, far, far too private. I wouldn't be mentioning it to *anyone*, except just possibly my Spiritual Director.

*Uncle Reginald, I wish I could have gone with you.*

Did I? Really? The pain I would've inflicted on Margo and

my parents and everyone.

*Lord, I don't seem to know what I want, do I?*

Yes, I did. *I want what you want, Lord.* There, simple.

But that ache, that longing, would it ever dim? Probably not. But if it had helped save Uncle Reginald, it was worth it. It wasn't like the Lord couldn't speak to me in other ways.

Enough moping. My Bible had made its way back onto the bedside cabinet—I managed to grab it and shift it to my lap. What had Uncle Reginald read after I'd fallen asleep, night before last? I'd never know, not until I saw him again. But I couldn't help wondering.

Awkwardly, I opened the book at the ribbon marker. It wasn't where I'd left it. Someone had ringed a verse of the Song of Songs in black pen: *Love is a fire no waters avail to quench, no floods to drown; for love, a man will give up all that he has in the world, and think nothing of his loss.*

Beside it was scrawled:

!Crazy Boy!

I read the words again, happiness bubbling in my chest. What thoughts had been going through his mind when he marked it? Had it simply reminded him strongly of me or had it touched him or even influenced his thinking later that night? The Lord spoke through his Word, after all.

Smiling, I re-opened the Bible at random. Hmm, what should I read?

But my eye fell on the verse right under my finger: *I am with you always, until the end of days.*

One more tear trickled down my cheek.

A tear of thankfulness.

A tear of consolation.

I closed the book, hugging it tightly to my chest as warm sunbeams shone through the window, caressing my face.

Seen or unseen, He was with me.

Until the end of my days.

And over that last horizon.

*Did you enjoy* The Siege of Reginald Hill*? Please consider leaving a review on Amazon, Goodreads or your favourite retailer. Thank you!*

*Corinna Turner*

# Have you read the I AM MARGARET companion volume?

# MARGO'S DIARY

> **9th June**
> Jane's had her little boy! They've named him Arthur Jayesh after U's brother and Jane's brother. He's the most darling little thing. U thinks he looks really like Jane but I think he looks a lot like U, too. And yes, there's a lot of 'he looks like U' jokes going on! Jane's already told me if I say that to her one more time she's going to slap me!
>
> **2nd August**
> Okay, so I was walking down the corridor earlier and who should I meet but Georg Friedrich! Well, Eduardo did say yesterday that he needed a word, but I was too busy to call him. Friedrich came rushing over and I kid you not, got down on his knees and I think he was aiming at kissing my feet, but I managed to get him up before he could do it. He kept saying, "I swore I would! First time I saw you! Should have done it before!" But I managed to dissuade him. Told him to find a statue of Our Lord and kiss his feet instead.

**MARGO'S DIARY covers six of the years in-between BANE'S EYES and THE SIEGE OF REGINALD HILL and also includes:**

UNDERGROUND LATIN PRIMER—MAPS—PSALMS—'PROCAMERA' MASS KIT DIAGRAM—PRAYERS—ETC.
(Plus a lot of graffiti from Bane!)

Paperback: ISBN 978-1-910806-04-3 / ePub: 978-1-910806-05-0 / Kindle: B06XZPP1BC

*Don't miss:*

# A SAINT IN THE FAMILY
## AND OTHER STORIES

**Containing:**

'The Underappreciated Virtues of Rusty Old Bicycles'

'Birthday Secrets'

'How Snakey Got His Name'

'An Unexpected Guest'

'Buttons'

A SAINT IN THE FAMILY (A Novella)*

'True To Form'*

'Persistence'*

'An Unlikely Comforter'*

***New** and **Unseen**

## COMING IN 2020!

Find out more at: www.UnSeenBooks.co.uk

**A prequel to the YESTERDAY & TOMORROW series**

# SOMEDAY

## CORINNA TURNER

### All proceeds go to *Aid to the Church in Need*

Ruth and Gemma have a Physics exam in the morning. Becky and Alleluia are revising for their A Levels. So it's an absolute nightmare to be woken by the fire alarm in dead of the night.

But for them, and for 272 other girls from Chisbrook Hall girls boarding school, the real nightmare is just beginning.

Because 'al-Qabda' are taking them all away. Whether they want to go or not.

### OUT NOW!

### READ 2 SNEAK PEEKS! ➔

Get SOMEDAY from Amazon or your favourite retailer today!

Paperback: ISBN 978-1-910806-02-9
Also available as an Ebook
(ePub: ISBN 978-1-910806-03-6 / Kindle: ASIN B01EAU6AT0)

Find out more at: www.UnSeenBooks.co.uk

*SNEAK PEEK 1—GEMMA*

I open my mouth to reply to Annabel...break off, eyes widening at the sight of a uniformed—armed!—soldier rushing up the stairwell.

"Outside!" he yells, in some sort of thick, inner-city accent. "Hurry up, everyone out!"

"Is there actually a fire?" gasps Annabel, her ridiculously long hair tumbling all around her again as she almost drops her hair tie. "Not just mice chewing wires again...."

But Ruth frowns slightly as she looks at the soldier—yeah, he's not a fireman.

He sees our expressions. "There's been a bomb threat. *Out*, now! Where is everyone else?"

"There isn't anyone else," Annabel says over her shoulder, taking off down the stairs as though...she's just heard there might be a bomb in the building.

The soldier looks annoyed—yells after her, "Where are the younger ones?"

"Year seven are at an adventure training camp," I reply, but I start down the stairs as well. Bomb threats are usually hoaxes but I'm so not risking it. Not the way things are at the moment. "Year eight, IT camp; year nine, French exchange; year ten, Venice, English trip. It's just us and the sixth form."

The soldier swears loudly, and starts herding us back down the stairs, giving me a push to hurry me along.

"Hey!" I protest. "If I fall and break something and you have to carry me, it's going to take even longer, isn't it?"

Ruth shoots the man another looks and trots on down the stairs, guiding Yoko with her, like she's more scared of the soldier than of the bomb. And though I'd never admit it, I do kind of respect her opinion—at least on anything that doesn't concern the divine Sky Fairy.

The man's scruffier than any soldier I've ever seen—and since when do they dispatch armed men to evacuate civilians?

*ALLELLUIA*
"Quit shoving, would you?" I snap at the man who's chivvying us towards the assembly point. "Think I wanna

stay in there with a bomb, huh?"

"Hurry up," he says.

That's all he's said since he met us outside the sixth form block and I'm sick of it.

"Jesus loves you too," I tell him.

He smacks me across the head and I gasp in pain. Did this soldier seriously just hit me? Then I see the assembly point ahead and the words evaporate from my mind.

There's a row of trucks and a couple of horse vans—horseboxes, they call them over here—pulled up in the parking lot, and more soldiers are forcing girls into them at gunpoint. Everyone looks scared—a few girls are crying. *Lord, what is going on?*

"Show us some ID!" Miss Trott is yelling. She's the senior housemistress. "You are not taking these girls unless we see some ID! Where are the police? Where's bomb disposal?" She grabs a soldier's arm, "ID, *now!*"

The soldier un-shoulders his rifle and casually smashes the butt into Miss Trott's face. She crumples to the ground in a horrible, boneless way. I jerk in a shocked breath—then grab Jill and Karen. "*Run!*"

I shove them towards the wood and dive at the soldier who hit me—after a moment of confusion, I'm rewarded by the sound of Jill and Karen's running footsteps on the gravel path. The soldier shoves me away so hard I fall, tearing pyjamas and knee. *Ow...* Blood oozes brightly across my black skin. But Jill and Karen disappear into the dark.

The soldier swings back to me—my heart freezes in my throat, everything freezes as he brings up the rifle and cocks it, hate filling his angry eyes...

*SNEAK PEEK 2—SAM*
We've spent hours trailing through any bit of woodland that can be accessed by road and we're scratched and footsore and frustrated. And hot. Of course we know ninety-nine percent of the searchers in the entire country won't find anything *and* we're being given the least likely areas, what with us being, like, the eighty-eighth line of defence or something—but I suppose we're all hoping—and dreading

what we might find, at the same time.

Movement up ahead...my mind snaps back to the job at hand, heart lurching in hope-fear. It'll be nothing...it'd better be nothing, we're all unarmed... Take more than this for them to issue live ammo to university students.

The biggest excitement of the morning approaches...in the form of a teenage boy riding bareback—and barefooted—on a black and white pony. He rides right on up to our fatigue-clad selves in a way that makes me pretty sure he's heard nothing about the terrorists.

I can't help asking, "Why aren't you in school?"

"I don't go to school. I'm home-schooled. Or..." He grins. "Caravan-schooled."

"Oh, you're a gyp...traveller, right?"

"Half. My dad's a hippie. Traveller-wannabee, as my mum would say."

"Right. Well... Have you seen any horseboxes or vans back there in the woods?"

He gives me a funny look. "You're soldiers, right? Why are you looking for vans?"

"Yes, territorial army, strictly speaking—but we're just university officer cadets. We're looking for the two hundred and seventy-six schoolgirls who were kidnapped this morning. Or rather, the vehicles they were taken in, almost certainly abandoned, by now."

The boy greets this with a nod. "So this is like a role-play, or something, right? That you're doing for training? Is it okay for me to tell you where they are, then, or are you supposed to find them yourselves?"

"No, they've really been taken. By Islamist fanatics... *Wait*, are you saying you've *seen* some vans back there?"

"Yeah," he says slowly, eyes very wide. Then he shakes his head as though to banish his shock and turns the pony, puts it to a canter, calling over his shoulder, "This way..."

"Wait!" I yell. "You need to wait for us. Those men are dangerous."

He pulls the pony to a halt and looks us up and down. "And what are you going to do, spit at them?"

I try not to grit my teeth too hard. "We can at least make

a cautious approach," I tell him, then call to the others, "Okay, stay in your line but we're following the pony. Double-time."

When the boy finally slips from the pony's back and throws his reins over a bush, we catch him up. "This way," he whispers, and glides off silently through the trees.

We follow, sounding like a herd of blundering elephants in comparison. But we soon come over a slight rise and there below us is a clearing...

My heart begins to pound. Three vehicles. Two white vans and a blue horsebox... God help us, it's an exact match! I hesitate, torn. We're under strict orders to call for armed backup if we find anything, but... I try the radio again. Nothing. No signal on my phone either. What have we got to report, anyway? There doesn't seem to be anyone here. It may be nothing to do with the kidnapping.

"Wrexham, come with me," I say softly. "We'll circle the clearing and see what we can see. Everyone else, stay here. Tanner, you're in charge. If someone shoots us, bug out and phone for help as soon as you can get a signal."

I pick up a sturdy branch and move down the slope towards the clearing. A stick's better than nothing, right? Henry Wrexham follows. The gypsy-boy has slipped all the way to the edge of the clearing and is peering from behind a bush. I'd better try and get him to stay back.

But as I move down towards him, I can see the backs of the vehicles, and they're all open, the roll backs up on the vans and the ramp down on the horsebox. A prickle of unease runs up my spine. Okay, so it's really hot today, but it could just as easily be pouring rain. Why would someone leave their vehicles open like that?

The boy glances at me when I stop beside him. "Someone brought two really big vehicles up into this clearing sometime this morning," he tells me softly, pointing. "You can see the tyre marks. Looks like articulated lorries. Totally unsuitable for that track."

Another cold prickle. "Change of plan, Henry," I say. "We'll..."

But then a thin cry comes from the horsebox: *"Help..."*

# DON'T MISS

# PLEASE DON'T FEED THE DINOSAURS

### IN A JURASSIC FUTURE, SOME STILL CHOOSE FREEDOM—DESPITE THE DANGERS.

It takes more than a T. rex scratching its back on his Habitat Vehicle to alarm young hunter Joshua—he's used to living close to nature. But a routine visit to the zoo to deliver a new velociraptor turns deadly when he comes face-to-face with an eleven-foot allosaur called Gold. He knew her when she was a tiny chick—is he a friend from the past—or dinner?

Meanwhile, Darryl and her brother, Harry, are taken completely by surprise when their father remarries. Their new step-mom is a glamorous fashion designer who's never been outside the city's electric fences. How will she cope with a life of dinosaur farming? All Darryl can do is try to get her new stepmom safely to the farm. But once you're unSPARKed, things don't always go to plan…

PLEASE NOTE: Please Don't Feed the Dinosaurs knits together the original unSPARKed book 1, DRIVE!, with the short story 'A Dino Whisperer at the Zoo,' along with a small amount of original material.

## OUT NOW!
### Read on for a SNEAK PEEK!

## JOSHUA

"Tell that hunter-boy to hurry up. I haven't got all day," snaps the man in the suit.

I glance out at the welcome party that stands on the obsoDeck. Ned Greyson, stocky and light-skinned, is Exception City Zoo's Head Raptor Keeper. I know him moderately well—the Wilson HabVi has supplied quite a few critters to this zoo over the years. The young Hispanic man—older than me but with that wet-behind-the-ears air most city-boys have—is an eager young underling, or intern, or some-such. The pretty lady—of Cheyenne heritage, I think—is the zoo vet. And there's the thin, pale man in a suit, looking down his nose at everyone, but especially at me in my camo-jacket and heavy boots. He hasn't even spoken to me. Keeps passing things through Ned.

Ned doesn't 'tell me' anything, he just screws up his face in apology and opens his hand in a 'let it go' gesture. He needn't worry. The guy's getting my goat but it takes more than that to blow my fuse.

"There we go." As Silky the velociraptor finally steps off my Habitat Vehicle's ramp into the zoo's holding pen, I press the button to lift the ramp and seal the rear door. He skitters away nervously, but by the time I've dropped out of the HabVi and climbed up to the obsoDeck to join the group standing looking down into the pen, he's run back up to the rear of the large grey vehicle where it's parked flush with the gateway, begging to be let back in, peeping plaintively like he's a juvenile again. "Sorry, Silky," I tell him, raising my voice. "This is your new home, now."

I ignore Suit-man and speak to Ned. "Yep, one velociraptor, male, adult, and zoo-tame."

Silky scratches at the 'Vi with one wing-arm claw, shoots a nervous look around at the strange pen, then calls pathetically.

"Ready to mate?" queries Ned, a twinkle in his eye.

I grin. "Yep. Though he ain't cutting a very manly figure this moment, is he? Too much new."

Ned grins too, but he looks pleased. Silky is young and healthy, virtually adult size—as tall as a wolf and several times longer from nose to tail tip—and into his adult plumage, his unusually soft, sleek charcoal grey feathers set off nicely by his dark blue ruff. A real beauty, and a perfect zoo animal.

But Suit-man steps up to the edge of the obsoDeck and peers down, making Silky start and bolt into the farthest corner of the pen. Suit-man frowns. "Well, this raptor doesn't seem very zoo-tame to me. It's terrified of everything."

"What d'you expect? He's never been in a place like this."

"We're paying extra for a raptor that isn't going to cower away from people and make the visitors think we're mistreating it. I've heard of you hunters' tricks. If you're trying to pass off some sub-standard creature on us, you won't get paid at all."

Ned winces and holds up a hand. "Now, Mr. Grundvick—"

But I don't care what Ned plans to say. Suit-man's suspicion is just one slur too many. He's gonna get punched if he keeps treating hunters like this—this guy could try even a hunter's self-restraint. But there are better ways to make a point.

"Not tame, huh?" I take two steps to the edge of the obsoDeck.

"Aw, heck, Joshua, don't you—"

I ignore Ned—and drop lightly down into the pen.

*DARRYL*

After knocking back my last swig of coffee, I slip on my denim jacket and pause on my way to the gun locker, checking my reflection in the hall mirror. Shoulder-length brown hair brushed—and loose, for once—face clean, blue eyes...glum. But this has happened, whether I like it or not, so I might as well make a good first impression.

"Harry, get down here, we're going to be late!"

The volume of Dad's latest bellow up the stairs shows that he means business. Well, *I'm* ready, at least.

I thought my younger brother had come around to the

'might as well make a good impression' viewpoint as well, but there's still no noise from upstairs. The fact is, when your dad comes back from a routine weekend market and supply trip to the city and announces that he's got honest-to-God *married* and that the woman—sorry, step-mom—will be coming to live with you, three weeks really isn't enough time to deal with it.

Harry totally lost it. Screamed Lord knows what at Dad, then ran off to the nearest barn. I managed not to do any screaming, but I had to go up and shut myself in the farmhouse's observation turret for almost an hour, and talk to myself *a lot.* You know: *Dad's been alone a long time, Darryl; if he's fallen in love that's wonderful, isn't it, Darryl; you want your father to be happy, don't you, Darryl?*

He totally sprung it on us, though. I guess he was so scared Potential Step-Mom—sorry, Carol—would come to her senses and decide that no handsome, propertied man of her own age was worth going and living unSPARKed on some farm. Carol's a city girl, all right.

When I finally managed to go back down and say something about being happy for Dad and try to show some interest in his new bride, he showed me a photo on his phone, and my heart didn't lift. Just sank even further. Manicured Carol looked like she'd never got within a mile of the city fence in her life, let alone stepped outside it. A less likely farmer's wife I had never seen.

Dad could tell what I was thinking, of course. Brain not completely scrambled by love. "I know Carol's no farmer, Darryl my girl," he told me, "but really, it doesn't matter, does it? We've run the farm by ourselves all this time. She can run her fashion design and consultancy business from the house—I'm getting a faster Net connection put in. And *we'll* run the farm, just as before. And you and Harry will inherit it, Darryl, no question. Carol has her own money."

I reach the gun locker and place my hand on the scanner. Much as I hated to hear Dad talking about *his will,* it's a relief to know the farm is safe. I could put up with a harem of step-moms if I had to, but if someone took the farm from me...

As I take my rifle from the rack I can't help smiling at the thought of Dad with a *harem* of Carols. No, not Dad. We're Catholic, you know. One spouse at a time. Carol's 'not religious,' apparently. I hope that won't matter. Dad did say he thinks she's 'open to it' so that's something.

I throw my ammunition sash on and check the pouches. Three hold full mags, but since we'll be traveling unSPARKed...I'll add the fourth pouch. I put my hand on the scanner to open the ammo box and take

a handful of HiPiRs, or Hide Piercing Rounds. Penetrate any hide up to T. rex, these will. Though for T. rex, I really would prefer a bigger gun. *Much* bigger.

"HARRY!" roars Dad, then heads over to me. "Whoa, girl, wait up. Come on, put the rifle away."

"What?" I turn an incredulous look on him. "We're travelling unSPARKed, Dad."

"Carol's nervous enough about the trip as it is, let alone living out here. If we turn up looking like Rambo-family, she's going to freak out. I'll have my rifle. Leave yours here. Just this once."

"But why have one rifle when you can have three?" I demand.

"Most people don't take *any* weapons when they travel, Darryl."

"*City* people. And sometimes when they break down or crash, they get eaten."
"Come on, Darryl, just this once. It will make Carol feel so much better."

Dad's pleading tone is too much. I unsling my rifle from my shoulder and put it back in its place. "All right. But we'd better not end up Raptor Food."

"Of course we won't." He sounds downright cheerful with relief.

## JOSHUA

"Hey, Silky-boy." I move out into the middle of the small space and drop into a crouch, making myself smaller and non-threatening as I pull a training treat from my pocket.

One knee I keep bent, blocking access to my stomach, while I tuck my left wrist under my chin, palm inwards, shielding my neck. Zoo-tame ain't all the way tame, not by a long shot. "Hey, Silky-boy, Mr. Suit thinks you ain't tame enough for his liking. Poor Silky-boy. Come on, then..."

"Joshua, just come out of there," urges Ned, in a low voice.

I ignore him, too busy saying friendly things in velociraptor-speak, though I need hardly bother. Silky is already running eagerly towards me, drawn as much by my familiarity as by the treat. When he pauses a few feet away, his head on the same level as mine since I'm crouched down, I toss him the meaty drop and pull out another one. He advances again, more confidently. When he's almost close enough to grab for it, I toss it into his mouth. "Good boy. Not scared of humans, are you? Just scared of new."

He takes the last few steps and rubs his head against me, like a hatchling begging a parent for food. Yes, he's very nervous of the strange place, and it's making him even friendlier than usual.

Crooning reassuringly like an adult to a chick—but keeping my knee and left wrist firmly in place—I stroke his charcoal grey back, healthy young velociraptor scent filling my nostrils. When he just carries on nudging me with his head and peeping anxiously, I slide an arm around him in a hug and ruffle his breast feathers, then glance at Mr. Suit.

"So, mister," I ask him, Silky's teeth inches from my face, "is this raptor tame enough for your liking?"

Get
**PLEASE DON'T FEED THE DINOSAURS**
from
**your favorite retailer today!**

## ACKNOWLEDGMENTS

Once again, I must thank my parents for all their support, and my mum for those ruthlessly honest critiques!

I'd like to thank Regina Doman, T. M. Gaouette, Elizabeth Amy Hajek, Theresa Linden, Victoria S., and Theo T. for all their excellent editorial input.

I'd also like to thank Fr de Malleray and Fr Tom Dubois for checking for any priestly errors!

And not forgetting the patrons of the book, Saint Margaret Clitherow, Saint Ignatius of Antioch, and Blessed Pier Giorgio Frassati!

## A NOTE FROM THE AUTHOR

At one point in THE SIEGE OF REGINALD HILL, Blessed Pier Giorgio Frassati is referred to as Saint Pier Giorgio Frassati. Since this story is set in the future, I have used artistic license in referring to him in this highly plausible way. However, just to avoid any confusion, Blessed Pier Giorgio Frassati remains, at the time of publication, a 'Blessed'.

## ABOUT THE AUTHOR

Corinna Turner has been writing since she was fourteen and likes strong protagonists with plenty of integrity. She has an MA in English from Oxford University, but has foolishly gone on to work with both children and animals! Juggling work with the disabled and being a midwife to sheep, she spends as much time as she can in a little hut at the bottom of the garden, writing.

She is a Catholic Christian with roots in the Methodist and Anglican churches. A keen cinema-goer, she lives in the UK. She used to have a Giant Snail called Peter with a 6½" long shell, but now makes do with a cactus and a campervan!

**Get in touch with Corinna...**

*Facebook*: Corinna Turner - *Twitter*: @CorinnaTAuthor

or sign up for news and free short stories, including 'Buttons' about Kyle travelling home to Vatican State, at: *www.UnSeenBooks.co.uk*

## DOWNLOAD YOUR EBOOK

If you own a paperback of *The Siege of Reginald Hill* you can download a free copy of the eBook.

1. Go to *www.UnSeenBooks.co.uk* or scan the QR code:

2. Enter this code: KRM333G

3. Enjoy your download!

All Free/Exclusive content subject to availability.

www.ingramcontent.com/pod-product-compliance
Ingram Content Group UK Ltd.
Pitfield, Milton Keynes, MK11 3LW, UK
UKHW041417180426
11947UKWH00007B/177